Y0-ACE-609

SPECIAL MESSAGE TO READERS

This book is published by

THE ULVERSCROFT FOUNDATION

a registered charity in the U.K., No. 264873

The Foundation was established in 1974 to provide funds to help towards research, diagnosis and treatment of eye diseases. Below are a few examples of contributions made by THE ULVERSCROFT FOUNDATION:

A new Children's Assessment Unit at Moorfield's Hospital, London.

•

Twin operating theatres at the Western Ophthalmic Hospital, London.

•

The Frederick Thorpe Ulverscroft Chair of Ophthalmology at the University of Leicester.

•

Eye Laser equipment to various eye hospitals.

If you would like to help further the work of the Foundation by making a donation or leaving a legacy, every contribution, no matter how small, is received with gratitude. Please write for details to:

THE ULVERSCROFT FOUNDATION,
The Green, Bradgate Road, Anstey, Leicester LE7 7FU. England
Telephone: (0533)364325

Love is
a time of enchantment:
in it all days are fair and all fields
green. Youth is blest by it,
old age made benign:
the eyes of love see
roses blooming in December,
and sunshine through rain. Verily
is the time of true-love
a time of enchantment — and
Oh! how eager is woman
to be bewitched!

DESTINY'S DAUGHTER

Sari Tregeer's only clue to her parentage was a brooch pinned to her shawl when she was found as a baby. When her foster parents died she left home, and was whirled into the thrilling life of the travelling circus, moving from village to village in nineteenth century Cornwall. There she was to find love, but that wasn't all, for she and the circus came to the great house of Boscarne, which changed her life forever.

Books by Mary Williams
in the Ulverscroft Large Print Series:

THE SECRET TOWER
THE MISTRESS OF BLACKSTONE

MARY WILLIAMS

DESTINY'S DAUGHTER

Complete and Unabridged

ULVERSCROFT
Leicester

First published in Great Britain in 1987 by
William Kimber & Co Limited
London

First Large Print Edition
published April 1992
by arrangement with
Harper Collins Publishers Limited
London

The right of Mary Williams to be identified as
the author of this work has been asserted by
her in accordance with the Copyright, Designs
and Patents Act, 1988

Copyright © 1987 by Mary Williams
All rights reserved

British Library CIP Data

Williams, Mary
    Destiny's Daughter.—Large print ed.—
Ulverscroft large print series: romance
I. Title
823.914 [F]

ISBN 0-7089-2635-5

Published by
F. A. Thorpe (Publishing) Ltd.
Anstey, Leicestershire
Set by Words & Graphics Ltd.
Anstey, Leicestershire
Printed and bound in Great Britain by
T. J. Press (Padstow) Ltd., Padstow, Cornwall

In memory of Mike

1

I REMEMBER the sound of roaring in my ears, and a silvery quiver of light overhead, spattered with darting white star shapes. These are the first memories of my life. I was a baby. The roaring must have been the pounding of waves breaking with myriad specks of foam against a clear sky — all else nothing but cold air and a gasping for breath.

Later, when I was a child old enough to understand, I learned that I had been rescued from a ship that had foundered and broken into pieces off the fearsome Craggan rocks on the Cornish coast. There were only two survivors — the mate, who later died of injuries to his head, and myself, a wailing infant lying on the wet sand. No one knew who I was. But Joanna Tregeer, the wife of Uter Tregeer, the farmer who took me in and adopted me, said the vessel had been a convict ship driven off course on

1

its journey to foreign parts.

"So you be lucky," Joanna said, not once but nearer a hundred times, during the years of my childhood, "with Uter an' me you have respectability an' a chance to make the best o' thyself. Van Diemen's Land? Hm! I've heard tell a real hell-hole it is, no fit place for any innocent chile to be."

She didn't tell me until I was six years old about the little brooch that had pinned the wet shawl round me. When I saw it I didn't think much of it at first. It was small, made of bronze probably, Joanna said. It didn't shine, or sparkle with any tiny jewels — and it was difficult to understand what it represented; there was a kind of head like a strange bird, entwined with leaves and lettering looking like an 'F' with a crown on it.

"It's the only thing you had on you to say who you was," Joanna continued, "and it told us naught. To my mind it's nothing of value, but Uter said we might keep it safe, because one day you'd maybe want to have it, seein' it's yours by right."

Because it was something special of my own, I cherished it, and was careful always to have it to be pinned somewhere on my clothing — pinafore, shawl, or at my neck. No one noticed it — it wasn't that kind of ornament — not even at the Dame school which I attended four mornings a week in Zaul until I was nine years old. After that I stayed at the farm to help Joanna about the house. She wasn't well; there was something wrong with her chest that made her cough a lot. 'Consumption,' Uter said. He worked very hard at the small-holding. We kept a pig, chickens and two white goats, and grew what vegetables were possible to have us adequately fed, with sufficient to sell for a little profit in Penzance Market, or at any available fair in the district. We had no horse or cart, and Uter had to walk the four miles cross-country into the town, with heavy sacks over his shoulders, unless he got a lift in Farmer Breague's cart. Farmer Breague was quite well off and had men working for him on his hundred acres of land.

I envied his prosperity; not for myself because I couldn't wear the fine clothes like his four daughters, who always looked very smart when they attended Zaul Chapel on Sundays. No, I'd no wish for fine clothes; our home was situated in so wild a spot — very near the edge of the cliffs amid a tangle of furze, gorse, huge boulders and tall waving bracken — that white frills and fancy hats would soon have got spoiled. Besides, I liked to be free and wander and climb about the coast whenever I had a spare moment. I had no desire at all to be a real 'little lady', like the Breague girls — it was only for Uter I was jealous sometimes, and hurt for him because he couldn't afford to give the small comforts and extra care necessary for Joanna's health.

Uter was such a kind man — very tall and strong, six feet in height, with a thatch of red hair and the brightest bluest eyes you ever saw. Joanna was small and thin, dark like most of the true Cornish folk, quick-moving, with a rather light high voice that could be shrill at times. But she meant well, and looked on me as the daughter she'd never had. Strangely, I never *really* felt I was one of them; from earliest days there was an instinctive inexplicable feeling in me that somewhere was another world where I truly belonged — a world quite beyond my knowledge that could lie fantastically round any bend of the moorland path. There were many of them leading between tangled undergrowth beneath the rugged hills where distant menhirs and carns stood stark against the open skyline, and an occasional mine-stack smoked.

Oddly, though, this sense of 'apartness' in no way lessened my affection for Joanna and Uter, rather enhanced it. I felt warm and loving towards them, and knew I had good reason to be grateful — to Uter especially. So it was terrible to me, when in 1834 six labourers of Tolpuddle, Dorset, who'd formed an active trade union, were sentenced for seven years transportation to Van Diemen's Land in Australia, and with them, Uter. He'd spoken out at a meeting near Redlake on their behalf, and because of that was made an 'example' by the court who judged him.

I was hotly, fiercely resentful; so was Joanna, partly because she was already ill, and didn't know how we were going to eke out a living without Uter; but she didn't fume and rebel outwardly like me, just worked on tirelessly, doing what she could about the small place and field, gradually getting more bent, and thinner as the days passed, and at night coughing the hours away drenched in her own sweat. Luckily I was strong, and managed to shoulder as much as any boy would have done. Farmer Breague, hearing of our plight, sent us a donkey, so I'd be able to ride to adjoining or not too far off districts where any festivity was going on, with bunches of wild flowers and brooms to sell.

"Save your legs and feet a bit," he said, when he called.

"Wish I could only do more for you, girl. If you wanted to come into service my wife'd find you a place, but — "

"Oh no, thank you very much," I said quickly. "With ma to look after, I couldn't. The donkey will be of help though. Oh, yes a big help. And he's a fine handsome donkey, aren't you, boy?" I patted the animal's neck gently.

The farmer laughed. "It's a 'she', child. Delilah's her name. Call her Del. And with all this undergrowth and turf to nibble she won't cost much in food either. Another thing — if you do want to sell that pig any time I'll give you a price; remember now. An' next time Dan goes to Penzance, he'll meet you at the crossroads eight in the morning, and you c'n have a lift." Dan was one of his labourers, a fine bargainer with a sound knowledge of livestock.

I thanked Mr Breague, and after he'd gone, leaving Del in one small field enclosure, I made friends with her and pulled some sweet grass for her to nibble. For some time I was lost in wonderment, and forgot the sadness and bitterness of Joanna's suffering. In a queer way the donkey seemed to understand the worries and loneliness thrust on us. She became my confidante and friend, and was certainly useful.

For three years we managed to survive, which was a wonder considering Joanna's progressive illness. Then the Tolpuddle Martyrs, as the convicted labourers were called by their supporters, were unexpectedly released and with them Uter. But he was a changed man. During the time spent in that dreadful place he had become old and broken. His red hair had thinned and turned white. His once jolly face was haggard and drawn, his back bent, scarred by terrible lines that showed he had been beaten, and he was thin, so thin. All the liveliness and life in him seemed drained away, leaving only bitterness, and a great sorrow for Joanna and me. He did his best to get the small farm thriving as it had once been, but it was no use.

One evening he did not return to the cottage, and when I went to look for him I found him slumped on the ground with his spade beside him, quite dead. He'd died, they said at the enquiry, from a heart attack. But I knew it was from injustice, and it was then I think that I first decided somehow to revenge myself on the powers that had sentenced and destroyed him — not only Uter, but Joanna. For she was to follow him within a month.

I was thirteen years old then, alone, except for Delilah, the two white goats, the few chickens, the pig, and the ramshackle small property that Uter had built himself on the patch of land rented to him by the Lord of the Manor, Squire Tremellick. He owned the moorland for miles around to the east, and lived in the great house, Boscarne Hall, in a vale below the first high ridge a mile beyond the coast.

The family had never troubled us during Uter's lifetime but I knew the present owner would now have right to claim the little farm, even rebuild or destroy it if he wished; Joanna owed rent. Besides, old Sir William — who'd spent much of his time up-country in Bodmin or London where he sat in court judging hard-working people like us for petty crimes and even some they hadn't committed — had been one of those responsible, I'd heard, for getting Uter sent to Van Diemen's Land.

Old Peter Nancegollan, a shepherd, had told me, and I'd hated everyone and everything to do with the Tremellicks or Boscarne ever since. Because of the Squire's power and wicked meanness and cruelty, Uter had died. One day, I'd thought childishly, time after time, I'd avenge the death of my kind good guardian. It wasn't right that any family so wealthy and able to live in such splendour should use power so cruelly. If *I'd* possessed money and a fine house like Boscarne, how different things would have been. I'd have — what would I have done? I didn't exactly know, only that somehow I'd have tried to understand and help the conditions of poor folk slaving in the mines or on the land without sufficient food to keep them healthy and warm. I'd have given parties, perhaps, for the miners and labourers at Christmas time or when there was any opportunity for celebration. I'd heard that rich people came down sometimes from London and foreign parts and that the Hall then rang with merrymaking and music.

Once, on such an occasion, I'd climbed the hill on a summer evening when there was a moon, and made my own way down the other side of the moor to a spot from where Boscarne was clearly visible in the weird lemon-pale light. It was a fascinating building, very old, that had been added to during the passing of the centuries. There were arched doors and

10

mullioned windows, gables and turrets, and tall, twisting chimneystacks that somehow gave it a mediaeval legendary look. One of the great doors was open wide, and under fancy lamps and chandeliers figures were moving to and fro, casting strange shadows streaking down terraces to the lawns. I crept nearer, and stood hidden behind the trunk of a dark yew tree, with the hood of my dark cloak pulled low over my head so I'd not be seen. Excitement mounted in me when a man fashionably clad in a grey satin coat and breeches ran out pulling a girl by the hand. She was dressed all in shimmering white, with her fair hair washed to silver in the moonlight. It was dressed high on her head in bunches of curls, glistening with tiny starlike jewels. They stole to a corner of the building where ugly jutting gargoyles cast shadows, taking them into darkness, but not before he'd pulled her close suddenly, and kissed her.

I was seized by a mixture of conflicting emotions holding a hint of envy not of the house itself or the wealth displayed, but of the beauty — I was sure she must be very beautiful — of the girl who could kindle such passion and romance in a rich gallant's heart. My own senses were intensified painfully, and suddenly into throbbing life beyond my years. Just for a few seconds I became that other — the young woman in the white dress made exquisite by rich satins and silks, and heady perfumes to stir a lover's desire. From where I waited I fancied the very air fragrant with her scent which would be more subtle than that of May blossom, heather, or brine blown from the sea. Wealth, I'd realised acutely then — wealth could bring so much. I knew Joanna would have disapproved of such thoughts or knowledge in me. But I'd made full use of my few years at the Dame school and learned how to read well. It was from books that I'd discovered there were two worlds — one of the poor, and one of the rich.

I was of the former. But one day — My thoughts broke off there. I'd turned suddenly and, with my head thrust forward under my hood, made my way back to the humble little farm by the cliff.

It was only a short time after that

incident that Uter died, and for the rest of Joanna's doomed existence I was too busy to have wild dreams of riches and power.

The day came, of course, after her death when I had to make up my mind what to do. I'd no fancy simply to stay in one spot eking out a hard living which might one day bring me to an early end, like Joanna. Neither had I a wish for serving as a kitchenmaid at Mr Breague's farm. There was nothing or no one here I cared about any more, except Delilah. With the donkey I could travel to other parts in Cornwall, taking any job for a day or maybe two, that came along. I could make posies, and small brooms, pick the wild spinach that grew round the headland, and take it in buckets to sell in Zaul. Oh, there was plenty I could find to do, especially at harvest time when most likely after a day's work, I'd be given dry shelter for the night in a barn. I'd have liked to take the two goats as well; they were gentle creatures, but too thin, and I knew they'd be better off with someone like Farmer Breague than with Delilah and me.

So one day I asked old Peter Nancegollan if he'd let Mr Breague know I was taking off, and if he wanted the pig and chickens, also the goats, he could have them gladly as payment for Delilah who'd been such a comfort. But the farmer was a just man and insisted on calling before I left and giving me two shining gold guineas.

The money was a real fortune to me. I put it in a little leather wallet that had been Uter's, and tied it round my waist under my woollen petticoat.

The next day I set off, with my few belongings harnessed round Delilah's neck, and leading her by a thin rope, left the shack that had been my home ever since Uter had found me as a baby on the wet sands beneath the cliffs.

It was an autumn morning, rich with the scents of damp undergrowth and tumbled leaves. As I climbed the hill towards the high ridge I looked back only once. Memories flooded me of early days when Uter worked so tirelessly at the stubborn earth, yet full of confidence and zeal. Joanna had not been sick then, or our stomachs hungry for food. Our lives,

14

though comparatively primitive, had been full of good simple things — milk from the goats, the smell of baking from the small kitchen, and of woodsmoke curling from bonfires outside. So many recollections of small intimate details of daily life that I was leaving forever. Emotion welled up in me, bringing a lump of pain to my heart.

Then I turned resolutely and went on, pushing brambles and gorse aside, with the donkey following. When we reached the summit of the moors I could just see in the distance the turrets of Boscarne rising towards the sky. I took the opposite direction joining the high lane that after a hundred yards or so divided in two directions, one leading east, and one to the west. I chose the latter. The time had not yet come for me to visit the big house. But one day I would, I told myself resolutely. One day, a deep sixth sense in me told me I would come face to face with the owner — no humble servant girl — but a proud woman determined somehow to seek vengeance for Uter's suffering and death.

The decision sent a fiery warm glow of

vitality to my body. I felt tall and strong, though I was but thirteen — nearly fourteen years old. Though autumn, the wind blew soft and gentle against my cheeks, driving my dark tawny hair free and wild behind me. Now the surface of the lane had smoothed I took off my boots and walked barefoot. Excitement deepened and flowed through my blood.

"We're on the way, Del, dear," I told Delilah, "going to some place, though I don't know where, just you and me, Del, you and me."

There seemed nothing strange about it, fearful or reckless. It seemed the most natural thing in the world to be walking away from poverty and grubbing about the soil, into an unknown future of new beginnings and adventure. At a bend in the lane I stopped for some minutes, took a 'taty cake' from a bundle and ate it, while the donkey nibbled the short turf bordering the track. The sky now was paper clear and glistening from early sun. On every side of us heather and wild thyme grew thick between patches of gorse, broom, and tangled brambles. A little ahead of us an ancient Celtic cross stood as a standing reminder of past days.

"Maybe folk worshipped here," I told Del, "or p'raps it's where the saints walked. There's an awful lot to learn, dear, don't you think so, Delilah?" I was talking my thoughts aloud, of course. But the donkey lifted its head for a moment, nuzzled me and gave me a little push with its head that sent me into the bracken. I laughed, sat up, and patted the grey neck. Life at that moment seemed all it should be, and just right. But as we walked on again I sobered and said to myself, "But it won't always be like this. You've things to do, Sari Tregeer. And one day all at Boscarne will know of it."

It was past noon when we reached Clooney Castle, a ruin so old that no one knew how many centuries it had seen. I'd heard it said by Dame Farne during my brief schooling that it was thought by knowledgeable men that Joseph of Arimathea might even have passed that way in the bygone past. When I'd told Uter and asked about it, he'd smiled his wise smile and said:

"Many tales be tole, chile, but no one c'n tell the right or wrong of en. All we c'n safely know is under our feet and in the sky above — the green grass pushin' round the stones of our great hills, an' the sun an' moon, an' stars shinin' when the night comes. An' rain an' storm, too. Oh ais. You c'n be sure of what you do see an' feel."

"Still, I *wonder*," I said.

He'd given me a long serious look before adding, "You be a one for wonderin', I do reckon. S'long as you kip y's feet on the ground it won't harm'ee. But don' go wishin' for things as can't come true. Best take what's at hand and enjoy it."

As much as possible I'd done that. But now with Uter and Joanna gone, and freedom ahead, my brain wouldn't stop buzzing with fancies; and I thought, looking at Clooney Castle, "Perhaps a king and queen lived there once, with crowns, and riches much more splendid than those at Boscarne. Perhaps I could be like that, with the power to make those cruel, greedy Tremellicks kneel at my feet and ask for mercy." Yes — in

18

such a way I would avenge the deaths of Uter and Joanna — *partly*, anyway. But I'd make them suffer first, although I didn't quite know how.

Through such wild imaginings I was brought to my senses abruptly by a sudden braying from Delilah.

"All right then," I said vaguely. "We'll get going again. You silly restless thing, you."

We went on and took another turn, to the left this time which dipped to a valley in the moors. On a hill opposite, overlooking the sea, the gaunt shape of a mine, Wheal Sally, stood derelict and abandoned, no more than an empty shell now, since the copper failed. There were a few granite cottages scattered about, but below, in the valley, was the village of Skillan crouched comfortably in a huddle of trees. I'd been there once or twice with Farmer Breague when there was a fair on, and had found it a prosperous little place with a market square, church, a hostelry, The Prowling Pig, a green with a duck pond, and two small stores. There was also a kiddleywink of doubtful repute on the outskirts.

"We'll go there," I told Delilah, giving the donkey a slap on the rump. "There's always something happening in Skillan."

As though sensing something good ahead, Delilah sharpened her pace considerably, forcing me to run to keep up with her. I was laughing when she slowed up halfway down the slope, by a thicket of trees. Smoke holding a good smell of cooking rose through the branches, and as we drew closer sunlight dappled the bright red and gold of a large vehicle drawn into a clearing.

At first I thought I'd stumbled on a group of gypsies. There was a fire burning in the patch of grass, with a large cooking pot on it. A tall fair-haired man emerged from the shadows carrying wood, followed by a woman in a scarlet skirt. She had something on her shoulder a monkey surely, that gave a sudden high scream ending in a curious chattering sound. I took a step forward. Delilah brayed loudly; the girl jerked round and came towards me with the animal still crouched by her cheek. She was young, with a mass of black hair falling almost to her waist.

"Who are *you*?" she asked in a deep, rather throaty voice. "What do you want?"

There was something a little aggressive about her that I didn't like, but she was handsome enough, with thickly lashed dark eyes and full sulky lips above a determined chin with a cleft in it. She *could* have been a gypsy, but I was mistaken. Before I could reply the fair man had come forward smiling, and said with a hand held out, "Don't be afraid. You're in good company, child, whoever you are. Welcome to Barney Goodfellow's Circus Theatre."

I gasped in wonderment. *Players!* but they weren't ordinary players either; they were circus people and must have animals and do funny tricks — there must be jugglers and acrobats, and dancing bears, perhaps. I'd read all about circuses at the Dame's School, but had never thought I'd really see one. I noticed then that there were other vans further back.

"Well — " I heard the girl insisting, "tell us your name and business."

"I'm Sari," I said.

21

"And this is Mylora," the man told me. "Allow me to introduce her pet monkey, Muncher. Mylora — " turning to the girl " — tell him to say how d'ye do." She whispered to the animal.

The monkey squeaked, doffed the little scarlet cap he was wearing and held out a paw.

I laughed. I couldn't help it. "Don't make fun of him," Mylora said. "He doesn't like it."

Neither did Delilah; suddenly she put her nose into the air and made the most dreadful 'hee haw' I'd ever heard. The kettle and other of my precious possessions rattled round her neck. The monkey continued gibbering.

I apologised for her.

The man smiled. "It's of no matter. We're used to strange language and odd ways here, aren't we, Mylora?"

"I suppose you could say that," Mylora agreed grudgingly, "but it won't do to have the animals worked up just when we've arrived, and remember the show opens tomorrow."

"Have you lots of animals?" I exclaimed quickly, before she could say anything more. "I mean, a bear that dances? And — and — "

"*One* bear," she interrupted, "this monkey and a dog — a dog that sings, that's all — except for the ponies. But if you're so interested, why don't y'wait till the performance?" The resentful note had crept back into her voice.

"Perhaps she'd like to join us," I heard her companion say. "Come to think of it, Mylora, why not? If she's agreeable. A donkey could be useful in many ways."

A beam of light cut across his face as he spoke. He was staring at me quizzically, and I noted how very handsome he was, with blue eyes of a lighter shade than Uter's had been, a mouth that could be twitching with laughter one moment, stern the next and hair curling back from his face so bleached by the elements, it shone almost white above his suntanned face. His features were strongly carved, but had a sensitive, almost noble look. At least that's what he appeared to me, and although I was not yet fourteen, my heart had a bumpy feeling, and I knew that if he really meant what he said, I would gladly go along with Barney

Goodfellow's Theatre.

"Come along," he said. "We'll have a talk with Barney himself."

The three of us wended our way into the copse past the clearing and the large red van which had large gold lettering on it saying 'Goodfellow's Circus Theatre' — to another grassy space where a second vehicle stood. There was a cage beyond it, with a big brown bear standing on its hind legs eating an apple. Round this second van figures were moving, shaking out fancy clothes, and hanging a few on lines of string to branches of trees. The largest, fattest woman I'd ever seen in my life was sitting on the steps smoking a pipe. She must have had about six chins, and her breasts were as large as balloons. I only discovered later that padding had been added to increase her size. She wore a gaudy scarlet flowered dress and had huge gold rings hanging below masses of curled yellow hair.

A quaint little figure whom I took at first to be a child perched by her side. But when he sprang from the steps to his feet I saw that in reality he was a very tiny man — a dwarf, and not really

24

young either. His head was rather large for his small body. He wore a check suit, and was holding a tall beaver hat. He gave a bow, fell over, turned a somersault and bowed again. His name, he said, was Mr Tobias Trout. He held up a tiny hand for me to shake; "How d'ye do," he said. His palm was rough, but so small it felt like a doll's.

For some odd reason I felt mildly embarrassed and was glad when my guide hurried me on to a tent further in the copse. It was quite a large tent and beside it was a wagon holding poles and canvasses and other equipment that I guessed would be used for any performance given. Other small tents were pitched at convenient places among the trees, and figures moved here and there — dispersing when Barney Goodfellow came to meet us from his own temporary dwelling.

Barney was a large man wearing a cut-away tailed coat and an embroidered waistcoat over his stout stomach. He was fastening his silk cravat with a diamond pin or perhaps it was glass, I don't know — and patting a forelock of ginger hair on to his forehead. My first impression was of extreme joviality. His small mouth beamed in his plump pink face; he had an air of good-fellowship, which, however, disappeared as if by magic when the fair-haired man introduced me saying, "This is Sari. Sari would like to go along with us. Sari" — to me — "meet Mr Goodfellow, the owner of this company.

Barney's bonhomie changed to one of shrewd appraisal. His small bright eyes narrowed to calculating slits, his mouth became primped into a tight button of doubt.

"A child?" he said, stroking his long chin. "What ye thinkin' 'bout, Dick? There's six of us already. Six mouths to feed and bodies to bed. And for what use? This one's nobbut a girl and a skinny one at that with no talent prob'bly. Only a great need for food to put some flesh on to her bones." He scowled.

A great desire seized me suddenly somehow to get him to change his mind. I couldn't exactly have said why at that point, but it was something to do with my new friend Dick — the bold, bright look of him, the kindliness in his bright blue eyes, and sense of adventure about him that reminded me of heroes I'd read about in school books.

"Oh, there's lots I can do," I protested quickly. "I can patch clothes and stitch, and I don't eat very much. I know lots of things you can cook too — where to find them growing, and I'm stronger than I look. I can scrub floors — " I broke off hopefully.

"There's no floors to scrub for us, the way *we* live," Barney Goodfellow said abruptly, "and you're a ragged-looking scrap of a thing anyway. Where'd you come from, eh? And what's that lean donkey for? Where'd you get him?"

"Not a he it's a she and she's my friend," I said simply. "My pa and ma's died now. They weren't really my kin, but they found me on the beach a long time ago after a wreck, and took me in when I was a baby. Then Uter — that's what my pa was called, was sent to that awful place over the seas in a convict ship "cos he was sorry for the union men, those at Tolpuddle; and when he

came back he was sick, *really* sick, and
— and — "

Suddenly I couldn't go on. I felt
lonely and lost, and very, very tired
after the nostalgic tedious business of
packing up, the long walk, and now
having to plead with this large gentleman,
Mr Goodfellow, to let me go along with
them. I was on the brink of crying, but
managed to contain my tears. There was
a comforting touch on my shoulder and I
heard Dick saying, "Come along, Barney.
Do me a favour. If you don't want her,
I can use her. And she's got potential.
Look at her."

I didn't know what 'potential' meant,
but Mr Goodfellow gave me another long
stare and said, "All right then, all right,
since you wish it, lad. But see she's fixed
up and cleaned proper before I have
to look on her again. Maybe she'll fit
in somewhere with Toby. But get that
donkey out of my sight. Set it free, and
give it a push."

He waved a hand disparagingly at
Delilah. I flung both arms round the
donkey's neck.

"No. I'm not going anywhere without

28

her. She's *mine. Nothing* ever will part us." I could feel my eyes flashing and cheeks flaming red.

Suddenly Barney Goodfellow laughed a loud sound that rumbled from his stomach like thunder.

"Aha! So we have a little spitfire among us. Well, we could have worse. Only don't use your temper on me, child, or you'll have my hand on your backside."

He turned away and went back into his tent. I was fuming, but Dick, the young man, with an arm about my shoulder said, "You asked for that, you know. You must learn to be polite with Mr Goodfellow. Don't worry, though, his bark's worse than his bite."

"He won't hurt Delilah, will he?" I asked anxiously.

"Lord no. He's not the hurting kind. But you must understand, Sari, that with the circus, he's master."

"Of you too?"

"Well — not in the same way exactly. I'm different — in a way."

I stared up at him. How handsome he was. Oh surely there could be no one in the world more handsome than Dick. "How are you different?" I asked. "Do you mean you're not really a circus man?"

"Not all the time," he said. "And stop asking so many questions. I'll take you to Fanny. She'll find you something fresh to wear and a place to sleep."

"Is Fanny the fat lady?"

"Yes. But to you Mrs Petra. Now that's enough, understand? You've been accepted. You're *here*. And tomorrow we perform at Skillan. So be happy, do as you're told, and sleep well. I'll see you in the morning."

A moment later he had gone.

In this manner I joined Barney Goodfellow's travelling circus.

2

MY first experience with Barney Goodfellow's travelling theatre was exciting but not easy. I spent the night on an improvised bed chiefly sacking, at the back of the van containing the 'props'. The van was half covered by canvas, and Delilah was tied by a tree, so close to me that I could pat her if I climbed on boxes and stood on tiptoe.

At first, although I was so tired, I couldn't sleep. I kept thinking such wild strange thoughts wondering what would happen the next day when the circus was to make its first appearance in Skillan. I screwed my eyes up tight, trying hard to slumber, because I wanted to be fresh in the morning, but I couldn't blot out the pictures that kept crowding my mind, remembering Fanny, the big fat woman, the dwarf, with his creased, round, funny face that was neither old nor young. There was Pom-Pom, too, whom I'd met before going to bed. He was supposed to be a clown, but his face was long and pale with a pulled-down mouth, and miserable looking.

Then the animals. The singing dog, Scrap, who belonged to Mr Goodfellow himself, and the bear. I'd had a peep at Bimbo the dancing bear in his cage, and seen two white spotted ponies under the trees. They were tiny ponies, and Fanny told me Mylora's monkey sometimes rode on their backs, jumping from one to another.

Most of all, though, I thought of Dick. He was so different, and had his own tent to sleep in. When I'd asked Fanny what he did, she'd put up a podgy finger and said, "Now you just stop asking questions, young 'un. What Master Dick does is none of your business. He's a gent, see? He does what he likes, and comes and goes as he pleases. But if you're goin' to be one of us you've got to toe the line, and be where you're wanted at the right time. Another thing — "

"Yes, Fanny?"

"An' no Fanny neither. Mrs Petra I am for the likes of you." She folded her ample arms, nodded her many chins and continued, "As I was sayin', child, you've got to learn to know your place, and not go putting on any fancy airs and graces. Mebbe in time you'll be of use one way or another. But a word o' warnin' — " She stared at me knowingly.

"Yes, Fanny — I mean Mrs Petra — ?"

"Take care not to anger Mylora. A great fancy for her Mr Goodfellow has, and she's a fiery temper. Wouldn't do to go upsettin' her. Neither would Mr Dick like it. Real friendly, they are — Mr Dick and 'Madam' Mylora."

By the emphasis put on the 'Madam', I'd sensed that Fanny Petra didn't particularly approve of the friendship, or of Mylora herself. There were two more in the company — Rom, a black-eyed brown-skinned dancer and who did other things too, like juggling with coloured balls and helping Mylora with the animals. From the beginning I knew there was a special bond between him and Mylora, just as I sensed that Mylora fancied Dick and kept her eyes on *him* as often as she could. These facts of course only really registered during the days that followed. For those few days at Skillan I was too busy trying to please — doing this and that, fetching and carrying at the command of everyone, being sworn at, having my toes trodden on and shouted at, or told to 'Get out of the way, brat', to think of anything but keeping free of trouble and seeing Delilah was safe.

We arrived in the village by nine o'clock. The duck pond in the green, which wasn't deep, had been covered by planks and a hole hammered through them so a tall pole could be stuck in and erected. While Rom and Mr Goodfellow were seeing the animals were taken safely into the yard of the hostelry opposite, Dick and Pom-Pom, with the help of the dwarf and two farm labourers, were already hammering and shouting and shrieking, just as though 'the devil was at their heels', as Joanna used to say. Fanny, I knew, was contentedly sitting at the back of the largest van with a big mug of beer in her hand, and Mylora was pretending to help Dick, though she didn't do much except arch her long neck and swing her hips, tossing

34

her black hair so it blew in an ebony stream on the wind.

The vans and cart had been pitched in a nearby field behind the inn with my donkey. In the bustle and confusion of so much going on, I crept off unseen to find Delilah. The field, though it was now autumn, had a fresh grassy smell about it, mingled with that of woodsmoke, heather and the salty tang of the sea beyond. Gorse still flamed in clumps nearer the cliffs. Large boulders dotted the earth here and there, and I thought back with a brief wave of nostalgia to times past when I was a child before Uter had been sent to Van Diemen's Land or Joanna had become so severely ill.

I sat on a stone for a moment, chin in hands, while Delilah nuzzled my cheek.

"It won't be for ever, Del dear," I said. "One day when I'm rich we'll be on our own, you and me; we'll come back then and go to the big house, Boscarne, and pay them out for what they did to Uter. I'll be a fine lady then, Delilah, and hold my head up like a Queen. Then I'll spit on them.

Yes, I will — *spit*, and crunch them into dust."

Just words, of course, but the spitting *did* rather appeal to me, especially imagining a crown on my head at the same time.

I was mulling over my fine future when I heard a harsh vibrant voice calling, "Come here, you. What do you think you're doing — lazing around while others are working?"

It was Mylora's voice. I sprang up hastily, wondering why she always had to be so angry with me. "You weren't brought along to laze about," she said crossly. "This afternoon or tomorrow you've got to show what you're made of — or else."

I scowled. "What do you mean 'or else'?"

"You'll be given your come-uppings."

I'd heard many strange expressions in my short life, Cornish of course, but never such an odd one as *that* 'come-uppings'.

"You'll be sent off," she told me, seeing I didn't understand, "without a coin in your pocket or a chunk of bread in your stomach you and that old nag of yours." And she stared contemptuously at Delilah.

"You're wrong," I couldn't help retorting, with a flood of warm anger filling me. "Dick wouldn't send me away, and I've got coins money from Farmer Breague; and Delilah isn't a nag. Delilah's *mine* — my friend." Although my chin was thrust out stubbornly, I was on the brink of tears.

Perhaps Mylora realised it, or perhaps she saw Dick in the distance, but her manner softened suddenly. "Oh, don't fret," she said casually. "My bark's worse than my bite often as not. But you must remember it's a great favour Barney's giving you, letting you join our troupe."

I nearly informed her that Dick, not Mr Goodfellow, had been responsible, but managed to hold my tongue, realising instinctively that Mylora wouldn't like it.

Later, when green canvas stuff had been pinned flat in a wide circle over the green, a large tent was pegged round, with an opening at one end where anyone wanting to see the performance had to pay. Outside were two wooden huts with a curtain drawn across one for Mylora to sit in dressed as a gypsy fortune-teller — she had a shawl half covering her face so no one would recognise her when she appeared afterwards as Princess Mylora and her famous monkey, accompanied by her 'snow-white steeds'. Fanny was sitting in the other; a notice outside said, 'Twopence for a peep at Buxom Bella — the bearded woman wonder of the world'.

I got a peep from the back before the show opened, and was astonished to see Fanny sitting on a kind of throne, wearing whiskers and a long beard reaching to her enormous padded breasts. It couldn't be real, I told myself. How could anyone, even a man, grow such a wealth of hair in such a short time? Especially a woman. I wondered what would happen if anyone gave it a tug; but of course no one *could*, because Tobias the dwarf had come to stand at one side of the hut, holding an ugly-looking knife, taller than himself — whether it was real or not I didn't know, — and Rom on the other, looking tremendously strong, with his brown chest bare, and a club in his hand.

I crept away fascinated, bewildered by the hubbub of the crowds already gathering outside the big tent — they'd come from near and far having heard of the travelling circus's arrival — by the confusion and orders shouted continually by Mr Goodfellow himself, and by wondering how everything was going to be fitted in. So many acts by so few people, all having to change quickly into someone else, and by the variety of animal turns — Bimbo Bear's dancing act, the monkey's scene with the ponies, and the dog's howling opera sing song, when he wore a top hat until Pom-Pom appeared and knocked it off. Pom-Pom's face was all white with a red blob of a nose and mouth; he was dressed in a spotted suit with baggy trousers, having a patch at the back. When he somersaulted the trousers fell off, and everyone laughed and clapped and shouted rude things, because underneath he was wearing frilly pink drawers.

I don't know who took the dwarfs place at Fanny's door guarding her, but someone must have done, probably

Barney, because when Mylora appeared wearing sparkling red satin covered by twinkling diamonds, she had a whip in her hand, and as she cracked it the two white ponies looking splendid with feathers on their heads trotted in; the dwarf was on one of them, the monkey on the other. Oh it was all so exciting I could hardly breathe, and once I nearly fell down from giddiness.

There was music too, pipes and a drum, and all round people were cheering and clapping, especially when the clown and Bimbo had a wrestling match. I wanted Bimbo to win, but didn't exactly want the clown hurt; so when the first chance came to escape I managed to push through the crowd and reach the field where the two largest vans were.

I crept to one side, and huddled myself on a rock by Delilah with my back against the trunk of an old May tree. Already the light was beginning to deepen to soft greyness. There were faint signs of thin evening mist rising. I didn't know how long this first performance would go on, and hoped that soon there'd be something to eat. My head felt light, and my legs were tired. An ostler from the inn appeared, carrying rubbish in a bucket that he dumped by the hedge. Delilah neighed; the man looked and saw me suddenly, stopped with brows raised in his round face.

"What's this now?" he said, "A young 'un like you. Trampin' the roads be 'ee? I do hope you bain't a thief or vagabond. Come, chile — or is it a real girl you be? Stand up an' face me proper."

I got to my feet and managed to say, with my head high. "Course I'm not a thief. I — I'm Sari, and travelling with the circus people for a bit, because my pa and ma — Uter and Joanna've died, an' I'm going to — to — " I broke off, not knowing quite what I was going to do.

The man scratched one ear, shook his head slowly in bewilderment, then said, "You look a bit wisht to me. Hungry, is that it? Wantin' somethin' in thy belly, do 'ee?"

I knew suddenly that I did. I nodded.

"Come wi' me then," he answered, "there's good broth in the stewpot. Liza'll give 'ee a bowl of it wi' pleasure. A good soul my missus is, wi' a likin' for all young things. Why, d'ye know midear, in our kitchen there's old Fuz, our ram, who sh'd've bin tekken t'market these many years afore, but Liz wouldn' have it. Fuz w's brought up here y'see — from bein' a tiny lamb without a mother — oh s'many winter's ago now I lost count. Liz fed en from bottle, and after that, each year I says to her — 'Liz midear, that sheep's goin' to be sold next month', an' she'd argue quite quiet-like, 'We'll see, man, we'll see', she told me. An' I knowed it were no good. She'd got a likin' an' love for the soft creature that went beyond common sense an' the need o' gold. An' so it was. Fuz is quite an old un now, sleeps a lot, an' ambles round after my old woman like as if she were God isself. When in a way so she is — to Fuz."

"I can understand," I replied, "I feel like that to Delilah. Will Delilah be all right left alone here?"

"No one'll touch'er while I'm around," the man said stoutly. "Come along now, and bring the donkey with 'ee if you do like. Mebbe there'll be a carrot or two waitin'. You never know what my good wife has in that kitchen of hers."

Together the three of us wandered to the back door of the inn and went through.

The smell that met us was a strange one, but very appetising, of baking, malt, spirits, and vegetables emitting a savoury odour, all blended together.

The kitchen was cosy and warm, with a large range, ovens beside a huge fireplace where logs burned and an immense black pot bubbled. In front of the fire a great woolly sheep lay stretched out comfortably like a huge dog. I felt suddenly at home, and wondered if Delilah and I wouldn't be happier living in a place like that which was half a farmhouse, and half an inn — than going along with the theatre and menagerie. Then I remembered Dick, and something stirred in me that was strange and new, and very bewildering.

However haughty Mylora was, however domineering fat Fanny, and wickedly mischievous the dwarf — however much the rest of the company might resent me, seeing me as just an encumbrance — Dick liked me; and he was different. He could have been a young king in a legend, so handsome he was. So tall and fair and strong. I wanted to know more about him — much, much more, so I'd put up with snubs from the rest, and in time make them proud to have me as one of their company. By then I'd be older and more beautiful. Somehow I'd have time to read more books and speak differently, so that one day — a great lump rose in my throat when I thought of the future — one day I'd walk through the gates and door of Boscarne and shame the great family of Tremellick for their terrible treatment of Uter. Just how I'd do it I still didn't know. But I *would*, I would, however difficult it proved to be and however long it took.

3

I DIDN'T like it the next day when Dick told me I had to rehearse in the morning with the dwarf for a new act.

"Don't worry," he said, "you'll find it exciting I guess. All you'll have to do is ride on Delilah's back, with Mr Tobias in front of you. You'll be dressed as a bride, and he as your groom. Everything will look splendid until Tobias takes a large carrot out of his pocket, and taps it on the donkey's head. Delilah will probably jerk round. Whether she does or not won't matter — Tobias will turn a somersault and fall off, and you'll — " he broke off, grinning and shrugging, " — well, we'll have to wait and see what happens next."

Something on my face must have disturbed him. He looked mildly worried.

"Who *arranged* all that?" I asked sharply. "I don't *want* to be such a silly little man's bride even in fun. I'll look silly, and Del won't like it either. I won't do it, I *won't*." I stared up at him with my chin stuck out aggressively. "Who *was* it?" I queried again. "Who thought of such a stupid thing? Mylora?"

Dick's face became stern. "Now why should you ask that? Don't you think you should be grateful for the chance to appear with the circus and all, in pretty clothes as well? If you're going into a temper when anything displeases you I can assure you there'll be trouble. It would be a pity if I had to beat you. But that's what happens to naughty little girls, so I've heard — "

I was very taken aback. My cheeks flamed. "You wouldn't. I know you *wouldn't*. Anyway, it isn't your circus, is it? And and — I'm not a little girl. I'm grown up — nearly. Fourteen."

"When you're fourteen you're not a child — " I paused because I was breathing so quickly, and my feelings were all mixed up with shame, excitement, anger, and a kind of longing that was very strange and new to me.

Dick studied me reflectively. I fancied there was a twitch of amusement about

46

his lips. "Not *quite* a child — mm," he agreed, "but then you're *not* fourteen yet, are you, Sari?"

"*Almost* I am," I told him defensively, wishing I didn't blush too easily. I wanted to add something like — "I could be married properly now, be a real wife; something happened to me last July that changed me." But of course he wouldn't have liked it, and I was far too shy. I was so shy that I suddenly wanted to run away and hide in the heather where he couldn't see the tell-tale look in my eyes, or guess at even a hint of my confusion.

I suppose it was at that moment I first fell in love with Dick Loraine, and the reason for my agreeing to do the silly act with Tobias and Delilah. I wanted to please him, and remain with the circus people so long as he was there too; and as it happened it wasn't after all such a terrible experience. I was dressed up in a white frilly dress, wearing a crown of artificial flowers that looked like water-lilies, and a long veil over my shoulders at the back. Before we tried out the turn, with the curtains of the big tent pulled close so no 'peeping Tom' could get a glimpse, Dick came in to have a look.

"Ah yes," he agreed. "She looks exactly right. Except for one thing — " he came close to where I was already seated on Delilah's back, and gently lifted the veil, so my long tawny-gold hair could spill to the front over my breasts. "There," he said stepping back. "A truly beautiful young bride. One day, nymph dear, I'll paint you like that, sitting by a silver pool. Undine, I'll call you. Do you know anything about Undine?"

I shook my head dumbly.

"One day I'll tell you," he said. "In the meantime he gave a slap to Delilah's flanks " — on with you. No. Wait. We're forgetting the groom."

Mr Tobias came running on his tiny legs across the canvas floor, and grumbling and swearing under his breath, climbed on the donkey's back before me.

So I didn't really have to act at all, and Delilah made everything more comical by refusing to move until the dwarf produced the carrot, then she gave a great rush to grab it, and Tobias plunged straight over her head to the ground, where he did his somersault, made a bow, and got on the donkey's back again.

Barney appeared just in time to see the somersault. "We'll keep it like that," he said. "Only three tumbles 'stead of four, Toby if your brain'll stand it."

The dwarf scowled, looking more like a grown-up gnome than ever. But he knew better than to argue. I'd heard from Fanny that a troupe of dwarves from Plymouth way were out of work and hankering to get jobs with Mr Goodfellow's show. So Tobias wasn't risking losing his place to them.

Everything went more pleasurably for me after that. Even Mylora was nicer to me; probably because she knew that once I was occupied in a funny turn with Tobias I wouldn't have so much time in Dick's company. It was the very next day, following my first public performance that I discovered what Dick's true profession really was. He was an artist who had become famous in London for his paintings of circus and show people. That's why he wanted to paint me as Undine, I supposed, and I was somehow disappointed. Oh, it was flattering that he thought me interesting enough, of course. But it simply meant that I was *useful* to him, and Mylora told me he had done lots of her; two were hanging in the Royal Academy.

"Is it very big?" I asked. "That place? The Academy?"

Mylora smiled a little pityingly. "You don't know much, do you? It's the most famous gallery in the world for artists. Folk come from all over everywhere to have a look. Thousands of pounds are given for a portrait sometimes."

I gasped. "*Thousands?*"

She shrugged, studying herself through a mirror in the van where we all dressed. "And more." I was staring at her critically. She *was* beautiful, with her bold features, golden skin, flashing dark eyes and wealth of black hair. The scarlet silk shawl draped carelessly over her shoulders somehow intensified and added to her attraction. I could imagine Dick wanting to paint her just like that — with the curve of one breast almost showing its nipple above the shiny material. I wished I had more bosom like Mylora, but one day I'd develop.

Perhaps when I was sixteen I'd be more voluptuous-looking — that's what Fanny called Mylora — *voluptuous*. And then — at such a point my mind became so mixed up by the idea of Dick admiring and wanting to kiss me, that I couldn't think properly any more at all, and had to turn my brain to something else.

So time passed. Dick did one or two drawings of me, but they were only sketches. "You'll just have to be patient, nymph dear," he said one day. "When the spring comes and we're all together again, I'll get down to doing a proper portrait — the Undine I told you about."

"But are you going away then?" I asked anxiously.

"For the winter I'll have to," he answered. "I have shows to attend in town, business, and other things."

I wanted to ask him what the other things were; but there was something mysterious about Dick that I sensed he wouldn't want me to probe into, so I held my tongue and tried not to feel miserable — or desperate, yes that was the word — desperate at the thought of him leaving.

Perhaps he guessed a tiny bit of what I was feeling, I don't know, but he suddenly added, "You won't be lonely for the few winter months. I've already arranged everything."

"*Arranged?* What?"

"There's an inn — a very respectable place — near Truro, where Mrs Geeke, the landlord's wife, will give you a home and find you something to do until the troupe opens again in the early spring. We always split up before December, you know. You'll be paid a wage too, and Delilah will be given a stable and plenty of fodder to keep her fit. Mrs Geeke's a kind good soul. She won't put on you; all you'll have to do is help her with the domestic side. Gentry stay there, nymph dear, and I'm sure you'll emerge as a very mannered, even sophisticated, young woman."

I thought hard. Dolefully.

"Like Mylora, do you mean?"

His expression changed, became somehow harder, withdrawn, as though I'd offended him.

"No. Not like Mylora at all."

"What is she doing when the — when

the circus breaks up?"

"I think that's Mylora's affair, don't you? *Now*, chit! stop asking questions and say 'thank you' for getting things all fixed up."

I felt suddenly stubborn.

"But I didn't ask you to. And I'm not sure I want to go to any old inn. Delilah and me — we're used to the open air and the moors, and the sea, and — and — oh everything was all right when Uter was alive. But — " I couldn't go on for the choky feeling in my throat.

His arm slipped round me.

"Now, now, don't be a cry-baby. That's not what I expect from my lovely Sari."

Something warm stirred and came to life in me, giving a delicious glow to my whole body.

"Am I *really*?"

He stared down at me.

"What?"

"*Lovely!* — and *yours*? Do I belong to you truly? *Am* I your Sari?"

He didn't reply for a moment, then he gave me a sharp slap on my buttocks and retorted half laughing, but with a catch in his voice, "Away with you, you wicked little thing. And don't ask such stupid questions. Just grow up and learn to behave, or there'll be no portrait. Understand?"

"Yes," I said meekly, "all right." But I didn't. Dick really wasn't easy to understand at all, and in the end, that autumn, I stopped trying, remembering other things — how I had determined to avenge myself on the family at Boscarne for Uter's death. That's why I'd left the smallholding in the first place, and a feeling of guilt came over me that I could have almost forgotten in so short a time.

October was a beautiful golden month that year; the fairs were well-attended, and I began to enjoy journeying the roads with the travellers. The days were mostly dry, filled with the rich tangy smells of ripe browning bracken and the smoke curling blue from farmlands and occasionally the moors, which caught alight in patches, following a warm day. For periods I rode on Delilah's back, walking sometimes to ease her, or sitting on the cart behind the vans. We had no trouble from highwaymen or the religious black-coated Methodists that could be nasty and even throw stones at players if they dared to appear on a Sunday.

The only bad thing that happened was at Redlake when Rom who'd had more ale than he should, took on a match with the local wrestler who was a huge fellow with tremendous arms and stomach. He was called 'Danny the Demon Giant', and Rom angered him by giving a punch in a tender place. This wasn't allowed, and there was a nasty fight between them that ended in Rom being knocked to the ground unconscious. I was terrified he was dead. But the next day he'd recovered except for a swollen black eye and a sprained leg. After that Dick said if Rom visited kiddleywinks in the day time he'd be kicked out of the show.

Sometimes I wondered who had the more power — Mr Goodfellow or Dick. When I asked Fanny she said, "Barney, o' course. It's *his* circus. But then Mr Loraine's got the — you-know-what — " and she rubbed her finger and thumb together meaningfully, " — the gold in his pocket. Rich he is, an' when you're rich like him folks is out to please 'em. Nat'rully."

I supposed she was right, and once more my mind turned to the future when somehow or other I'd have gold too; enough of it to flaunt before the proud noses of the Tremellicks at Boscarne the folk that had treated Uter so cruelly — and tell them just what I thought. Perhaps it wasn't quite fair to judge them *all* so harshly. The old squire could easily be dead now, but I'd heard that the whole family had a bad name as tyrants and oppressors of the poor. It was only right that they should suffer a bit too.

Deep, deep down behind all thoughts of revenge I knew there wasn't *much*, practically, that I could do. But to be rich! — yes, being rich mattered; as Fanny had pointed out, money meant power; and when you had power there were so many chances and ways of using it. So many opportunities for doing good or evil, and for levelling the differences between the wealthy and poverty-stricken hard-working people like Uter and Joanna had been. And for other things too. For being beautiful — having lovely shining gowns like the girl I'd seen dancing along the terrace in the moonlight that evening at Boscarne. I'd never forgotten, and never would — the way the young gallant had drawn her into his arms. Oh! — if that could only happen to Dick and me as usual my trend of thoughts inevitably ended in dreams and longing for Dick. And now — quite soon, he was going away, the circus would be disbanded until the early spring when we were all to meet up again at Redlake.

October passed into November, and at the end of the month the vans were taken to a builder's place near Penjust for storing, and the company split up. Fanny travelled upcountry to be with her brother and his wife who lived on a barge. It was a fine big boat, she said, and carried coal and other cargo for various business companies who hired them. They travelled by rivers and canals all the year round, from Wales to the West Country and back. "A splendid life it was, she boasted, and she'd half a mind to join up with them for good instead of sitting padded up like a balloon for folk to grin and jeer at. I didn't believe her, though. She was fond of the circus people, and earned quite a good salary from being on show.

Where Mr Tobias went I didn't know; but Pom-Pom the clown had been taken on at an Exeter theatre for a month of pantomime in December, and Mylora was going to stay with her step-sister in Plymouth who ran a tea-shop. Rom was paid a sum by Dick to take the horses to a farm in Devon where he'd also have a job as cattleman. Mr Goodfellow himself was going to take charge of Bimbo Bear, the monkey, Muncher, and the singing dog.

One by one they all went until only Dick and I were left, and that was not for long. The same evening he took me to the inn at Truro — The Golden Cow — where I was to help with the domestic work, for my food and lodgings, and with a little payment as well. Delilah had already been stabled there by Rom before he took off with the horses.

Oh, it was a strange, exciting, half-sad time, because I couldn't be sure when I'd see Dick again, and although he kissed me on the cheek when he left me standing at the door with Mrs Geeke, it wasn't the kiss I'd wanted and I knew he didn't understand one bit how I felt, or how the deep newly-aroused woman-feeling in me longed so passionately for a sign from him that he'd be looking forward to the spring when we could be together once more.

All he said before turning and walking smartly to the wagon was, "Be a good girl, nymph, and keep that wild little temper of yours under control. We'll meet again." And he was gone.

But would we? *Would* we? How could anyone tell? So many things could happen in the months ahead.

Mrs Geeke was a pink-faced, comely, kind woman. She seemed to sense my reluctance, putting it down to shyness.

"Don't be afraid, child," she said. "We're going to be good friends, you an' me. I'm sure you're goin' to be a great help to me."

I *did* try, although it was strange having to wear aprons and say 'yes surr' and 'no madam' and more polite little remarks like that to any fine lady or gentleman who arrived at the inn. The

Golden Cow was an old building where once, I was told, Queen Elizabeth had slept. The bedroom was a very special one, and it was one of my duties to see that the quilt was always tidy on the great four-poster bed, and that no speck of dust was left on the floor or furniture. I helped Connie, the kitchenmaid, peel the vegetables too, and was only allowed in the hotel side of the inn, never in the bar. Oh, my life was busy, and I had good food, and was even given a new blue dress and mob cap to wear. There was nothing I could complain about except missing Dick.

In my spare time I went walking towards the moors, and sometimes took Delilah. She had a small field to nibble in next to the inn, but I'm sure, like me, she felt the grass of the moorlands smelt sweeter, and the damp earth had a fresher scent.

When I had my free half day and it was fine, we'd climb a bit of a hill and stare over the landscape into the distance where the view stretched lonely and hazed with thin mist to the west. I'd remember the wilder places then: the narrow lanes curving seawards that had been hushed and still and thick with foxgloves, bluebells, and tall, curling bracken in the summertime; the small grey farmsteads huddled in valleys, and the pumping rods of mine stacks moving against the sky; the ancient dolmens crowning the rugged heights bordering the wild north coast, and the Celtic crosses tangled with briars and gorse standing like guardians of the past at crossroads, or in unexpected places. Oh, it was all so wild and sweet remembering — almost as overpowering, as my passionate longing for Dick.

Not that I was unhappy in any way at The Golden Cow. It was just that living was something to be got through rather than enjoyed; only half of me there, in Truro. The other half was away in a dream wandering and jogging down secret byways, pitching tents for a night or two, then moving on again with the circus people to different places, where we did our acts never knowing quite what could happen next, or when Mr Goodfellow would think up some fresh turn for Tobias and Delilah, or for Mylora, Pom-Pom, and of course Rom.

I wondered a lot about Mylora, because I knew she and Dick were friendly, and it made me a bit jealous, I couldn't help it. He'd told me about a picture of her he'd done called 'The Dancer', which would have a place of honour in his new exhibition in London because it had won an award and had already been purchased by a rich American for a lot of money.

I'd wished so much the painting had been of me, and that my hair had been lustrous black like Mylora's. Once I'd borrowed a pair of earrings from Fanny — she'd pierced my ears for me the day before, unknown to Dick, and put little gold things in to keep the holes open. I'd given one yell and she'd shaken me, saying, "Shut up, girl, or you'll have us both in trouble." The next day I'd taken the tiny rings out and put Fanny's dangling gold ones in. There was a mirror in the van. One look at myself had told me that I did, indeed, look much more grown-up, though not really like Mylora. My face was the elfin kind, Rom had once said, adding, "Don't you go spoiling it with paint and powder or those silly gee-gaws tarts wear. You're fine as you are, and just you remember.

"What about Mylora?" I'd asked pertly. "She wears lots of bracelets and rings, and things in her ears."

"Mylora's different."

Yes, Mylora *was* 'different', I'd thought enviously. She knew how to get a man to desire her, and have her portrait painted by Dick who'd got it into the Academy. He'd *said* he'd paint me, 'Undine' it would be called, but I didn't know anything about Undine. Would she wear earrings? Or was she just a child? Someone very young who'd have to look good and sweet in a white dress? I wasn't *really* the good and sweet kind. My hair, though light tawny-gold, was long and silky, and my eyes were green. Funny! — until the day I'd put Fanny's long gold earrings on, I'd never noticed how truly green they were, or how they slanted upwards under darker flyaway brows. I'd twisted my head this way and that, feeling in an odd way quite vain and proud of myself. But when Dick had seen me later he'd said, "What the devil have you been doing to yourself?

Take those tawdry things off at once, or I'll do it myself, and give you a good walloping into the bargain."

I'd stared at him defiantly for a moment or two, disappointment and rage seething in me. Then suddenly and mutely, I'd pulled the rings out, thrown them into his face, and rushed away down the slope towards the sea. I'd crouched by a great boulder hidden by heather and undergrowth, half fearing, half hoping, that Dick would find me. I wouldn't have minded being walloped — not really — by Dick. But I *would* have hated him to see the tears spilling from my eyes all over my cheeks. I was so disappointed and ashamed because he'd once more succeeded in making me feel like a naughty child.

He hadn't come though, and next time I saw him, *without* the jingly earrings, he didn't say anything, just acted as though nothing had happened, which made things, if possible, even more humiliating.

Remembering such incidents brought the past very close during those long winter months, and increased my longing for spring when the troupe all came together again, with Barney Goodfellow in charge, but Dick taking command when he felt like it, because of the means he had of supporting the circus and helping to pay any debts that arose, should trade become bad.

I still had some of the money given to me by Farmer Breague when I'd first set off from the smallholding with Delilah following Joanna's death, added to which were the wages paid by Mrs Geeke. The brooch, too — the precious relic found pinning my shawl when I was a baby — was always somewhere about my person. Once, when there'd been a shindy between an Irishman and a Cornish miner after a fair at Zaul, a drunken man had lurched forward, grasped me and pulled up my skirts revealing my red woollen petticoat. But he hadn't discovered the wallet. I'd bitten his hand hard; he'd yelled and tumbled down. I'd run away, and luckily Dick had appeared.

"You shouldn't wander off alone," he'd said, "or get talking to strange men. You haven't yet learned a mite of sense about some things, have you? — In spite of all your braggardly talk about being grown-up. Why — any decent servant girl would know better than to get involved in a brawl of that kind."

"It wasn't my fault, and I wasn't involved," I had told him sharply, "and no harm was done anyway. I bit him hard."

"Good," Dick had exclaimed, and I'd fancied there was a twitch of amusement about his lips. "But just see you're more careful in future."

We'd walked away from the scene together, with no further conversation between us. It had often been like that — he'd slip into silence, some other world, of thoughts unknown to me, dealing I guessed more with his sophisticated life in London and art, than with a travelling circus company needing his patronage. Perhaps even he could have been wondering about Mylora. I'd already learned to accept that he admired her in a funny kind of way, perhaps even desirously. I didn't *want* to believe that; the very idea was a torment. I was fiercely jealous, and day by day did my best to appear more beautiful and adult.

4

I WAS fifteen, almost sixteen, and still with the troupe when an occasion arose that was to change my whole life.

By then a new act had been evolved for me to dance partnered by Rom in a colourful, wild semi-acrobatic scene wearing a very short frilly Columbine kind of dress, with my partner looking spectacular as Harlequin in multi-coloured patched attire and a black mask. I had grown inches taller during the past two years, and had filled out, Dick said, in all the right places — no one could take me for a child any more. My shape was still slender, and my breasts, though not so voluptuous as Mylora's, were firm and uptilted and looked enticing enough, I hoped, in the tight satin bodice.

Dancing came naturally to me, as it did to Rom. When I performed before audiences I forgot about the canvas tent and that I was doing it to put money into Mr Goodfellow's pocket — I danced to the wind and rain and high moors outside the tent, imagining the sky overhead, and the gulls rising and dipping again to the heather. My tawny hair would be flying and my feet have wings. Oh, I loved the feel of it — the swing and rhythm and magic of movement of letting my senses and imagination blend in a wonderful output of feeling and emotional response.

I was aware also that Dick at that time was beginning to admire me more. He no longer chided or treated me so much as a child, and I was allowing myself to feel that in the end he'd forget all about Mylora and take me as I wanted him to take me — in passion and love.

Mylora was jealous, of course. She pretended not to be, and hadn't yet any cause, because Dick still painted her, and I couldn't help knowing by then that they spent long hours together during the spring and summer evenings, and everyone seemed to accept them as a kind of team. All the same his blue eyes would frequently stray from hers where they were together, to mine, lingering in a watchful warm way that set my pulses dancing and leaping in my blood.

It was in Maytime that Dick started his first real painting of me. It had to be done in odd half hours and any extra leisure moments we had because we were busy working new turns into the programme just then, and everyone seemed rather at 'sixes and sevens', as Fanny put it. Fanny was talking of retiring from the circus, at the end of the year, and going to live permanently on the barge. Mr Goodfellow was already looking for another fat woman but in the meantime took on another dwarf, smaller even than Mr Tobias, a tiny lady midget called Princess Titania who was only two feet high, but perfectly formed, with yellow curls and her own wardrobe of silk and satin dresses, and minute rings and bracelets for her dimpled tiny hands. She was much sought after by show people, and Barney had to pay her more than the rest of us just to make an appearance and double that for taking on my scene with Tobias as her newly wedded husband.

Delilah was dispersed with for the act,

and Pom-Pom brought in. The clown had a knockabout scene with Tobias and in the end captured the bride and put her in his baggy pocket with only her tiny yellow head sticking out. At first Princess Titania protested. She thought it undignified, until Rom as a young gallant came in and rescued her and put her on a tiny throne where she was crowned as the most beautiful Midget Queen in the World.

Oh, there were so many things going on then, and although I enjoyed the excitement of it all, it was wonderful having moments alone with Dick at secret places on the moor, where he sat on some available boulder with his brushes and paints ready to 'capture me forever' he said on canvas. I wore a long green skirt at such times, and had my hair all loose and flowing. I thought he was going to picture me as Undine, by a pool. But for some reason or other he'd changed his mind.

"Later," he'd said, "if I feel like it. At the moment you're just nymph."

I'd shrugged and pouted. "But you've *always* called me that. It should be something else now. Soon I'll be sixteen."

"That's the point," Dick had said abruptly.

"What do you mean?"

"Nymphs aren't children. As you well know — hussy. And don't look at me like that from those wicked green eyes of yours."

"What do you mean 'wicked'?"

"Shut up," he said quite rudely, "or I'll — "

"What? What will you do?"

"Kiss or beat you, one or the other, I don't know. Or maybe I'll pack up and take off. Models aren't supposed to talk. Understand? And that's what you are; just my model. So don't forget it."

Realising I was somehow upsetting him, and secretly gratified by my power to do it, I settled into the position he wanted, with my head half-turned to one side, presumably staring at a clump of wild white cherry blossom. The sky had been misty blue that day shot with pale silver light from the sun. Everywhere was windless and hushed. We could have been the only two people in the world. In the distance faint sounds came from

71

the circus folk beyond the high lane, but that was all except for the crying of a gull and sudden full-throated chortle of song from a blackbird nearby. Boulders between clumps of gorse and heather glittered with dew; a few yards away an ancient menhir stood as relic and guardian of the distant past when the first small dark Celts trod the wilds of Cornwall.

A tremor of excitement and primitive joy shook me. Hardly knowing what I was doing, I moved towards Dick, and on my knees stared up at him smiling.

"Oh, Dick," I said, "Oh, Dick, please — "

I didn't say 'kiss me', but he laid his brush down, paused a moment with a queer penetrating look in his eyes. Then his two arms came out, and my head was forced back. His mouth was on mine, hard, and one hand was trembling as it travelled from the back of my skull down my shoulders to the soft flesh where my breasts pricked, with a longing I'd never felt before. My whole body seemed alight and yearned towards him.

Then suddenly, it was over. He

pushed me away, got up quickly, and his expression, though stern, was kind of sorrowful, too. He shook his head.

"You shouldn't have done that, nymph."

"But I — I — " I felt so humiliated the proper words wouldn't come.

He pulled himself together. "I know, I know. Forget it — it was my own fault."

"But why? Was it wrong then? Didn't you — don't you *like* me?"

"*Like?*" he suddenly looked much older. "Oh, Sari. Is it possible anyone could be so naive as you? — And provocative, damn you."

The unexpected anger in the last few words shocked me into apologising weakly. "I'm sorry — I didn't know — I didn't want to annoy you."

"Then in future when and *if* we have any more painting sessions, we'll keep strictly to business shall we, and no more girlish tricks."

He started to pack up his things.

"It wasn't a trick," I told him miserably. "Perhaps I was silly, but I truly thought you — I — "

73

"Cared for each other?" he finished for me more gently. "So we do — But when you're grown up a bit more you'll realise there are many different ways of caring. Come now. Forget it." He passed me a handkerchief. "Dry your eyes, nymph. Methinks I catch the glint of tears ready to sprinkle thy lovely cheeks."

He was smiling hopefully, quoting something from a play in the manner of a true actor. I tried to match his mood, and presently felt better.

We walked back amicably to the vans together, although an awkward silence remained. 'Never mind,' I told myself, 'tomorrow it will be different. And when next he throws me an admiring glance or wants to be appreciative I'll be nice to him, of course, but distant walk away perhaps in a casual manner, with a shrug of my shoulders like Mylora.'

I was careful after that incident to be on my most dignified behaviour when Dick was around, and to give him no further chance of snubbing me like a child. I'm sure he noticed. Sometimes in a spare moment I'd catch his eye on me, holding a puzzled calculating look which showed he was still interested in me. 'Interested'; — what a stupid word, when I knew, however he acted now that he'd wanted me that day in the heather when he'd kissed me. Then why couldn't he be honest, as I had been with him? Perhaps he had a wife somewhere tucked away, although I felt instinctively he hadn't. Or was he in some way pledged to Mylora? Oh, there were so many questions to which I had no way of finding any answers. So many 'ifs' and "perhapses', that in the end I stopped ruminating, and concentrated more on my dancing act with Rom.

It was in mid-June that it happened — the unexpected event that was so drastically to alter the course of my future. June was a lovely month that year. At the end of May it had rained; but when the clouds cleared everything suddenly sprang to new life again, lush and verdant. The ferns and flowers of hedgerows pushed properly through greenery bordering the winding lanes, birds trilled, the sturdy spears of valerian and foxgloves took on a richer glow and the moors stretched deep purple sprinkled with the flame of gorse under newly washed skies.

I slept in the open then, enjoying the fresh air pungent with the mingled scents of earth and growing things. Sometimes a fox barked, and Delilah, lying near to me, would lift her head lazily in the quiet starlight then lower it quietly to sleep again.

There were occasions when Rom was restless and flung himself down a few yards away. Once he rolled over and touched my hand then kissed me gently on the cheek. It was kind of nice, after Dick's rebuffs, and I wondered what it would be like to let Rom love me; he was young and strong and nice to look at, and we had fun together. We could laugh. But I knew my heart wouldn't be in it — it wouldn't work, because I didn't love him. It was only Dick who mattered in such a way, and I sensed that Rom was secretly aware of it, because he never tried to force himself on me or appear in any way serious.

One day Mr Goodfellow got a message from Boscarne asking if the troupe would please the Squire by appearing for an evening in the grounds of the Big House. We had already been at Skillan for three days and were due to travel westwards the following afternoon to a summer fair near Redlake. But Barney told us we could well afford to spend a few hours at Master Tremellick's. He'd promised splendid payment, and it was an honour to have been asked.

"The dancers 'specially he wants," he told us, with a meaningful glance at Rom and me. "He saw the act yesterday apparently, and was impressed. Good girl!" he nodded approvingly in my direction. "Y'r doing well."

If he'd known the sudden rush of power and exhilaration — not entirely well meaning — that filled me then, he might not have considered me so good. This was my chance, I thought; my chance of getting a foot into the Big House, of finding a way somehow of avenging myself for Uter's sad death — or at least of proving in some manner that folk of humbler origin than that haughty family had arts of a certain kind denied to them. Oh, I didn't exactly know what my plans were — only that it would be a fine thing to parade before them, having them awed into wonderment by my achievement. I think, deep inside me, I was still remembering the girl in the white dress with the young gallant's arm round her on the terrace.

So I told Rom he must be specially good in our act together the following night. Perhaps my eyes were greener than usual, my cheeks more vividly flushed, I don't know. But something must have shown, because Rom said, "What's the idea, Sari? Got your eye on some lord or other? Wanting a rich man to bed you — is that it?"

"Hold your tongue," I snapped quite rudely. "Shut up. You're just stupid, *silly*."

"Oh, yes," he replied, still teasing me. "I'm that, all right. But don't think I haven't noticed."

"*What?*"

"The way you look at Dick when you think no one's seeing. You've bitten the apple, haven't you — and so far it's been sour. Never mind, love, there's plenty more of a sweeter kind."

For fear of losing my temper too

fiercely, I checked the hot words on my lips and walked away with my head in the air, hearing Rom laughing mischievously as I went. I wished Dick was near at hand, then maybe the vengeful thoughts in me wouldn't have been so intense. But he was away for a week — something to do with his painting, and wouldn't be back until days following the show at Boscarne. A pity. I'd have liked him to see that I well knew how to act before so-called gentry. And in another particular way too, his presence could have made quite a difference to what followed.

The great house, which had originally been built in Tudor times, was E-shaped, with enormous bay windows projecting at each side from both wings. During the course of years parts of the building had been replaced, modernised to a later period, but most of the square-topped chimneys remained; the drive led straight between clipped yews and lawns to the front of the Hall, dividing in both directions along the front of the house to courts, and the back quarters.

At a later era probably Georgian — a terrace had been built from wing to wing, with steps cutting immediately centre to the imposing porch. The roof which had been restored at some earlier era had been given small towers poking at odd angles in a confusing manner reminiscent of the Gothic style which nevertheless added an air of fantasy that I found enchanting, despite the grudge I bore to its inheritors.

It rained on the evening of the troupe's performance — thin rain that drove in a shroud of grey across the moors as vans and wagons made their creaking way along the rough lanes leading over the high ridges towards the valley. Candles and lamps were already twinkling from the mullioned windows when we approached the big house, and streams of golden light filtered from the open door, casting long shadowed shapes from bushes and trees across the velvet lawns.

Later, probably, the mist would lift, and the clouds clear. Already the dim blurr of a climbing watery moon was struggling wanly over the horizon. The air was chill; in my thin gauzy Columbine dress, despite the blue cloak I wore over it, I shivered. Rom, who was sitting next to me, put an arm round my waist, and whispered, "What's the matter, love? Not frit, are you?"

Abruptly I sat up straight, and pushed his hand away. "Of course not. What's there to be afraid of?"

"Hm! well, we don't know, do we? Mebbe the Lord of the Manor'll tek a fancy to you, an' carry you to his bed. On the other hand, mebbe he'll fall to his knees and beg you to wed him. We can't tell, can we? You look real beautiful tonight. Know that, sweeting?"

"Oh don't be silly, Rom," I replied. "And don't push, you'll knock my wreath off."

I put a hand to my head impetuously where the light crown of artificial flowers was held by wire and pins over my knot of silky hair. I'd wanted to wear it loose, but Fanny and Mylora wouldn't have it. Mylora had been quite contemptuous.

"You'd look any cheap little tart showing off," she said. "It's dignity you need. Why do you want that mane of yours flying everywhere? You've a lot to learn, and that's a fact."

Mrs Petra agreed, but I thought to myself of Mylora — "I know you. You're jealous of my hair. It was the same the first time when Dick was going to paint me. You wanted my hair screwed away under a cap.

Still, I didn't argue, knowing that if it came to quarrelling Barney Goodfellow would support Mylora and Fanny. Anyway, I guessed it would be quite easy during the dance to loosen my locks so I could be free and wild in movement, feeling and being my own true self. As the company and vans came to a halt near the stables and large court at the back I'd almost forgotten my hostility to the Tremellicks, so excited was I.

Because the master of the house had been especially entranced with the dancing act when he'd watched unknown to us the performance at Skillan, it had been arranged for Rom and myself to appear twice during the showing at Boscarne. Once near the beginning, then at the very conclusion of the event.

A room had been allotted to us at the

back of the house for changing, and for the assembling of any necessary props. The night before we'd had to devise a new turn for Fanny and the two midgets. Delilah and the horses had had to be dispensed with on this special occasion, but Bimbo had been brought to fill in the gaps, also Mr Tobias, who'd been cajoled into doing a number of comical conjuring turns which included the singing dog. Hours had been spent thinking up new tricks and the whole of the morning after had been taken up in rehearsing.

"I hope it's worth it," Mylora had commented rather sourly.

I knew she was annoyed and disappointed when Barney suggested her sole contribution to the performance should be a public display as a fortune teller with a crystal ball and pack of cards. "Who'll be there to want their fortune told?" she'd complained. "*Servants?* Or is there a house party on perhaps?"

"Oh, that's for sure," Mr Goodfellow had replied. "And you'll be bedecked out all beautiful like an Egyptian Queen. In fact, you shall have an announcement from me personally — 'Wonderful

Mylora, Queen of Magic and the Mystic Powers.' How's that, eh?"

Mylora had become slightly mollified, and when she was dressed up in sparkling scarlet and purple silk, with a gauze veil over her black hair encircled on her forehead by a silver band, and long gold earrings dangling from her ears, she did look quite spectacular.

Memories now of this first contact with Boscarne are confused and somehow a little unreal, although despite the hurry of adjusting make-up, pirouetting a little, and the chatter of the troupe making a last quick rehearsal of their lines as they powdered cheeks, pushed, swore, and jostled each other, a few highlights register clearly still in my mind.

The great hall, for instance.

It was very large — large as an immense room, and entered by guests immediately through the front door; at one end was the beautiful bay overlooking the grounds — at the other a door leading to a smaller passage from which an immense spiralled stone staircase wound upwards to the large gallery and numerous bedrooms. I wasn't aware of any detailed architecture of course that first night — The company was ushered into the house from the courtyard at the back. What fascinated me and took my breath away was the exquisite modelling of plasterwork, thrown into brilliant relief from the candlelight of numerous crystal chandeliers and side lamps. Goddesses, cherubs, nymphs, satyrs and unicorns were depicted on the ceiling of the great interior known by the household as 'the Hall' or the 'big parlour'. The walls were covered by wooden panelling carved with fantastic designs. At the far end of the room a kind of dais ran the whole length of the interior in a direct line with the entrance to the smaller passage and stairs. This 'stage', I gathered, was where musicians and occasional players gave their performances.

I couldn't help thinking after a bemused glance round how wonderful it must be to own such a magnificient place which seemed to be more like a palace or castle than a dwelling for merely a rich family. I was standing at a small side door opposite the one leading to the passage and staircase, waiting for

Mr Tobias to leave the stage following the opening turn with Mylora's monkey on his shoulder.

My heart was beating uncomfortably quickly against my ribs. I hated waiting, and wished Rom would hurry up and join me. He wouldn't be late, would he? Oh, surely not. It would be terrible having to appear alone before such a crowd of gentry. There must have been forty or fifty guests seated on chairs and benches in front of the dais, and behind them a number of servants. I'd heard the rattle of carriage wheels along the drive and caught glimpses through curtains of richly coloured gowns silks, satins and velvet cloaks, with the quiver of expensive jewellery when a flicker of light caught them.

Ospreys curled from elaborate coiffures the men too were fashionably and extravagantly clad in velvet-collared coats, embroidered waistcoats, frilly white neckcloths, and breeches of an elegant cut — It was only afterwards, of course, that I recalled such details; at the time, during those few moments of wonderment and excited anticipation, I was conscious merely of the extreme luxury, and heavy perfume cloying the warm air. Someone was playing a fiddle from the other side of the dais, just out of sight. I guessed it was Pom-Pom, who fancied himself as a bit of a musician and had brought his instrument along to accompany the singing dog, and my turn with Rom.

Rom! — oh, why didn't he appear? I stopped jigging my toes for a moment and took a deep breath. Someone touched me on the shoulder.

"Are you nervous?" a man's voice said. "There's no need to be."

Startled, I turned, and lifted my head. The face looking down on me was thin, youngish, with a high-bridged nose and a strong cleft chin. His eyes were brilliantly dark under heavy brows. I'd never seen him before, but in an instant I knew. He was the owner of Boscarne he must be. The one person in the world I had come to detest, and whom I'd childishly vowed to revenge myself upon for Uter's untimely death. His elegantly cut coat of a yellow-brown shade had the sheen of heavy satin. He was clean-shaven, except for thick sideburns; crisp dark curls waved back from a wide forehead — his whole air obviously was of one used to ruling his domain — proud, dominating, yet at the same time reserved as though holding himself apart inwardly from the fashionable throng. Not exactly handsome, I told myself critically. The mouth, though well formed, was somehow aggressive, the features a trifle too blunt. Challenging; yes, that was an apt description, and if I was correct concerning his identity I knew it would be no easy task in any way to humiliate him.

It was strange how speedily the thoughts flashed through my mind, and odd, too, that no anger stirred in me during that short time — only a sense of mounting exhilaration in having come face to face at last with an opponent I'd hated since childhood.

"Well?" I heard him query. "Are you dumb, girl?"

I pulled myself together.

"No, sir, and I'm not frightened either. That's what you wanted to know, isn't it? I'm just — just — "

"Yes?"

88

I swallowed, feeling the warm colour flood my face, and trying wildly to stop it. It would be dreadful if I became too hot and started perspiring before the dance properly started. The kohl might spread from my eyes to my cheeks which must already be pink. So I said on the spur of the moment, "I'm thirsty, sir — master, master — ?" I broke off with the question.

"Tremellick," he told me, shortly.

So I was right. "Thank you, Mr Tremellick, sir. I'm thirsty, I'd like a — "

"Glass of wine?"

I shook my head.

"Rom will be here any moment, and it will be time for our dance. But if I could have a glass of water it would be nice."

All pretence of dignity had slipped from me. I was aware of speaking childishly, but my one desire just then was to get him out of the way so I could compose myself and concentrate only on my act.

"Certainly," came the answer. He disappeared for a second or two, and the next minute a maidservant came scurrying to my side carrying a crystal goblet of sparkling water. I accepted it gratefully, but had only time to take a sip before Rom arrived, looking wickedly handsome in his Harlequin mask and multi-coloured garment.

A minute afterwards, following Tobias's exit with the monkey seated on his head, Rom and I had taken the centre of the stage, and to the sounds of pipe and fiddle were dancing.

Oh, how I danced that night — triumphantly, with abandon, ignoring any controlled steps of the conventional Columbine, but as flowers danced to the wild Cornish winds of the moors, freely, with an exultance to which Rom responded, becoming for that brief time both partner and lover — spirits of nature belonging only to ourselves and the elemental urges of sea, flying clouds, earth and sky, all the thrusting ungovernable whims and forces of nature.

I knew I was good that evening, and through my daze of delight was aware of Rom's brilliant eyes flashing and the gleam of his teeth, the beauty and rhythm of his lithe body that made him momentarily a god, rather than man. Forgotten was the sophisticated audience of fashion and wealth, of well-fed pampered women and scented snuff-taking men. None of it registered, except at one point, a hazy recollection of hard, strongly carved watchful features impelling me to an even wilder display of emotion.

When it was over there was a short pause followed by thunderous applause. My heart was pounding under my satin bodice, but I managed breathlessly, to bow and mutter, "Thank you — you — " while Rom, holding my hand, did the same.

"Encore!" someone shouted. "Encore, mademoiselle."

But I had neither the energy, nor wish, to comply, and after another little gesture, more of a curtsey this time, fled from the dais to the sanctuary of the anteroom, where I half-collapsed on a bench.

"There'll be no holding you down after that," Mylora remarked as I pulled off my dancing shoes, "I admit I'm quite envious."

This was an admission from her I'd never expected to hear. I looked up at her, and was puzzled by the thoughtful, questioning look in her dark eyes. "Where did you learn the tricks?" she asked bluntly.

"Tricks?"

"The seductive part — movement, the gestures."

I shrugged. "Nowhere. It's just — I dance as I feel. Even when I was little — " I broke off. There was something still subtly hostile about Mylora that cautioned me to keep the secrets of my childhood my own. Even if I'd tried to explain to her, how, when I was a small girl, before Uter had been sent to Van Diemen's Land — I'd skipped and run before him as we wandered along the pale sands, breaking into a dance with my toes wet, where the frothy waves ebbed and flowed in curling ripples of foam, she wouldn't understand.

Or was she wiser than I imagined? — did she guess for instance one tiny bit of the happiness I felt when I was with Dick? I'd have liked to confide in her, but there was no trust between us, and I knew she felt she had a proprietary claim on Dick's attentions.

"When you were little? Yes? What about it?" Mylora continued. "What were you going to say?"

"Oh nothing. I forget now. Nothing important."

Mylora laughed shortly. "There's something sly about you, Sari. Ever since your arrival on that donkey I've had a feeling you've told none of us the real truth about yourself."

"There's nothing to tell," I answered. "Except about Uter being sent away."

She turned her back on me and started to comb her thick hair from her face. I knew she didn't believe me, and it occurred to me at that point that there *were* things in my life no-one knew about including myself. I'd no idea who my real parents were where the ship had sailed from that had thrown me up on the wild Cornish beach those years before, or for where it was bound. The only clue I had was the strange, rather grotesque little brooch that I still wore — only as a pendant now, threaded on a cord so it could hang from my neck safely hidden under my clothes, resting in the soft hollow between my breasts. I'd taken it off for my Columbine dance, of course, and put it in the pochette I wore round my waist with my few precious guineas in it. I'd have trusted it nowhere else.

Remembering it suddenly, I went to a shadowed corner of the room, and unfastened the tiny wallet, opened it and looked inside. The brooch wasn't there. The guineas were safe, but my precious memento was gone. Someone must have taken it; someone — but how *could* they, when it had been securely fastened on my person?

I rushed from the changing room, through the small hall past the winding staircase, making my way speedily and carelessly to the Great Hall itself. Most of the guests — except for the few who were staying for the night, had left; the rest were either in the powder closet or the drawing room — Servants were starting to clear up. I bumped into a footman, hastily apologised, and then — it happened. Suddenly a tall, broadly-built form loomed before me — that of a man clad in a golden-brown jacket, with fiery eyes staring down on me from an imperious face. Master Tremellick.

I stopped sharply, breathless and confused.

"I'm sorry. I — I didn't see you. But I was in a hurry. You see, I — I — "

"Yes?"

"I've lost something. My brooch. I thought it was in my pochette, but it isn't."

"And where do you keep your pochette?"

I blushed.

"Round my waist. Because it's safer. At least I thought so."

"Oh! but then you should be *certain*, shouldn't you? Precious things should be put at no risk at all. Perhaps there was a hole in the purse. If so, any tiny object might drop through it under certain circumstances. During a particularly energetic dance, for instance?" I fancied there was a hint of humour in his voice — a twinkle at the corners of his eyes. But why should he be amused? He was treating me as a child, like the others did, like Dick.

"I stiffened and said with what I hoped

95

was a certain dignity, "Do you mind if I go to the stage and have a search, sir?"

He laughed then.

"There's no need. Here it is, I think, your brooch, and very interesting too. It was found by a servant and handed to me."

He uncurled his fist and there it lay. Relief filled me, but I was also bewildered. A hand rested on my shoulder briefly, while he emphasised again. "I do advise you to examine your purse — pochette — whatever it is. Another time you might not be so lucky in retrieving your little relic. By the way, young lady — " He paused, staring at me thoughtfully as though wondering what to say next.

"Yes, sir?"

He tore his eyes from mine. "I enjoyed your dancing immensely. So did the Vicomtesse."

"Vicomtesse."

"She's a very old lady a relative, and was seated in her special chair which had been taken to a bend in the staircase to watch. From there it's possible to have a fairly good view of what's going on below. She was much impressed."

"Thank you."

"If ever you get wearied of travelling about the countryside," he said in polite, practical tones, "I'm quite sure you could be found a position here. Lady Le Villemont, my old relative, is frequently lonely and at times can be difficult when she's bored. A little youthful company would be good for her — and the whole household, for that matter. If you care to consider the proposition and let me know — "

"Oh *thank* you," I interrupted quickly. "It's kind of you, but I'm happy with the circus and there's Delilah, you see, my donkey, and — " I nearly added Dick, but had the sense and was quick enough not to mention personalities.

He nodded gravely. "I quite understand. It is just a thought, but as you are quite content we'll say nothing further. However, do remember the offer, and contact me if a time comes when you wish for a change."

I told him I would, and there the incident ended.

It was only the next day when the

troupe was on the road once more moving westward for our next destination at a fair near Frinkle that I chided myself for my weakened friendly attitude to the master of Boscarne. He had retrieved my brooch, true; and also offered me a post at the great mansion, the very name of which had previously stood for all I detested. But the grudge was still deep in me. In spite of the praises and politenesses afforded me, the position was the same; if ever I had the chance to damage in any way the reputation of the family responsible for so much misery of poor hard-working folk, I would do it to the best of my ability. Master Tremellick had got round me by flattery and elegant manners. I'd been temporarily bewildered and overawed by the glamour and richness of the surroundings, letting fancy and imagination overcome commonsense. Instead of thanking the owner so humbly for the restoration of my possession I should have been haughty and aloof, shown him his fine manners of speech carried no weight with me. I still disliked, even hated, all that he stood for. And in the future I must remember it, and keep the flame of anger still burning strongly in my mind and heart. This was a vow I'd made to myself when Uter died. To break it would prove I was a weakling willing to betray trust and love by succumbing to the power of wealth. I would never lower myself into becoming a mere puppet to the glib ways and bribery of folk like the Tremellicks. As for being a companion to some demanding old dowager wanting a slave to cater to her moods and needs — it was ludicrous, unthinkable.

I laughed and patted Delilah affectionately on her neck. "We'll never be slaves, Del dear," I said, "never, *never*, even if we ride these lanes for the rest of our lives."

I jumped off her back, to lead her up a sudden steep slope. The moorland breeze blew fresh against my face. All the scents of earth and summer growth were sweet in the air. Rom, who was walking by the van ahead of me, looked round and waited.

"What were you going on about, talking to the birds and bees?" he enquired. "An' what's that gleam in your eyes mean?"

I tossed my hair in the wind. "It means goodbye to all those fancy folk at the big house," I answered gaily. "Oh, Rom, I couldn't be one of them, for all the riches in the world."

Rom, taking a grass he was chewing from his mouth, said, "You seemed in fine feather last night anyways. An' the Lord o' the Manor or whatever he is, seemed t've taken quite a fancy to you."

"But he isn't a lord, is he? He's just a — a person. One who's got rich at the expense of other needy folk."

"You're an odd kind of girl and that's for sure," Rom told me, with an overt glance. "Quite political you sound sometimes, an' with an air about you I can't make out. Does it matter whether Master Tremellick's a lord or not?"

I looked away. "No, not really."

"He isn't though. I learned a bit o' history last night from one o' the servants — a groom. The old man, the owner of Boscarne, died about ten months ago, and this one's a nephew or something, cos Sir William wasn' married."

"Master Tremellick then — does he inherit the 'sir'?"

"I reckon so — or mebbe not. Sirs aren't lords, you know.

"Then why is the old lady, is she his grandmother? or what — ? called *Lady* Susannah?"

Rom looked surprised. "I didn't hear a thing 'bout an old lady."

"It's true," I affirmed. "*He* told me, the master — *Sir* whatever-his-name-is — Tremellick, when he found my brooch for me. I'd lost it, and someone had found it and given it to him."

"Hm — You're a deep one, Sari, havin' secret conversations with the gentry."

"It wasn't secret," I answered coldly. "I was very upset. And you haven't answered my question about the lady business."

"How do *I* know?" Rom exclaimed impatiently. "It's not my business to go foraging into family trees. She could be a ladyship in her own right I s'pose. Some of them are — a few. Anyway you'd better keep such learned questions for Mr Dick. Mr Goodfellow tells me

101

he's joining up with us again in another fortnight — "

Dick — *Dick*. My heart lurched, and jumped into life madly, bubbling and racing as though the whole world was singing. In a flash, for those first joyous moments after hearing the news, my curiosity and hostile feelings towards the Tremellicks vanished. Nothing registered for me but the memory of Dick's handsome blue-eyed face, of his voice teasing, laughing, and bullying me in turn — and of that one exciting incident when he'd betrayed his true feelings for me by kissing me.

Oh, I was in love, in love.

I really believed it, but in the month following much was to change, because of Mylora.

5

DICK, after all, didn't rejoin the circus troupe until mid-August, due to an unexpected important commission he'd received from a famous society beauty, Lady Vance-Carew. He sent the news to Barney in a letter, who casually told Fanny.

"Makes no difference," he said. "These new acts of ours are doing nicely, very nicely. Money's better than it was, and we've got to remember that it's a privilege having a man of Dick's fame with us at all. I reckon he's making the Goodfellow circus famous too, with all those paintings of his. Pictures of the countryside he's turned to as well, not only people. Says something about impression — " he screwed his eyes up to peer more closely at Dick's rather straggly handwriting, continuing, " — *istic!* that's the word. *Impressionistic.* I've never heard of it meself. A tree's a tree to my fancy, and a rock's a rock, call it what else you like.

103

Educated folks is different though," he chuckled. "What d'you say, old dear?"

Fanny, scowling slightly, glanced at Barney disapprovingly. It wasn't his habit to call her 'old dear', and her tremendous bulk felt momentarily affronted.

"It depends on what you call eddication," she announced. "If you mean the difference between folk who mix with uppity ladida speakin' people an' those like you'n me — yes you an *me*, Mr Goodfellow, I s'pose you're right. For myself — " she lifted her head, folding her enormous arms over her more-than-ample bosom " — for *myself* I consider ordinary everyday decent livin' folk such as ourselves every bit as good as those high-and-mighty ones living in Lunnon an' such places where they go in for art an' speakin' in riddles."

Barney gave a twist to his moustache, a habit of his. "Didn't know you had such knowledge in you, Fanny," he said. "I don't recall your mentionin' you knew anything about highclass society before."

"There are a lot of things I don't let on about myself, Mr Goodfellow, and that *you* don't know neither. It's right

104

we should all have our little secrets. Even young Sari's found that out."

"Sari? What's Sari got to do with it?"

"With what, Mr Goodfellow?"

Barney, red in the face, scratched one ear. "You're making a play on words, Mrs Petra. Being just obstinate. That's what you are — obstinate."

Fanny's mildly aggressive mood concerning the 'old girl' referenced quickly faded. "Oh, it ain't nothin'," she replied agreeably, "Tek no notice of me. Don't mean a bloomin' thing — except I was taken aback, affronted-like, at what you dubbed me just now, 'old girl'. I'm not so aged as all that, you know. And I have my vanities "spite o' my size."

"Sure, sure," Barney agreed. "And taken all in all we've got on splendid together during the years you've worked for me. But that girl — Sari. She's an asset to us. A real asset. You were implying she was hiding something, though. Not plotting to leave or anythin' is she? If so, it's your duty to say — confidentially, of course. Just what did you mean about her havin' secrets?"

"Don't you worry," Fanny said, "There

was nothing behind it — nothing at all, 'cept that none of us know 'xactly where she come from, or what she rightly is. Prob'ly she don't know nothing herself. But I tell you this — " She leaned forward confidently.

"Yes?"

"She's got an air, that girl. She'll get somewhere one day. Those green eyes of hers, and the way she carries on in front of the men! — 'Specially Master Dick! — you'd think she was aiming to make a real catch there. *Oh* yes." Fanny's voice swelled with self-satisfaction into a kind of boom that made me want to giggle. "An' another thing — Mylora's noticed too. Ask her."

Barney waved a hand as though he didn't believe a word. "Listenin' to women's prattle ain't my way. And for all I care the girl can bed or be bedded by any lusting male around, providing she stays with the troupe. So the sooner you stop putting wrong ideas into folks' heads, the better, s'far as I'm concerned."

Mrs Petra lifted her numerous chins, turned her back on Mr Goodfellow and waddled away, but not before a final thrust of "You watch her, Mr Goodfellow, you just watch, or you'll be sorry, and don't say I didn't warn you."

I hadn't *meant* to listen to the conversation in the beginning — it just happened. Fanny had thought she and Barney were quite alone sorting out props by the large waggon, and didn't know I was there quite near but hidden from them by a large clump of gorse, where I'd gone to have a few moments on my own thinking of Dick. The mention of his name had instantly made my ears prick, and I'd been all attention — so sharp my head rang. I may have missed a few things out, but written down I think I've got the conversation right. Nothing about it surprised me. I knew Mr Goodfellow wanted to keep me with his circus just as I knew how Mylora resented me, and was jealous.

I wasn't upset at all. In a funny way the gossip was flattering, and added to a sense of power developing in me, making me feel more of an adult, and a proper woman.

On the afternoon of Dick's return the

weather was sultry and mostly overhung by a thin veil of cloud. There was no sign of rain, but the air was thunderous, close. No one quite knew the day or hour of his arrival, but I'd been hopeful and watchful from time to time during all that week, restless with happiness and the exciting awareness that at any moment I might catch sight of his tall figure either walking or riding down over the rim of the hill towards St Rozzack where we were giving a show before moving on to St Clunack, a few miles away. St Clunack stood on the coast in a bay of the North Coast cut deep between two giant headlands with cottages clustered beneath massive granite cliffs. It had a long established fishing community — as well as two or three working copper and tin mines in the area. Artists were beginning to visit the area for long periods in the summertime, and Barney Goodfellow expected good audiences for the troupe there.

"That's the place where Dick'll appear," he said. "You just wait and see if I'm not right."

We didn't have to wait long. He

appeared the first evening when we'd just finished pitching camp on the rugged, jutting hill forming one arm of the bay. This was a favourite area for larger circuses than Goodfellows. Elephants had been there in the past, and the 'big top' — an immense tent providing coverage for spectacular animal acts had been erected on the grasslands forming the base of the hill. On the highest point was the relic — mostly ruined, of an ancient Celtic shrine, and a few miles out to sea a lighthouse stood to give warning of the savage Cragga Rocks where so many ships had foundered and mariners died.

Most of the troupe were resting a while following the energetic business of unpacking and getting props and things into order for the following day, but I didn't feel like resting. There was an adventurous kind of expectancy churning my heart, so I left the vans and waggons, and climbed round rocks and stunted undergrowth to a high point on the headland and took a long look toward the coastal road winding westwards from the small town. Fishermen were busy about the quay getting ready for a night at sea.

Some of the boats had already set out. It was the weather, I knew, when they could have a good catch. But I wasn't specially concerned about the fishing. All I could think of was Dick — Dick — as my eyes went searching through the yellowing light. Unconsciously, almost, I clutched the little emblem, the pendant, hanging against the warm skin under my cotton bodice, and I wished and *wished*.

Then, suddenly, I saw him. There was no mistaking Dick's strong form, even from such a considerable distance, as he appeared at the far end of the Wharf riding erectly astride his white mare, Ivory. With a little gasp of delight, I started racing and jumping down the slope, with skirts and hair flying, taking no notice of the shouts from the company as I passed.

"Dick," I cried when I reached the bottom. "Oh, Dick!" I was laughing with happiness. He reined, grinned, jumped from his horse and planted a kiss soundly on my right cheek.

"Hello, nymph. My goodness! you've grown, even in these few weeks. What's all the excitement about, eh? Got yourself a new admirer or something?"

The first question curiously flattened me. What a thing to ask, even in fun — when he must know how I felt.

"Don't be stupid," I said, somewhat truculently.

His expression sobered. He raised his brows in a wry, half-comical gesture. "Sorry, Sari. I was only teasing. It was your exuberance! — like a — "

"Child?" I queried, lifting my head proudly, and staring him straight in the face. His glance rested on my eyes first, then lowered to my curving up-tilted breasts and slender waist.

"No," he said seriously. "Child no longer."

"Then — ?" I waited hopefully, wondering if he'd kiss my lips, but he simply took my hand in one of his, and with the other leading Ivory by the bridle, started walking and chatting with me about what he'd been doing — the paintings, and galleries where his work was being shown, about how he'd missed the nomad life — that's what he called us, nomads — even during the short time he'd been away. I remember vaguely his reference to Lady Vance-Carew, and some remarks concerning a duchess who'd pretended to be interested in a work of his, but as it turned out was only trying to capture an up-and-coming famous painter for a husband.

"She was very rich," he said, "and had already had three matrimonial disasters. I'd no fancy, I can assure you, of being the fourth victim."

"I suppose all that money would've been a help to your your career?" I suggested slyly, anxious for his reaction.

He gave me a 'knowing' look.

"Most certainly. And maybe I was a fool not to get the ring on her finger and the money bags in my pocket, then blown her a kiss and said 'Goodbye madam, it's been fun knowing you'. But how could I with you on my mind, nymph?"

Although I knew he was teasing I could feel the tell-tale blush creeping to my cheeks most annoyingly.

"I don't believe I've been on your mind at all," I said pertly.

"Oh, but you have." My heart quickened. "You *all* have — " he added, spoiling everything again. "How's everyone, by the way? Mylora?"

Trying to keep my voice steady, showing no betrayal of my quick jealousy, I answered, "Mylora's all right. At least, I think so. We don't talk to each other much, though. She prefers Rom's company to mine."

Now why did I say that? I knew the next second it had been wrong. Dick's expression darkened. His voice was cool when he said, "Indeed! — well, she's her own mistress. We all have minds of our own, and that's something *you* should remember, Sari. Be yourself. Never care too deeply for anyone or you may land yourself in the hell of a muddle."

I didn't know who or what he was referring to, and why he should have spoken in such a manner at a time like that when I'd longed so much for us to be happy together.

Mylora, of course. He was thinking of Mylora; and at that moment I detested her.

So things didn't turn out as I'd wildly hoped and expected.

During the next few weeks it became clear to me that he and Mylora were even closer friends than they used to be. It was mostly on her side; I knew that. Whenever there was an opportunity she was lingering about somewhere near to him, although she was clever enough not to appear to be intruding.

I'd expected and hoped so much that he'd start on the promised portrait of me as Undine, once he was settled in his own caravan with his paints and canvasses ready. But instead he told me his first commitment was to do a painting of Mylora sitting on a great stone looking like a gypsy, with a baby in her arms. The baby, of course, would really be a doll, and Mylora would be holding it draped in a shawl. "I was asked to paint her that way as a favour by a wealthy patron in London," he explained. "It's to be titled 'Moorland Madonna' — The gentleman who ordered it was obviously impressed by her looks. Well — I suppose she's got something — a striking quality."

I couldn't help blurting out, "*You* are too, aren't you?"

"What?"

"Impressed. You think she's beautiful."

"Certainly," he agreed, impersonally,

almost coldly. "In her own way — which isn't yours, dear nymph," and his eyes changed, became almost amused.

"I know that," I said sharply. "I'm just — "

"Very lovely," he interrupted, "and will be more so when you're grown up — or rather more matured, I should say."

"Mature's a very dull word."

"Only to youth," he said, depressing me once more.

However, gloomy moods never lasted long with me, and I had a moment of triumph one day when Dick told me he'd been having vivid accounts of my success at Boscarne. "I just danced," I said indifferently, "with Rom."

"And charmed the Lord of the Manor into the bargain."

I didn't mention about being offered a post there as companion to old Lady whoever-she-was. I didn't want to talk about the family at all. After all — they were the ones responsible for Uter's tragic end, and the suffering and death of Joanna. I must never forget that — *never*. For a time I'd been under a spell at the great house, enchanted

115

by the wealth and elegance, the beauty of the vast rooms and hall and even by the courtesy of Master Tremellick. I'd enjoyed being admired, by the obvious appreciation of his glowing dark eyes. But afterwards, very gradually, I'd seen things in perspective again and myself for what I was — a kind of Cinderella leaving her fairy tale behind. Only in my case there'd be no Prince with a glass slipper kneeling at my feet — only a rekindling of the grudge I bore and a determination never in the future to think well of those in power who used it for wrong ends.

It would not be true to say that I consciously *hated* the Tremellicks any more. Hatred is too strong an emotion to foster forever, and inevitably, as time passed, my childlike sorrow and first wild grief had faded to acceptance, which is the way of life. Apart from that I was too deeply concerned with Dick to let anything interfere with our happy moments together. Yes, I *was* happy for much of that lovely summer. August passed into September, and Dick started on his painting of 'Undine'. I was pictured half kneeling, half lying, by a moorland tarn, resting on one elbow, with my hair loose, staring into the water. I was then sixteen — in my seventeenth year. Dick by that time had grown to realise it, which resulted often in long silences between us, free of the banter that had previously so irritated me. I was puzzled, but not disappointed, by his intense concentration in a work which he hoped would prove to be a masterpiece. He painted the background first in order, he told me, to catch the pool's light as it was at the time.

"We've only a few days to get your figure just as it is now," he told me, "with the sun dappling the water, and catching the pale stream of your hair. Once I have the essential effect I can carry on at the next place we visit. We'll find a convenient spot on the moors again — not exactly the same as this, of course — but imagination plays an important part in any worthwhile artistic creation."

He paused, staring at me with a thoughtful half-abstracted look in his blue eyes, "You don't understand one bit what I'm talking about, do you? And why the devil should you! What I'm trying to do is to capture the essentials of a certain mood — the transient beauty of nature — of a figure's grace and movement in a moment of time — so it will be there for ever. I think most artists feel that way. A search for the impossible; and, of course, that's what it is. How can anyone stop the clock, even for a second? You can revive a memory, but the memory at the best can only be an impression; whereas *you* are the reality, Sari."

He laid his brush down, moved towards me and kissed the top of my head. "Rest a bit now. Here I've been nattering on, and you must be stiff and bored to death."

I eased myself up, and stretched my arm to the soft air.

"I *am* a bit stiff," I agreed, "but not bored. You couldn't possibly bore me, Dick, not ever."

The faint smile on his lips faded; the brilliance of his blue eyes seemed to darken and become still — very still and intent. He seated himself by me, and put his arm round my shoulders. "You think so, but I would, you know. There are so many different — aspects — of my life that you wouldn't understand and enjoy. I'm not an easy person to live with. A kind of loner, I suppose — " His voice trailed off.

I snuggled closer, resting my head on his shoulder. "I'm a loner too," I told him, "except for Delilah, of course. So I understand. And, oh Dick — if you love me — "

"Love?" The word at that moment had a sad sound on his lips. "You mustn't let yourself think that way — not about me, Sari — "

"But why? *Why?* You do care, don't you?"

The pressure of his arm tightened. Suddenly his mouth was urgent, warm and demanding against my cheek, throat and on my cool shoulder where the white dress had loosened and fallen away.

"Of course I care, you ridiculous chit — " he admitted, and the hot husky note in his voice thrilled me.

"Then please — "

"*No.*" He tore himself away and strode a few paces from me, with his face turned deliberately towards the sea. His pose was rigid and tense. But behind the rock-like

119

exterior I sensed how shaken he was. "Dick — " I begged, moving towards him and touching his back, "please don't push me away — "

He turned sharply, staring down on me, and his expression was unfeeling, stern.

"Tidy yourself," I heard him saying coldly. "It's no use, understand? We could never belong, and that's final."

"Then why didn't you say so before? Why did you let me think — ?" I broke off in a whirl of anger and heavy disappointment.

"Pull yourself together, Sari," the command was like the stab of a knife wound. "I didn't *ask* you to care for me. In fact, I've tried several times to keep our — affection — on a controlled and reasonable footing. But you're so stubborn and over-emotional, so *demanding*."

"You mean you don't want me at all?"

"Not in the way you seem to think."

"Thank you. Oh, thank you very *much*. I'm sorry I've been a nuisance — "

"I didn't say that."

"No. You said much worse," I stated with fury mounting in me. "You've made me feel cheap — *cheap*. And I hate you for it, Dick — Dick whoever-you-are. I may have been stupid not to have taken your hints. But then that's just what I am an ignorant country girl who thought your kisses were genuine and you wanted me. Now I'm ashamed; of myself, and most of all for you. You're nothing but — "

"The devil incarnate," he supplied for me. "Quite right." His manner softened suddenly. "Oh, don't be so intense, nymph — "

"I'm not your nymph, and I don't want to be in that wretched painting at all. You've humiliated and shamed me. So — "

Suddenly I reached for his canvas, the half-done picture of Undine, and ripped it across; then, before he'd properly realised what I was doing, I'd thrown it into the tarn, and turned to rush blindly from him up the hill, clutching tumps of heather and undergrowth as I went.

I heard him shouting, and stupidly half-hoped he'd follow so there could be an impact — some wild emotional conflict that could miraculously end in reunion. But he didn't, and I never looked back. When we met the next morning before moving on to St Clunack, he treated me with chill politeness, as though addressing a stranger.

That same day he left the troupe giving the excuse that he had an appointment in Exeter. He'd be back when he felt like it, he told Barney, probably in a fortnight's time.

I felt stunned, almost dumb with misery, and I fancied that Mr Goodfellow noticed it, and in a vague way felt I'd been partially responsible for Dick's leaving so soon.

Mylora, on the contrary, had a smug self-satisfied air about her, holding a tinge of malice that did not escape me. I guessed she'd discovered through her usual devious methods something of what had occurred between Dick and me.

"Cheer up," she said, when she caught me alone at the back of the wagon, before starting off. "You've asked for it, you know."

"I don't know what you're talking

about," I said, not glancing at her.

"*Really!*" the tone was contemptuous. Well, let me tell you all the rest of them do. You've been making a real exhibition of yourself ever since you joined up with us. Dick this — Dick that! — following him around with your cat's eyes and sly-puss ways — " she broke off; I still determinedly kept my back to her. She came nearer. So near I could hear her heavy breathing. "*Look at me,*" she said harshly, pulling me round with unexpected force. I stared in astonishment. Her handsome face that Dick had thought beautiful was blazing with angry colour. I opened my mouth to speak, but was prevented by the hard sting of her hand on one cheek. "I've been wanting to do that for quite a time," she said then. "It's what you deserve, and more. Because of you Dick's taken off. And if you've any sense you won't be here when he gets back. Do you know why? Because he despises you. Not only that — " she drew herself up before continuing more quietly " — we're getting married soon."

"Married?" I couldn't believe it, and

yet half of me was clearly beginning to.

"As soon as possible. You see — there's a reason. Can't you guess?" She smiled, and when I didn't answer, went on, "In a way, Sari, I'm almost sorry for you. You're so naive. Hadn't you noticed anything about me — something different lately?" She dropped the shawl from her body revealing the slight protuberance of her stomach under the brilliantly patterned skirt. I shook my head slowly, not wishing to understand; only half-comprehending.

"I'm having a baby," she said flatly. "*His*."

"I don't believe you." My voice was a whisper.

"I think you do; he's always wanted and needed me — even since the first day at Goodfellow's. True, I may not be quite in his class, but I know how to make him happy and at ease, and I shall understand when he has to be back with his fine friends in London. I shan't pester him, or go crawling begging for kisses when he wants to be alone — "

"Don't!" My cry was shrill. "You're being beastly — *cruel*."

124

She shrugged. "The world can be a cruel place until you learn a bit about it. Now look here — " her manner became quieter, more conciliatory, " — I didn't mean to slap you. Fact is, I don't grudge you anything, I've no need to. All I want'll be mine — the free life, Dick's arms about me from time to time, to ease the hunger in us, and his baby. But *you* — you've got to find yourself yet, and make your own course. You've got looks and a way with you in front of an audience that most women'd envy. If I were you, I'd leave this charade and aim for something more ambitious. Most towns are on the lookout for girls of your kind. And it's getting near pantomime time. Understand what I mean?"

Yes, I understood, and I knew she was right about leaving.

To have remained with Barney's troupe seeing Mylora and Dick as a married couple would have been too hard to bear.

So that evening, after the circus had reached the site three miles south of St Rozzack, I left secretly, leaving only a note for Barney, which read, " — Sorry,

125

thanks for all you've done. But I need a change so I'm going. Don't try and find me, and don't worry. I'll be all right. Sari."

The night was dark when I set off with Delilah, walking at first, taking instinctively a moorland track in the direction of Boscarne. That was where I was going; fate had played into my hands. There was no one in the world I cared about any more, except the two now dead — Uter and Joanna. My mind was once more coldly clear, my purpose defined. I would get a foothold in the Tremellick family home and prove I was not just a nobody. I'd learn, and accept anything that came my way, as my right, giving nothing of my heart in return. And if a Tremellick became hurt through any action of mine I wouldn't care. In this manner I'd avenge the past, and in the future, with luck, have the power to humiliate others, in return partly for the humiliation forced on me by Dick.

6

IT took me that night and almost the whole of the next day to reach St Rozzack. I spent a few hours sleeping in a farm barn conveniently left open, and lay with the donkey beside me in some hay left in a corner. At dawn, we went on again; there were plenty of blackberries ripe in the hedges, and mushrooms showing their pearly heads in the fields. I gathered a number of these and later, feeling hungry, peeled them ready for eating. An old vagabond met me by chance, and kindled a fire for me, providing me also with a tin plate from his sack.

"Use that," he said, "an' mebbe a tater or two wouldn' come amiss. Throw em on the flames an' they'll cook beautiful, girl." He produced two large potatoes which I took gratefully.

I thanked him and did as he said. Never had food tasted better.

"Where'ee goin' to?" he asked as he

squatted beside me, poking the sticks.

I explained, asking if I was on the right route for the Hall.

"Ais," he said. "I bin there meself did a bit o' clearin' up — outside work — for a good breakfast in me belly. Kip straight on, only see as you bear to the right. Know this part at all, do 'ee?"

I didn't disclose that I'd been found as a baby many years ago on the wild Cornish beach below the moors; but simply replied, "I know parts. But I've been away for some years, and all these tracks can be bewildering."

He said nothing to that, just glanced at Delilah nibbling nearby, and remarked, "Got a friend there, I s'pose. But looks to me as he's gettin' on in life. Ancient — like me." And he gave a cackle of laughter.

"Delilah's all right," I said. "And she's not a 'he', she's a female."

"Ah." He winked. "That explains it."

"What?"

"The stubborn look on her. An' kind o' crafty-lookin'. Still a wumman's comp'ny can be useful — even the mulish sort.

Me though, I prefers me own. Used to it, y'see."

He went on muttering for a time while I finished eating the potatoes and mushrooms. Then, after thanking him again I roused Delilah, and continued on my way, leaving the vagabond to go the other.

When at last I reached a high point overlooking the distant gaunt coast stretching westwards towards the rugged toe of Land's End, the shape of Boscarne emerged dark under the fading rim of greenish sky in its valley below. Any tiredness I'd felt vanished in a wave of anticipation holding only a tinge of doubt. For the last mile or two I'd been riding Delilah; I swung myself off her back, patted and rested my head momentarily against her grey one, then stood for a minute or two staring.

"That's where we're going, Del dear," I whispered, "just you and me as it was when we left the farm. Only this time it will be different. I'll be a fine lady when they've grown to know me, and you'll have a place to sleep in as grand as any highbred horse — even a field maybe, with buttercups all yellow in the Spring. I'll see you have a good home, Delilah, and it won't be all silks and satins I'll wear. Sometimes I'll creep out in these old skirts and be in the long grass with you near me just as we've always been — "

I let the nonsense on my tongue die — she was looking at me so oddly, with a kind of pitying love in her soft brown eyes that told me I was just a fool of a girl who didn't know what on earth she was rambling on about.

I laughed, patted her neck, and said more briskly, "Come along now, or it'll be dark before we get there."

I shook my hair back behind my shoulders, tied it neatly with a ribbon, lifted my skirt, and from my pochette took a clean small square of linen to wipe my face clean of any dust or grime. Earlier we'd come to a stream where I'd washed my feet and hands and pinned the shawl at my waist with my cherished brooch, to hide a rip in the front of my gown. I wished I had a mirror to look into, one of the kind Mylora always carried. But they were costly to buy, and

I'd clung to my remaining few guineas, never knowing when they'd be of use.

Once, during the journey I'd stared into a moorland pool and seen my reflection appearing like someone half drowned, all swimmy and strange, with my long hair spreading like waving weeds in the water. An ache of memory had overcome me," because I'd inevitably thought of Dick as his 'Undine' — the Undine now that never would be. The pain had been only momentary. Dick had never loved me. He'd said so, and the recollection of his rejection spurred me to continue on the journey briskly putting all longing and weakness behind me.

An hour later I was leading Delilah up the drive towards the great house. No one seemed about, for which I was grateful. Only a single candle or lamp flickered from an upstairs window; I kept in the shadows as much as possible, then took the curve to the right leading to the back of the house and the courtyards.

There was more light and movement there. Blinds were just being pulled down, and servants crossing to and fro. I rattled the heavy knocker of the vast oak door.

There was the murmur of voices and sound of footsteps from inside. Then the door opened. A woman's face in a mob cap confronted me.

"What do you want?" she said. "And what's that theer donkey critter doin' here?"

I lifted my head proudly, and remembering to speak clearly in the proper English tongue I'd studied in my spare moments during my travels, said, "My name is Sari, and I'd be obliged if you'd inform Master Tremellick of my arrival. He invited me to call one day on a matter of business."

The woman looked confused, irritated, yet a little wary at the same time. Obviously my manner had disconcerted her.

"You'd better come in," she said grudgingly, "only not that animal. You just shoo him off to the stables somewhere."

I shook my head.

"I'll wait outside until the master arrives, and Delilah with me."

She screwed her eyes up more closely, and a hint of memory seemed to dawn in her. "You're one of they players, edn' you? I seem to remember."

I nodded.

She shrugged, shook her head, and still muttering under her breath, made her way through the small scullery place and cut through another door.

Delilah gave a sudden hee-haw. I patted her neck encouragingly. "Don't worry, Del dear. We're here — and going to stay."

And that's what happened.

We did.

I didn't talk with the master of Boscarne that evening, but hearing of my arrival he gave directions I should be given a suitable bedroom for the night after which, the next day, he'd interview me. I felt slightly rebuffed. Surely he could have given me a tentative welcome.

"He *does* know who I am — she did tell him, didn't she?" I queried of the housekeeper, who seemed a rather worried but fairly amiable woman. "The — the person who opened the door to me — "

"The cook you mean, Mrs Jelly?"

Perhaps I was overtired, but the name Jelly gave me an absurd impulse to laugh, it seemed so apt. I swallowed hard. "Yes — the cook; thank you. She — she *did* say I was Sari — the dancer, I hope? Master Tremellick told me that at any time I could call — and it didn't annoy him about Delilah, I hope — the donkey?"

Her pale, rather drawn-looking face, assumed a kind but slightly pitying expression. "Mrs Jelly informed *me* who you were, and *I* told the master. He remembered you quite well; I didn't think it necessary to bother him about the well-being of your animal. It's already in a groom's capable hands, and I can assure you will be well-cared for. Now follow me, and when you've washed and tidied yourself you can come to the kitchen for a meal, it adjoins my own parlour. I'm sure you must be hungry, and perhaps a change of clothing?"

After lighting a candle, she paused, her shrewd glance scanning my colourful but obviously peasant attire: the orange-coloured skirt with the muddied hem, the bedraggled shawl draping my black laced bodice, and the shabby toes of my boots. I felt suddenly conscious of how unsuitable my appearance was to the neat kitchen. The red ribbon tying my hair gave no confidence any more. I felt vagabondish, completely out of place, and wished for a fleeting few seconds I was back with Delilah on the moors. My fit of dejection must have registered. She patted my shoulder reassuringly.

"Come, girl, miss — whatever your name is. I know naught about you yet, except that you were with the circus troupe. But it's getting late now. A good rest is what you need. In the morning no doubt, after he's seen you, Master Tremellick will put me in the picture. But there's no need for explanations. Come along now, do as you're bid, and I'll find a fresh gown to make you feel a bit better."

I followed her from the kitchen into a passage with a door at the end. It was rather dark.

"Be careful you don't trip in that dragging skirt of yours, she said. "Watch your feet now."

She turned briefly, lowering the candle

so a flickering gleam of light showed uneven gaps in the slab floor. I lifted my dress above my ankles, stepping carefully. A few yards ahead the corridor branched off to an opening from which a narrow flight of stone stairs led steeply upwards. She proceeded ahead of me and as I was about to take the turn I glanced to my right and saw the distant door at the far end of the passage open briefly, revealing a tall figure watching. Surprise and nerves jerked my heart to a quick race. Then I recognised him. In a beam of warm lamplight his rugged features were unmistakable, and I think he smiled. The sudden trembling of my legs steadied. Tension eased. The door closed again; it was the barrier I supposed dividing the servants quarters from those of the family. Mrs Pratt looked back at me.

"Don't dawdle, girl," she said, a trifle sharply. "All of us want a bit of rest this night." I did my best to obey, although the steps were tricky. Halfway up we came to a wider curtained interior containing bath tubs and toilet accessories, obviously a wash place for maids. Immediately on the other side, the steps wound up again, until we came to a wider landing.

Mrs Pratt paused to take a bunch of keys from the pocket of her starched gown then beckoned me ahead. The corridor was long and dark except for candles burning on the sill of a narrow window. At the end of it, as on the ground floor, was a similar barrier shutting off one part of the house from the other, menials from gentry. It was only after passing a number of doors, servants' bedrooms possibly, that my guide stopped and inserted a key into a lock. She entered the room first and from her own candle lighted several others.

"Here we are," she said, turning. "This room may be only temporary. It's kept for any emergency or unexpected — person — arriving. I think you should be comfortable."

The inflection on the word 'person' didn't escape me. But I supposed to her, I was just that, and a poor one into the bargain. However, what she said about the room was true. The oak bedstead had a yellow quilt on it. The floor, though of boarded wood, was polished, and had two large mats on it also in a buttercup colour. There were curtains on either side of the small window to pull across the blind in case of draughts a chair, small chest, wash-stand and dressing table. The walls were panelled in light oak which I thought quite sumptuous, and above the bed a hand-worked sampler in a heavy frame.

"You'd better put your bundle down," I heard Mrs Pratt saying, "and if there's anything decent in it lay it in the chest. I'll send a girl up with some water for you to wash in, and go myself now to find you a nightshift and gown. And it's crossed my mind you might like to eat on your own tonight after all. What about a bowl of broth up here?"

"Oh, yes. That *would* be kind of you," I said.

She nodded and went out, reappearing presently with the shift and dress, followed by a rosy-cheeked girl wearing an apron and mobcap. The girl put the can of water by the basin, bobbed to Mrs Pratt, and left. Meanwhile the housekeeper laid the dress on the bed, straightened its folds carefully, and said,

"What you've got on under that red thing I don't know. But be careful not to pull this gown about too much. It's fresh and clean, but not new. Belonged to my niece at one time. Not fashionable, of course, but it's use that matters, and to look neat and tidy."

"Of course," I agreed. Joanna, my foster-mother taught me that. We may have been poor, but everything in our home was as spotless as possible."

"Then how come — " she broke off. "Oh well, tisn't my business. Must have been hard sometimes with those circus folk, what drove you to join them's beyond me. Still, that's between you and the master. *My* job is to see you're presentable when you meet him."

"Yes, Mrs Pratt," I agreed, "and thank you for the gown."

When she'd gone I examined the dress. It was of blue cotton in the old-fashioned Empire style, very high-waisted, having an apron front, with a coarse lace collar tied at the throat with a bow. I tried it on. It was rather short, showing more of my ankles than it was meant to, and a little tight over the bust. Oh dear, I thought, however could I meet Master Tremellick with dignity, looking more like a gawky, developing girl who'd grown out of her clothes than a young woman seeking a position?

And footwear! — I'd nothing but my boots and the pair of slippers worn for my dancing act with Rom. Luckily I'd brought the latter along. They'd have to do, and when I dressed in the morning I'd put on a white cotton petticoat I'd hastily packed with my other possessions, and somehow fix it so it hung below the hem of the blue gown.

My reflection, through the rather poor mirror, didn't please me. With my hair pulled back I looked prim and quite out of date. But the funny side didn't escape me. "All you need," I told myself, "is a high bonnet on your head tied under the chin with blue ribbons."

Any sense of humour soon vanished. I felt tired suddenly, more tired than at any moment since joining the circus.

That night, following a meal of a large bowl of broth brought to me by the maidservant, I went to bed thankfully and slept soundly until the morning.

When I woke sunlight filtered through a chink in the curtains, and from outside came the screaming of gulls. I lay for minutes thinking back and remembering, recalling with a spurt of excitement that in an hour or two, perhaps less, I was to meet Master Tremellick, the owner of Boscarne.

At last.

My chance had come.

7

MY first formal interview with the Master of Boscarne took place in his study shortly after breakfast. I'd endeavoured to make myself as attractive as possible, but the clothes didn't help.

"You may find our household a little — complicated at first," he said in rather remote cool tones. "But if you decide to accept my offer, I'm sure you will adapt yourself successfully in time. I live very much my own life here — there are many things concerning the estate to attend to, and get into order. There is also the mine needing investigations and possibly further development. We're bound to meet on occasions, of course, but your duties will be mostly with Lady Le Villemont — Lady Susannah, my ancient relative."

I studied him thoughtfully, noting the unswerving glance of his dark eyes, and strongly carved features above the cream silk neckscarf, and expensive cloth of his well-cut fawn coat. The sideburns of his crisp hair were well trimmed, his whole manner was one of aloof interest concerning only our mutual suitability — for the arrangement. I wondered whether I dared put a question, and decided I would.

"Your reference to Lady Susannah means your — your grandmother perhaps, sir?"

There was a short pause before he answered. "You can *call* her my — step-great aunt, if you wish. Not that it should make any difference. She's become part of the household, we think of her as the matriarch. She has a separate suite of rooms in the west wing. A certain dependent of hers has two rooms nearby and lives there in complete seclusion. You will have nothing to do with him at all."

"Oh. Is he — ?"

"My wishes are very firm on this point," Master Tremellick stated unemotionally, but firmly. "You won't need further emphasis from me, I hope. I shan't interfere with your life and duties if we come to a satisfactory understanding about the position. But on this one point I must insist. Keep to your own duties with her ladyship, which will be merely to be at hand when you're required to read to her a little if she feels like it — even dance a few steps when she feels particularly lively. She had a knowledge of the art, and gets frequently bored and irritated that she's confined to such a dull existence."

"I understand," I said stiffly.

"She's almost a hundred years old," he added nonchalantly.

I gasped. "A *hundred*?"

"Yes, and still bright, over bright sometimes, in the head."

"Oh but I don't think — " I broke off feeling suddenly inadequate, unable to accept completely that anyone could live to quite such an age.

His voice was more personal, warmer, when he said, "The idea frightens you? Yes, I can understand. You are, obviously, very young — "

"It's the dress," I blurted out, forgetting my determination to appear dignified before the master of Boscarne. "I feel

144

wrong in it — Mrs Pratt made me wear it, but it's much too short and tight, and I feel stupid. And this cap — " I touched the balloon-like headgear she'd forced me to wear at the last minute before going to the library for my interview. "I *never* wear caps," I stated in a wave of irritation. Almost before I realised what I was doing, I pulled the silly contraption off, and with it pins were dislodged leaving a mass of hair to fall loose over my shoulders. "Oh," I put a hand to my lips. "I shouldn't have done that. I'm sorry, but I've always been so free, and I don't think — "

A laugh interrupted my hasty words.

"Neither do I," he exclaimed. "I don't think such outlandish prudish concoctions enhance your type of looks in any way. In fact — it's quite an abomination. But Mrs Pratt's rather a stickler for convention. I'm sure she meant well."

My heart steadied with a feeling of relief. "Perhaps. But she's the housekeeper, isn't she, and if she tells me to dress in her way, I'll have to, won't I?"

"No. It's Lady Susannah who matters,

and you'll find her extremely individualistic. I'm quite sure she wouldn't approve of the cap any more than I do, and if you decide to accept the post I'll send to Truro or Penzance at the first opportunity for a collection of clothes to be sent, so you can try them and choose what you want. What about it?"

I was so dazed I could hardly think clearly at first. When he saw my bewilderment he mentioned the wage he was prepared to pay, and I was quite astonished. It was so much more than I'd ever have anticipated or even imagined. At last after a few more practical considerations had been discussed and settled, I accepted Master Tremellick's offer, and my new life at Boscarne began.

Fitting into a fresh life and completely new routine so suddenly would have been extremely difficult, if I hadn't felt myself in a kind of dream from which I might suddenly wake, to hear the chatter of men's voices including Rom's shouting round the horses, and Mrs Petra's grumbling mingled with Delilah's hee-hawing and the grating and bumping of props being moved.

My duties at the big house at first seemed few. Lady Le Villemont was apparently suffering from one of her 'moods', and did not wish me to meet her at all during the first week. Such fits of solitude were quite normal for her, Master Tremellick told me, and the natural result of her great age; very shortly, when we were introduced, I would be surprised — even mildly shocked possibly, by her vitality.

"Is she French?" I queried. "Her name sounds like it."

"No," he replied curtly. "Her husband was. He's been dead many years, and we don't discuss the past with her. It's important you remember that your position here is merely mainly to amuse her, and keep her from brooding." He flung me a peculiarly searching look. "Too many memories aren't always good. The present and future are far more important to the living."

Perhaps he was right, I thought, knowing though that there were things I could never possibly forget, and did not intend to. Memories that had played a large part in my even contemplating taking a position in the Tremellick household, of Uter and Joanna — my stubborn desire for revenge, and of Dick too. Dick who had meant so much to me, and humiliated and forsaken me for Mylora. I would never forgive him — *never*. And one day I'd make him sorry — realise that when he turned me away he'd insulted someone who wasn't just a nobody, but a woman of purpose and pride despite my youth.

Oh yes. Beneath my facade of obedience and show of good behaviour and wishing to learn, the fiery rebel still remained. Even Mrs Pratt was impressed. "You're doing quite well," she said grudgingly one day. "In fact, I'll admit I'm agreeably surprised. When you arrived looking like a wild gypsy girl with that old donkey of yours I had misgivings, I can tell you. But it's clear to see now that you have decent blood in your veins somewhere, and can put on obliging airs when necessary. I'll go so far as to say that you may fit in as companion-maid to Lady Susannah quite adequately."

"Not *maid*, if you please, Mrs Pratt," I corrected her. "Master Tremellick's made that quite clear."

"Hm! well, your arrangements with the Master are your own I suppose, but don't expect me not to give a word of advice when it's needed."

"Of course not. I know the importance of your opinion." A suspicious, shrewd look flashed from her eyes for a moment. Whether she saw through my subtle flattery I don't know. I tried to keep my face straight and expressionless, and after a moment, apparently satisfied, she remarked, "That being so, I've a tip or two that could be useful. Your gown — !"

"Yes?"

"Oh it's becoming enough in its way, but maybe a bit fancy for mornings. Mauve's a bit delicate and soils easily. And, gracious me, nothing looks so bad as a soiled gown. Then the neck's a bit too low for my liking. That collar could be taken up a bit, and it doesn't need lace edging. The braid's enough. Then the cut of the bodice — the pointed front, oh, I know it's fashionable. But in *your* case

— it *does* give emphasis to the figure, if you know what I mean. A modest woman doesn't need to emphasise what's — well, I don't have to give a name. But I'm sure you understand."

I nodded. "Yes, Mrs Pratt. If Master Tremellick hadn't already seen me wearing it, I might take up your suggestion of — of moderating certain small things here and there. But I haven't really time, and as you must know the dress came with others from the costumier's. I chose three, and when I came downstairs today he saw me wearing this, and quite approved." I suddenly smiled; it sounded so stuffy talking in such a manner. "Oh, don't let's worry. He — the master — said Lady Susannah liked pretty clothes and still went through any fashion magazines she could find."

"So she may do," came the answer primly. "But you must realise she doesn't belong to the present. Half her time she's back in the past with those fine ancestors of hers — or her husband's, I should say — in that dreadful France, where they had the Revolution. Which proves, doesn't it, that it's risky to be too vain. You never know what politicians are going to get up to. Even in England there's a deal of ill feeling from the lower classes."

"Not without reason," I said tartly. "Have you ever heard of the Tolpuddle Martyrs, Mrs Pratt?"

"*Tolpuddle?*" she threw up her hands. "Gracious no. Where is it, and what are they? *Tolpuddle?* such a name! no, I've certainly heard nothing of them."

"They were poor people with little to eat who were trying to form a method of protection for themselves and a living wage so they could exist without dying from bad conditions or ill-nourishment," I told her. "They wished to harm nobody, but simply asked for their rights, and were sentenced for transportation to Van Diemen's Land and savage imprisonment there."

"Dear me. No. I never heard o' that. But then I wouldn't, would I? Living in a respectable household like the Tremellick family's."

"Exactly," I said ironically.

"Well, then, why make such a song of

151

it, or bother your brain about matters that aren't women's affairs, when you've got plenty else to think about, like learning how to act with her ladyship?"

I didn't reply. There seemed no point, and that same afternoon I met Lady Susannah Le Villemont.

I was conducted by Mrs Pratt to her quarters which were composed of a completely separate wing looking westwards on the first floor. There was no mistaking the privacy of the apartments which were shut off by an immense carved door with a heavy brass knocker on it. As Mrs Pratt knocked, I glanced behind me. The corridor to this special domain branched off from the main gallery halfway up the principal staircase of the house, and was only slightly narrower; tapestries, and immense portraits of bygone ancestors or historical characters stared superciliously down from heavy frames.

Through the elusive candlelight, features took on a curious semblance of life. Vague unease stirred me. It was as though the fitful shadows were symbolic of my days ahead, warning me I was about to enter another world, a completely new sphere of existence built and founded on memories of a past age. But when the heavy door opened with the sound of bolts being drawn, sudden golden light splashed across the marble floor of a hallway revealing rugs of a rich Persian design, tastefully blending into the colour scheme of the wall, soft blues and cream pannelled in gilt. The ceiling was encrusted ornately with baby cherubs, stars and clouds. It was like entering a sunlit palace from a shadowed wood. Oval mirrors were hung in recesses, reflecting brilliance. The movement of air caused a tinkling of crystal chandeliers, and at first I was so bemused I could hardly move. Then I heard Mrs Pratt saying, "This is the girl — Miss Tregeer — the one her ladyship wishes to meet.

I became aware for the first time of a short, stout figure silhouetted against the light. She moved, indicating us to enter, and I saw then that she was middle-aged — perhaps older. Her hair, so intensely black it could have been dyed, was parted in the middle, and drawn severely back from a pale plump face. Quick bird-like eyes darted from Mrs Pratt to me and back again; she offered me her hand, and it was comforting, warm and firm.

"Very well," she said, "follow me."

We walked in a line, down the passage, one behind the other, reminding me suddenly with a spurt of humour of ducks in a row — the leader plump and upright, in heavy black satin, with a shred of white lace on her head, followed by Mrs Pratt, a smaller edition also in black — then me, the duckling with its feathers not completely sprouted, a yard behind.

"I hope all is well today," I heard Mrs Pratt saying politely, "and that her ladyship has fully recovered from the megrims, and that you also are fit, Mrs Delaney."

"We have nothing to complain about," the other woman answered, "and as to my health it is as good as possible, so it is. 'Twould be no use otherwise, as you must know, Mrs Pratt."

Her voice had a slight accent — probably Irish, I thought. "And you yourself?" she continued. "Is the master satisfied with arrangements now?"

"I've had no complaints," Mrs Pratt replied.

At this point the brief conversation ended. We took a sudden turn to the left, and entered a room — at least Mrs Delaney and I did. Mrs Pratt, after a brief word of advice to me to do my best and remember always my new employer was a *lady* — gave a nod to her fellow housekeeper and departed.

Feeling more than ever at that moment like a character from a book rather than real life, I took a quick glance round the interior. It was that of a sitting room, furnished elegantly in what I guessed was French style. There again, was a good deal of gilt and crystal about. From this room we went through yet another and into a third, which had an immense bay window overlooking gardens and a distant vista of moors and sea beyond. The bed, though, caught my first attention. It was immense — a great canopied four-poster with satin curtains patterned with roses, and quilt and pillows to match. Lights seemed to twinkle from every possible recess, and converge upon the figure propped comfortably in the sumptuous mass of frills and fine sheets. A perfume of roses filled the air; it was like stepping into a fantastic dream. I stared as Mrs Delaney approached the bed, bent down and whispered something. There was a sudden alert stiffening of muscles and movement, the lifting of a white gnarled figure and of a thin voice saying, "Come here, girl."

Mrs Delaney stepped aside, and I moved forward. Except for the circus midget I'd never seen such an exquisite, small figure before. Old? Yes. But the features, though drawn and etched with tiny lines, could have been of finest porcelain, her skin was so white, almost translucent, and pale as ivory. A frilly lace bonnet trimmed with pink ribbons was tied under her chin which pointed at an immediate angle towards the tip of her finely chiselled high-bridged nose. She gave a faint flicker of a smile, and extended a thin hand sparkling with rings. It felt so bony and paper-frail in mine I hardly dare clasp it for fear of it breaking.

"So you're — what is your name, child?"

"Tregeer," I answered. "Sari Tregeer."

"Hm." As though suddenly tired she lay back for a moment or two with her eyes closed. Then just as quickly she perked up again and remarked more brightly, "You were the one who came dancing that night. *I* saw you. But you didn't see *me*, did you?"

I shook my head. "No, but then — "

"Go on, go on; can't abear anyone not finishing a sentence."

"I was going to say I never *do* see anyone when I'm dancing," I told her. "I just think of moors, and sea, and flying clouds, and being free." Perhaps it was a stupid way to talk. But she didn't appear to think so. Indeed she patted my wrist and nodded.

"Ah. We're two of a kind, you and I. You at one end of life, and me at the other. Sad, is it not, that the dance cannot go on forever?" She sighed. When I was trying hard to think of a suitable reply, she queried more tartly, "Answer me — what did you say your name was — ?"

157

"Sari."

"Hm. A funny name; foreign. Sounds Indian."

"Oh no. I'm not Indian. I'm — "

"I know that. I heard your tale — forget who from now — about you being brought up by the tide. All drivel. Still, it don't matter. You haven't answered my question. What do you think of it, eh? Of life? When you get to my age and look back you wonder sometimes." She sighed once more.

Not wishing to be scolded again for keeping silent, I replied, "I haven't lived long enough to have a clever answer. I just think it can be very good, because every day's different, and you never know what lovely things are going to happen.

She nodded slowly and appeared to be puzzling over what I'd said, then she murmured, "Ah, yes. That's because you're young. Something new waiting round every corner.

"And some*body* perhaps?" A tinge of roguishness entered her voice.

Against my will I thought of Dick, but resolutely packed the memory of him away. I shrugged: "People come and go, don't they? There are nice ones and nasty, but mostly nice, I suppose."

"That depends, child. That depends. But tell me do you think you'll find *me* nice? Are you prepared to read to me when I want you to? And dance, maybe, sometimes by my window when a mood threatens? I have a musical box given to me by a foreign prince when I was young, and on the stage. I should like to see you dance to my music."

"I didn't know you had been on the stage," I said, with surprise and excitement rising in me.

"Oh yes. I was once famous. And then I married." She lay back against her frilly pillow, lids closed over her old eyes.

"One day I'll tell you all about it," she said in a whisper. "But leave me now. I'm tired. I wish to sleep."

Mrs Delaney appeared from the shadows, treading softly with two fingers to her lips, and gesturing for me to go.

I tiptoed from the room, with her beside me holding the keys, passing through the lounge, breakfast room or whatever it was, into the ornate hall, where Mrs Pratt was hovering about.

"I hope the meeting went well, and that Sari — Miss Tregeer, pleased?" she said questioningly.

"Indeed so," the other woman answered pleasantly. "But her ladyship is a little weary now, so she is. Tomorrow, perhaps in the morning, it will be possible for this young miss and the dear old soul to have another chat," and she beamed at me in a most friendly way. On the surface, Mrs Delaney appeared a really amiable and comfortable person, but I sensed that internally she could be strong; strong as iron. Why I got that impression I don't know. Perhaps it was her response to the sound of footsteps above, which must have been heavy to penetrate so clearly. This unexpected noise was followed by a rumble of male laughter — more of a boom, then silence.

Mrs Delaney flung up her hands, with an upwards glance of her round eyes displaying the whites. "That'll be *him*," she said. "Playing the king again."

For a second she must have forgotten me. When she remembered, she clucked, shook her head as though impatient with herself, and rather red in the face said,

"We've a great big oaf of a footman who insists on having his little joke sometimes. Take no heed, Miss Tregeer. For sure you'll be hearing it more than once, I'll be bound."

I pretended to accept her explanation, but I didn't wholly believe her, and was mystified.

Once Mrs Pratt and I were in the long gallery with the dividing door safely shut and bolted behind us, the housekeeper started planning the rest of the day's programme for me. She was interrupted by the unexpected appearance of Master Tremellick at the head of the main staircase. He dismissed her with a discreet gesture, and striding quickly towards me said, "Ah. I take it you've been getting acquainted with my — grandmother, and also with the curious geography of this house." He smiled, and the smile changed the stern, rather haggard, features briefly to those of a younger man. At the most, I thought, he couldn't be more than thirty.

He was attired in high boots, knee breeches, and an elegantly cut brown velvet jacket and stock, as though he had been riding. He was even taller than I'd first thought, with a boldness about him that sent a curious electrical awareness through my whole body.

This annoyed me slightly. I had not come to Boscarne to be in any way influenced personally by a powerful member of the Tremellick family, but as a challenge, and to be in my own way in command of the situation. Of course, it was probably sheer vanity on my part to have such ambitious thoughts; but I sensed — *knew* — in those fleeting seconds that we were already opponents as I'd intended us to be — supporters of rival causes; he of the aristocracy and ruling élite, myself as upholder of a principle: that of fairness to everyone, especially those who'd been oppressed, like Joanna and Uter. Did he sense it too? Feel the intense resentment behind the magnetism and shocked surprise of impact? How could I know?

All that registered was the heady physical awareness between us that held both hatred and longing; hatred reinforced by memories of the past, and my desire for vengeance. The longing? But that was for Dick. For Dick only, and an ability to fill the emptiness left by his rejection and deceit.

Oh, it was impossible during that short time to analyse my own feelings. They were so confused with excitement, anticipation and the old bitterness. Noting my silence Master Tremellick suddenly broke the spell by saying, "You haven't answered me. About Lady Susannah. How did you get on?"

"Oh, I — " I pulled myself together. "Very well indeed, sir — I *think*. But she got tired. She's wonderful for her age, isn't she? And so interesting. I hope she liked me."

"I'm sure she did. And now, what are you intending to do before dinner? You'll dine with me, I hope, for this first night."

"If you wish me to," I answered. "Thank you."

He appeared mildly puzzled, and I wondered why; the next moment I knew.

"You have great politeness of speech when you feel like it — " he said speculatively, "for one so young, and of your background. How did you come by it?"

"I had education," I replied stiffly, "of a kind, at the Dame School. And I read books when I had the chance. I was only ten, of course, when I left there — I was needed to help my foster mother, Joanna, especially after Uter died. But what you learn when you're young remains with you, I suppose. I still have a little book of poetry — Mr Keats'." I paused, before continuing, "All humble people aren't ignorant, you know."

"I'm fully aware of it. But their chances are limited."

I nearly commented, 'Thanks to the cruel law of England, and great families like yours — the rich Tremellicks', but containing my hot temper I put on a front of dignity and answered, "Naturally, sir. When days are spent in scrubbing and digging and working from morn to night trying to eke a living from a poor patch of ground where nothing grows but potatoes and turnips and a few straggly greens — well, you can't expect to have time left, or energy, for much learning, can you? We had goats, of course, and at one

164

time a pig. Then when — when — " I broke off, not wishing to confide more at that moment.

"Yes?" he persisted. "When?"

I looked away. "I'd rather not go into the past just now, if you don't mind. I'm sure it wouldn't particularly interest you."

My touch of bitterness didn't escape him.

"Don't pride yourself you can see into my own mind, young lady," he retorted sharply. "However, we'll leave reminiscing at this juncture, and get down to practical matters. Dinner is at seven, as Mrs Pratt will also doubtless inform you. As Lady Susannah eats in her private apartments except for very rare occasions, I am generally on my own, so the smaller parlour leading from the main hall is used. I shall look forward to meeting you there." He drew a diamond-studded watch on a fob from a side pocket, glanced at it and said, "That's all then. I won't keep you. You haven't overlong to dress and make yourself beautiful for our meal. Especially as Mrs Pratt has arranged for you to have a different bedroom." He looked me straight in the eyes. His own were expressionless, but I could feel mine burning.

"Thank you for telling me," I said. "I'll find out for myself."

I didn't have to. A second later, as though she had been listening, Mrs Pratt appeared, bobbed to the master, gave a meaningful glance at me as though to say, 'Bob, girl, bob. Or curtsey'.

I did neither, just turned and before she could say anything, *or* him for that matter, remarked, "I hear I'm sleeping in another room tonight, Mrs Pratt."

Looking both furious and flurried, she answered, "Yes. Well — come along then."

My glance for a fleeting moment wavered and met the unswerving glint of Master Tremellick's. It was as though swords clashed between us, despite the hint of wry amusement twitching his lips. Then he'd turned on his heel and walked smartly away, leaving me in confrontation with the outraged housekeeper.

"I must say I'm surprised at you, Sari — Miss *Tregeer*," she told me coldly.

"Your haughty manner was in bad taste, especially as you've been here but a day. Didn't you know, girl, that it's the custom for all staff to show respect to the master of the house?"

"By bobbing and bowing?"

"By showing at least a hint of good manners.

"Oh, I don't think I was in any way rude," I murmured casually. "I'm sure Master Tremellick understood."

She muttered something under her breath that I couldn't make out, then after a jerk of the head and gesture of one arm, directed me to follow, and together we walked ahead towards the main staircase and my new sleeping quarters.

8

LOOKING back now my first fortnight at Boscarne reflects the unreal but nostalgic qualities of a strange dream of wandering among a wilderness of conflicting emotions, and images of people not previously known in life, against a background of familiarity that was almost frightening. It seemed that I was always searching though for what I didn't know.

I suppose the haunted feeling could have been due to the locality — the closeness, comparatively, of Boscarne to the farm shack where I'd spent my first youth with Uter and Joanna. Sometimes when I was walking the long corridors to my bedroom or Lady Susannah's apartments, I'd pause by a long window, staring across the brown moorlands and high ridge above the sea, thinking about the past — half expecting to see Uter's tall form take shape against the horizon where at that time of the year so many massed forms of dark clouds were driven wildly against the windblown sky. Then I'd move on, jerked into the present by the voice of Mrs Delaney or Mrs Pratt calling me to attend Lady Susannah, or by the occasional wish of Master Tremellick wanting to learn of my progress in the household and if I was happy there.

Mostly I *was* happy, in an ambitious, self-seeking manner; except in heedless moments when my thoughts turned to Dick, then truth would hit me painfully, and a longing for his love sweep over me in a tide of resentment. Handsome, carefree, selfish Dick, who'd humiliated and cast me aside for the fiery hot-tempered Mylora. One day he'd have a shock though, I told myself in a swift rush of pride. If we ever met again — and surely it must happen one day — I'd be in the position to flaunt myself before his gaze and make him realise his mistake. I was so confident we had been meant for each other, as confident as I was that fate had interceded and driven me to leave the circus for one cause only somehow to right a dreadful wrong by bringing me to Boscarne.

Naturally I wasn't aware of the persistent grudge gnawing me *all* the time. There were both fascinating and boring periods during my sessions with old Lady Susannah when I was conscious only of wishing to please, and actually enjoyed the times when I danced to her tinkling music-box in the great bay overlooking the gardens and beyond to the distant headland pushing like a giant finger into the Atlantic.

Once, after a more than usual energetic display I flung myself on to the chaise-longue temporarily breathless, she exclaimed, "Ah! you are a wild one, Sari," and she chuckled audibly, "a wild one like I once was, only you have not the lovers, have you?" she sighed. "I had so many. So many rich gallant gentlemen at my feet. Whereas you — poor *petite* — have none — nothing but that great bore of a man, my stepgrandson, for company."

She leaned forward in her chair and wagged a finger; she was sitting up that day fully dressed, I remember, wearing a wig of silverish gold curls instead of the lace cap. Her gown of cream satin was intricately beaded with tiny starlike jewels; rings flashed from her white claw-like fingers. "You should rouse that man," she told me, "taunt him a little — show an enticing touch of what you've got beneath those prim clothes you're so fond of." She stuck her pointed chin forward and whispered meaningfully, "Make him jealous. You could do it. And perk yourself up a bit. As a ballet girl — *now* — yes, you are very sweet, *ma chérie*. But too much sweetness can cloy a man. And he *doesn't* see you, does he? — even as the dancer. Me only," she sighed and looked away. "Go now. I've had enough. And — " with a sudden widening of her eyes, almost a glare, "get yourself something more colourful for everyday. Be brilliant, bright. Don't listen to *her* — " as Mrs Delaney came forward " — or that dull creature Pratt. They know nothing of the world or men. I *do*. D'ye hear? And I wish for more variety. That's what you're here for, ain't it? To amuse. Very well, do it." She turned her face from me, tapping the floor with a tiny foot. "Get yourself a

171

new wardrobe. And that's a command."

I was about to try and explain that I had already done so, and that the gowns I appeared in for reading to her or for conversation had been sent to Boscarne on the orders of Master Tremellick himself, but was disconcerted by loud male laughter from either the same floor, or above, reducing me to temporary silence.

Mrs Delaney, after a quick glance round, touched my arm. "Come. Her ladyship is weary. And I may be needed — " She didn't finish. There was a sharp sound like that of a heavy stick being thumped overhead, followed by the echoing tread of footsteps. Then again laughter.

A feeling of unease, almost fear, seized me. Everything seemed so uncanny; not threatening exactly, but unfathomable and mysterious.

"What was that?" I asked Mrs Delaney as she ushered me from the room into the hall. "I heard voices before — once. But not so loudly." I didn't mention the 'footman', not wishing to be considered impertinent.

"Don't worry," I was told ambiguously. "There's nothing to harm you in this household. It's her ladyship's relative. He's a — theatrical kind of character, and enjoys playing a part sometimes. With his manservant — " Her voice trailed off.

"But why? And why doesn't the relative ever appear?" I asked stubbornly. "It seems very odd."

Instantly the woman became on the defensive. "It's not odd at all, at all," she told me, with her colour heightening. "You're business is with Lady Susannah only, and to a certain extent with the master, I suppose. Any other member of the household has a right to his own privacy. Remember if you please, and another thing — "

"Yes?"

"If her ladyship wishes you to appear as a dressed-up doll — do it. I don't approve, I believe in folk dressing according to their position in life. But I'm merely her attendant employed to see that her wishes are observed as accurately as possible Now — " Her tone lightened, and she half-pushed me through the door leading into the main gallery, "Why don't you forget what's just happened, get out of that frilly thing, change, and go into the gardens for a breath of fresh air. I can assure you you won't be needed by her ladyship any more today. Or perhaps Mrs Pratt will find something for you to do."

The door closed, taking her plump figure with it. I felt a surge of relief, and hurried to my room, luckily without meeting anyone on the way.

Mrs Delaney's suggestion of fresh air seemed a good one, so I discarded my dance dress for an everyday gown, put on my new cape — it was of an attractive but discreet shade of greenish-blue, changed from slippers into light ankle-length boots, and tucked my hair under a velvet bonnet that had been sent along with the boxes of clothes ordered by Master Tremellick. After a hasty glance at myself through the mirror which told me I looked like a prim housewife or upper-class lady's maid — I went downstairs as quietly as possible and out of a side door leading from the back hall and kitchen quarters.

There appeared to be no one about except for a gardener working at the front of the house, and he never saw me. I was filled with relief. Why? Perhaps because ever since my arrival at Boscarne I'd had an uncomfortable sense of being watched — not only openly, but by unseen eyes. During the brief time of trying to please and do my best to win approval of my employer and those under him, complete freedom had been denied me. It was true that in Lady Susannah's presence I'd enjoyed some sessions of dancing, and even appreciated her wry fits of humour. But always in the background somewhere there'd been the knowledge that Mrs Delaney or Mrs Pratt were at hand nearby to see I didn't exceed my rights.

My strolls about the terraces, lawns, and neglected rose gardens which were now being put into order again following the old master's death, had generally been in the company of Mrs Pratt, or the master himself — polite short interludes of conventional conversation that had been a strain rather than a pleasure. Now, at last, for the first time, and at the suggestion of the housekeeper, I was alone to make my own exploration and take stock of my surroundings.

I thought at first of wandering down to the valley side of the estate in its cluster of trees, but on impulse changed my mind and from the side drive cut to my right and through a gate which led between hedges of thorn, sycamore and larch to the moors. Behind me, at the far end of the court and stables, the whistling of a groom gradually grew fainter, leaving only the intermittent screaming of gulls rising and dying on the fresh wind.

I turned once to stare back at the house before moving on, and it was then I had a shock. At one corner of the building, in the proximity of Lady Susannah's apartment, but higher up, was a wide disc-like face watching, pressed close against the glass of a protruding tower window. Immediately below was a terrace railed off by stone balusters. Curiosity mingled with a tinge of fear stirred me. Who on earth was it? The mysterious relative? And why was the face so unmoving, so somehow — blank? I rubbed my eyes, thinking possibly I was imagining what wasn't there, that the cold air, following the warmth of Boscarne, had temporarily affected my sight; but when I glanced up again the countenance was still obvious, suddenly clarified by a beam of cold winter sunlight streaming through the clouds.

Actual features, of course, didn't register from the distance, but there was no mistaking the wig which was silver-white against the shadowed background. There was something menacing about the silent communication of glances between us that steeled my spine, and set my heart thumping. I turned quickly away, and forced myself, half-running, half-walking up the moorland path leading towards the ridge of hills out of vision of Boscarne. The air was chill, but wild and tangy, pungent with the scent of damp turf, heather, and the last leaves of late autumn underfoot, mingled with moss, and blown brine from the sea. Misgivings and brief despondency were swept away, as I continued further than I'd intended, to the first high ridge of moor overlooking the familiar landscape of my childhood. In the far distance the line of breaking waves on the shore was lit to pale silver by a fitful streak of dying sunlight. Standing there I remembered so many things; memories that took me from earliest days with Uter and Joanna, to the time when I set off like any vagabond gipsy girl with my donkey, Delilah, not knowing what the future would hold — where I was going, or what kind of life awaited me. Little I'd guessed then that a young man called Dick would appear with a travelling circus to steal all my youthful heart, and so change the whole of my existence. It wasn't so long ago really, of course, but thinking back made it appear an age. And here I was, back again, driven by some strange power of fate to the very household I'd vowed to hate forever.

My determination for revenge, during that short interval, seemed suddenly and inexplicably rather futile. What could I do? There was no one in the personal menage of the family I could see myself hating. The ancient Lady Susannah was so old and frail that my only instinct was to care for her and pander to her whimsical moods. The servants were dull creatures, but merely doing their duty, and the Master of Boscarne, Mark Tremellick, had as yet only shown a wish to make my employment there comfortable. All the same — there was something in him — a challenging quality that defied understanding. Beneath his polite exterior I sensed a will of iron that could be hard and unrelenting in the face of opposition. In such a mood could he be capable of sitting in judgement on others without the means of defence, such as Uter had been? Yes. If he considered he was in the right, I was sure of it; and the knowledge reinforced the old grudge in me.

I lifted my chin high, and the sharpening wind took the bonnet off my head, leaving it swinging by its ribbons from my shoulders. I shook my hair free of its combs, and the long drift of it on the wind gave a heady sense of excitement. I lifted my arm wide, leaving the cape loose, billowing wildly on the whirling currents of air. An impulse to dance flooded me, to dance with the elements of wind, sea and sky — and to love — *love*! to have a man's arms about me, taking me to ultimate ecstasy and fulfilment.

Dick!

"Oh, Dick, where are you?" I almost cried, but no words left my lips; for there could be no response, and deep in my heart I knew it. Then, suddenly as my senses sobered a little I heard it — the pounding thump — thump of hooves from the west. Startled, I stared — recalling in a second of alarm the watchful face at the window of Boscarne — wondering if I'd been followed, or if the looming grey figure on the dark animal approaching was cloud merely — a figment of the imagination.

Brushing a lock of hair from my eyes, and with the other hand trying ineffectually to draw the cloak round me, I screwed up my eyes against the salty wind. I was suffering from no illusion. The shapes were real, and a few seconds later horse and rider were close; a gasp of astonishment escaped me as the latter reined drawing his mount to a rapid halt.

He dismounted and exclaimed, "So we had the same impulse and need for solitude. I hope you've enjoyed it."

Master Tremellick!

"Yes," I shouted back. "I came further than I thought. But — I used to live over there — " I pointed to the cliffs overlooking the long-deserted farmstead " — with Uter and Joanna, my foster-parents."

"I see. I understand," he answered.

"But you don't," I thought. "That's just it. You've never known the struggle we had, and what Uter went through."

"You never will, because you're rich and powerful. But one day — one day — " I checked the wild imaginings racing through my brain, and forced myself down to earth and commonsense. "I must be getting back," I said. "I'm afraid Mrs Pratt may be needing me."

"Do you ride?"

I shook my head. "Only a donkey."

He laughed. "Then Pluto shall be donkey, and sufficiently strong to carry both of us."

This was how I came to ride back to Boscarne with Master Mark Tremellick that late winter afternoon, sitting before him on his grey stallion, my hair and spirits free as the open Cornish moors under the fading sky. We didn't take the direct straight course, but circled further west following a coastal route, and the wild story returned to me, which had been a legend when I was a child — of the dark demon huntsman who rode with his hounds seeking a bride of his choice. At last against a high mound, Master Tremellick drew the steed to a halt, staring eastwards towards the distant towers and turrets of Boscarne in the valley below. He dismounted, and lifted me down. The touch of his hands under my arms gave me a curious tingly feeling.

When I'd regained my breath and composure, I heaved a great sigh and glanced at my companion's face. The black hair was ruffled and unruly about the wide forehead, the flash of his eyes brilliant above the dominant nose and thrust of chin; in spite of the cold air, the animal's shining coat steamed, one hoof pounded the ground impatiently. At a word of command, however, Pluto was brought under control. "A good view," Mark said.

"Yes."

"I enjoyed the gallop," he remarked, "and I hope you weren't afraid."

"*Afraid?* Me?" I laughed.

He turned his head and looked down straight into my eyes. "No, I can see you're not. It would take more than a spirited canter over the moors to scare you. You're the wild kind, aren't you — Sari?"

It was the first time he'd addressed me by any name but 'Miss Tregeer'.

"Perhaps," I answered guardedly. "There was *something* upsetting though, today — before I came out."

"What?"

I hadn't meant to refer to the watcher in the tower room, but the opening had arisen so naturally, and I took the chance to enlighten him. When I'd explained briefly, he said lightly, *over* lightly I thought, "Oh that's nothing. There's no secret about it. I think I told you of our dependent relative. He's a joker given to playing pranks. An invalid, and incarcerated up there through no fault of his own, poor man. A favourite with the old lady, though, which is a mercy."

I left the subject there without telling him of Mrs Delaney's references to a footman's tricks concerning the strange bumping and laughter overhead on my first visit to Lady Susannah's apartments. Following a short silence, with excitement faded, Mark Tremellick — I was already beginning to think of him as Mark — in more formal remote tones said, "Come along, up with you." He helped me mount again, saying, "We'll cut down to the left now. I'll escort you from the stables myself, and inform Mrs Pratt, if any questions are asked, which I'm sure there won't be, that I had taken you on a short tour of the territory."

"Thank you."

"There's no need for thanks, Miss Tregeer — Sari. Shortly, though, I will arrange for you to have proper riding lessons, which will enable us possibly to have a canter together sometimes."

That was the beginning.

Anticipation filled me. A sense of triumph, and plans for the future in which I'd achieve what I aimed for a respected footing and power in the house of Boscarne.

9

FOR weeks following the episode on the moor with Mark Tremellick I saw little of him, and when we met his attitude was of polite formality, no more. My meals were taken mostly in the small parlour, unless the Master requested my presence at his table. These occasions were rare, and although I did my best to appear attractive, wearing the smartest of the gowns in my new wardrobe, he didn't seem impressed. There *was* one occasion when he said with a sudden glint of appraisal in his dark eyes, "That sea-green colour — or blue — suits you. You should wear it more often."

Stupidly I blushed, reminding myself afterwards that his opinion was of no personal importance whatsoever, except as a means of gaining more power in the household. And the latter, just then seemed exceedingly doubtful, except where Lady Susannah was concerned. I became aware that she was beginning to depend on me entirely for diversion, and although in my own way I'd developed a certain fondness for her, the wearying periods of reading to her from Richardson or Jane Austen, interspersed with her endless recollections of the past which I was hoping to learn by heart, became eventually no more than boring sessions of stoical endurance on my part.

I missed the variety of my days with the travellers — the circus folk, and of course, Dick. However hardened my heart was against him, at unguarded moments his image returned, and could only be allayed by a hot and angry determination somehow to cause an impression on society and make him sorry for his false and careless treatment. So the vengeful bitterness towards the house of Tremellick became curiously mixed up with my jealousy of Mylora and wish to hurt Dick.

Such moods were rare, of course. I was not by nature a vengeful person, and during my leisure hours when I was free to go walking, or practise horse riding in the paddock, life could be comparatively enjoyable. There was the mystery and curiosity concerning Lady Susannah's peculiar relative. We never met; he remained closely confined in his apartments, and walking the terrace gardens by the stone balusters, hands behind his back, talking to himself, looking at the sky, or booming with low laughter. I had to accept the information firmly given to me that he fancied himself an actor.

But the strange circumstances of his behaviour and incarceration indicated there was far more in the situation than that. He was deranged in some way, and had to be kept under some form of restraint. His clothing itself was too bizarre for any normal human being, belonging to a past decade of brilliant colours, curled white wigs, and pompous bearing. On two occasions when the weather was fine and warm for the time of the year, I looked upwards from the drive, and saw him parading to and fro, to and fro, his enormous stomach a splash of scarlet in the sunlight. He looked down once, but from where I stood I could see nothing of his features but smudged shadows between mounds of flesh. Once he was wearing a crown, looking quite absurd, and somehow — unnerving. I knew he'd seen me and was interested. It was an interest, though, that I didn't wish to encounter again. And from that time I avoided passing that particular portion of Boscarne, taking the route round the opposite side of the house when I went out, which brought me to the court and adjoining paddock almost as quickly, and from there to the moors.

Winter was mostly a wild one that year. In early January high gales swept the coast, bringing a fury of storm and enormous waves lashing the rocks. Boscarne then felt like a fortress against the elements, or else a prison, I didn't know which. There were several wrecks that month, and at such times Mark Tremellick, curiously, was frequently out, at the scene of the disaster or embroiled in mysterious business with men — ostensibly concerned with the Revenue. If we chanced to meet then he would be short-tempered and abrupt and I wondered in what way he was concerned.

I knew smuggling went on, of course, and that rare cases of deliberate wrecking were not unknown. But Mark — the master of Boscarne — no, surely he would never be tempted with such barbarism. On the other hand, how did I know? Human life could be cheap to autocrats in authority. I must remember this and not allow myself for one moment to have false illusions concerning any member of the Tremellick family. So I hardened my heart against any slight softening of feeling, and coldly, deliberately set out to entrap the master of Boscarne, and play up to him with every feminine wile I could muster — so charm and entrance him that he would feel he could not do without me — until he *had* to.

It wasn't an easy ambition or an advisable one to pursue; I realise this now, and knew, even at the time, that Uter certainly wouldn't have approved! Occasionally I felt secretly ashamed and if there'd been a chance of happiness with Dick I'd have given in and enjoyed what I could in peace, of my new life. But by then I'd become convinced of Dick's duplicity. The troupe had not been anywhere near the vicinity for months. Once I casually asked a gardener — a native of Skillan, if he'd heard anything of the circus recently, and he'd told me no — that a sister of his near Truro had said Mr Goodfellow's company were keeping to more northerly regions thereabouts at the moment as the fairs there seemed more profitable.

On advice, I'd thought bitterly. He didn't wish there to be any contact with me, or risk of recriminations. I tried deviously to discover whether Dick and Mylora were married, but the man seemed to know nothing of the travellers personally except that the Fat Woman had left to live on a boat, which I already knew, and that the tiny Princess Titania was a great favourite with audiences.

So once again I had to accept the inevitable and concentrated with forced enthusiasm on my objective. The salary I was paid enabled me to spend more than I would ever have dreamed possible on new clothes, and during the first months of early spring I made trips to Falmouth, Truro and Penzance, with Lady Susannah's advice and connivance, being driven there in the family chaise, for, she told Mark, certain herbs, lotions and feminine accessories that she had a fancy for.

"Women of status need their fripperies and fal-als," she told her grandson acerbically, with amazing strength for one so old. "Also pills and potions and little beautifiers you men have no knowledge of. And the gal — young Sari — she's worth better things than the dull creations you sent for. Now don't you argue, or I'll get a temper on me and a fit of the megrims. D'yer hear?" And she rapped her ivory fan on her small shining side table fiercely. "There's a wig-maker in Penzance I'm told — a new one. Next time she goes, and Lili can travel with her — " Lili was her special personal maid — "she can bring me a couple. A white and a red." She chuckled. "I fancy red for a change, like Queen Elizabeth, eh?"

Master Tremellick — or Mark as I now thought of him — agreed in a conciliatory fashion. "Very well. It's your money you're spending."

"Aye. *Mine!*" She tapped her thin

breast with a grotesquely gnarled finger. "And don't you forget it. A good thing it wasn't a tired old pauper you had to take on with that — that prancing independent o' mine upstairs." All energy suddenly seemed to drain from her. "Poor Georges."

As I'd overheard the encounter I wished I dared question her further concerning the mysterious resident of Boscarne, but I knew any probing of mine might bring on a fit of temper, which from the old lady could be quite frightening.

So I fitted into her scheme willingly, pleasing both her Ladyship, and with great benefit to myself.

During February and early March I gradually assumed more confidence in playing the 'young lady', wearing silks and satins mostly of pastel shades that suited my tawny gold hair and delicate complexion, teaching myself to walk more gracefully, in styles fashionably calculated to accentuate the slender shapeliness of my figure to full advantage.

While pretending not to be outwardly impressed, Mark's eyes were frequently upon me whenever we met, either by chance or arrangement. One day in late February he requested my appearance at the dinner table at a future date.

"I have a friend — a prominent Revenue Official — in the Preventative Service arriving," he told me. "He'll be staying overnight, and I'm sure you are capable now of acting as hostess. I thought I would inform you in good time."

I felt flattered, triumphant, and a little uneasy at the same time. "If you think my presence is really necessary — "

"I shouldn't have mentioned it if I hadn't thought it at least — propitious," he interrupted. "There are times when a woman's presence can give a little flamboyance and gaiety to an occasion."

"I see." My voice was purposefully stiff. "So you consider me flamboyant."

"I didn't say that." He regarded me with eyebrows quizzically raised. "And obviously you missed the compliment I paid you in referring to you as a woman." He paused before adding, "How old *are* you now, Sari?"

The direct question brought a glow to my cheeks.

"Sixteen — nearly seventeen."

"Quite an age. Old enough to be married."

"I don't see that's got anything to do with it."

"No," he smiled slightly. "But it has a point."

"If you're thinking — "

"Of trying to marry you off to some worthy and obliging suitor or have aspirations in that direction myself," he remarked, "I can assure you you're wrong. You're very useful to me here. Indeed I should be very sorry to see you go."

"Thank you." For some stupid reason the almost business-like statement depressed me.

"Just try and behave less impetuously," he went on, "and don't be so quick to take offence. I can enjoy a wild ride over the moors as much as you, but life has another side. There's business, and the social duties that go with it. If you intend remaining at Boscarne you must accept all that it entails."

"I've tried to do what you asked me to — entertain Lady Susannah."

194

"Ah! yes. I know you have, and you've succeeded very well. But you can't forget the circus, can you? There are times when you long for it."

"Not the circus exactly," I retorted.

"Then *who*? — that artist fellow you talked about — does your torch for him still burn as strong and bright?"

I was completely taken aback. How had he guessed — even gathered an inkling of my feelings for Dick, especially as I'd stifled them so effectively from my life — or thought I had. His name had only cropped up on the rare occasions when the past had casually been referred to, and I'd been very careful to show indifference. Perhaps too much.

In a stubborn wave of defiance I said, "Dick's nothing to me now. He painted me, and helped me when I first joined the troupe and I — I admired him very much. He was that sort of person. And as you've pointed out more than once, I was then merely a child — in your opinion; though what this has to do with my meeting some stuffy Revenue Official, I can't imagine."

There! I'd done it again! lost my

temper and destroyed any show of dignity I'd assumed in the last months. I pulled myself together abruptly, and said, "I'm sorry. I shouldn't have said that. Perhaps now you'll realise it wouldn't be at all fitting for me to play the part of hostess."

"On the contrary, Miss Tregeer," his tones were mildly sarcastic, "I consider you a very good actress indeed, and quite capable of playing *any* part, if you've a mind to. And I can assure you, you won't find it half so onerous as you may imagine. Captain Ffaulks has a way with him for any pretty woman — even a young one. So I shall expect you at my table on Saturday evening. Now I must attend to other matters. By the way — "

I lifted my head high. "Yes?"

"Have you any knowledge of a man called Pete Bottran living in this area? He's a native and must have spent most of his life in the vicinity, part farmer, part — well, shall we say a man of many parts? — He has a small plot of land to the north of Skillan. Your foster-father, Uter, may have spoken of him some time.

Or don't you remember?"

I thought back, then replied, "Nothing much really. He wasn't the sort of person Uter liked. There were things going on like cock-fighting, and oh! — I don't know. He spent a lot of time at the kiddleywink and the Prowling Pig. That's all I can remember."

"Thank you. It's enough to be useful."

"In what way?"

"Nothing to worry your head about. I just mean to do a little cleaning up in this locality."

"*You*," I thought with indignation, "*cleaning up?* What right has any Tremellick to put himself in the position of God — of judging other people and lording it over them? You and your kind who did that awful thing to Uter and men like him?" I was not so stupid, of course, as to voice such thoughts, and a moment or two later, when I was alone again, realised that my grudge concerning his attitude to the cock-fighting and Pete Bottran had not only been unfair, but quite wrong of me. Pete had been a scoundrel of the worst kind — that's what Uter had said — involved in many unsavoury activities that decent folk avoided like the plague. Somehow, though, due to his extreme cunning, he'd never been caught. If Mark Tremellick *really* meant to expose him — but did he? *Did* he? — or was he merely sounding me out because of some devious purpose of his own?

I was confused; not only by the mysterious undertones of life at Boscarne, but by the workings of my own mind that at one moment were violently resentful and suspicious of Mark and his motives, at the next unwillingly excited by his presence, and in a strange way attracted. Perhaps it was partly the attraction I felt that made me so determined to provoke, or stimulate, his attention. He was so sure of himself; so certain that once he set his mind on an object he'd obtain it. If I could make him want *me* for instance — and then defy and deny him, it would be an achievement indeed.

What he'd admitted *was* true — I was no longer a child; day by day I grew more conscious of passionate longings that were subtly obvious in my appearance. My lips had a more sensuous curve to them, my complexion seemed to have a richer glow, my eyes shone brighter, and my breasts pricked full beneath the bodice of my new gowns. Occasionally, when I passed Mark in the corridor, strange desirous sensations stirred about my body and the ripening curves of my thighs. I knew I needed something desperately. If Mark were Dick now! But Dick was no longer in my life, and somehow remembering him was not sufficient to subdue the electrical awareness of Mark's physical presence. So while my will and mind rejected him my body didn't, and this made my project easier, and to me more possible.

From that moment — the moment of truth, of facing myself honestly, I set out wilfully to have Mark 'at my feet' — although the simile in my case was quite ridiculous. However wildly he might desire any woman he was certainly not the type to kneel. And I would not have had him otherwise. There would have been no satisfaction in the achievement of conquest.

Oh, how wicked I was. Suddenly I realised how Joanna would have chided me, and Uter have been ashamed. They had both been such really good and nice people, and for the first time, I realised, how different from me. There was no point any longer in pretending that my future actions were to be solely philanthropic — vengeance on their behalf. Emotionally, I was also obeying my own instincts. The whys and wherefores just didn't enter into the scheme of things any more. I was using Uter's sad fate as an excuse.

"And it's your fault, partly, Dick," I told myself, in an attempt at self-exoneration. "If you hadn't humiliated me so, I wouldn't be at Boscarne at all — I'd be with you, and the circus perhaps, because I *did* love you, truly."

Thinking so made me feel better, and I proceeded to cultivate my looks and manners in every possible way, taking care to observe any hints given to me by Lady Susannah on subtle make-up, perfumes and salves.

The evening of my dinner with Mark and Captain Ffaulks arrived. I wore a sea-green satin gown, with my hair dressed high, entwined with ribbons and a minute silver-jewelled butterfly given to me by the old lady. The dress was cut low, revealing the subtle, shadowed dip above my breasts. I felt, and looked, quite grown up.

The Captain's looks disappointed me. He was short, rather burly, with a high complexion, and blunt features that could have been passable in youth but in middle-age had thickened almost to coarseness. In manner he was affable, with a flattering approach suggesting he was used to having his way with women. Well, in my case, of course, this would not apply. At Boscarne, in Mark's presence he would be given no chance for dallying with me alone. If he *had* — then he would have received a shock, maybe a slap on the cheek. However wise and sophisticated I might be becoming in the modes of social behaviour, I had no intention of becoming any man's plaything. The fierce pride in me inherited, I suppose, from some unknown forbear, would never, *never* submit to any cheap second-rate relationship. The hurt I'd so innocently been subjected to as a young girl in showing my fondness for

Dick had ensured me against ever again being placed in such a position — least of all with any lascivious-looking portly little Revenue Officer.

It was like a game of cards in which I held the winning ace or else left the table. I would win the Captain's admiration, so obviously that Mark would be roused to jealousy, without in any way committing myself. I knew by then that I could make him jealous. During the last few days my efforts to allure him hadn't been in vain. His glance when he thought I was not aware of it was frequently on me, holding a mixture of curiosity, and deepening admiration which fanned my developing sense of power and excitement.

If anyone had said to me, 'You must be in love', I'd have laughed the suggestion to scorn. Love meant trust, the romantic unsullied devotion I'd so guilelessly offered to Dick. The awakening of my senses to Mark Tremellick was something quite different, and not wholly good or what would be expected of a young woman brought up on the high principles instilled into me by Uter and Joanna, peasants though they were. But then I wasn't their child. Who *was* I?

That evening before going downstairs to dine, driven by some strange instinct I didn't bother to fathom, I took the memento — my precious brooch, and wore it close to one shoulder, by a froth of lace. In the flickering candlelight, and reflected glow of the green satin, it took on a bronze hue. I saw, when I took my place at the table, that Mark briefly noticed it. A bewildered slight frown creased his brows for a second, then he quickly looked away, to speak to the Captain whose eyes were also upon me.

The meal was rich that night, the wine heady, and the conversation falsely light and contrived. Quite consciously, and with a confidence and aptitude I'd not relished or realised I possessed before, I played up to the two men — oh, shamefully.

Lady Susannah, of course, had primed me well. When I thought about it later, it seemed odd that I, who had been employed to divert and amuse *her*, had become in reality more of a pupil to the old autocrat.

Certainly on this first occasion and

test of my feminine powers, I succeeded more than my wildest dreams could have imagined.

At the hour suggested by her ladyship that I should retire, leaving the two men to any discussion concerning male affairs, I bid the Captain and Mark goodnight, and took my leave for my bedroom. To my surprise Mark followed me to the foot of the stairs. His gaze was fiery under his dark brows, his mouth grim.

"Thank *you*," he said, "for a most revealing evening."

His eyes strayed momentarily to my bodice which had slipped an inch lower. "I'd no idea you could be so intriguing a mistress of such a conventional occasion. Your act was superb, your appearance — quite dramatic. In future I'll recall it, should you attempt to play the innocent."

He took my hand, raised it to his lips, then suddenly, to my amazement, placed his mouth on mine, hard. There was no one about, and in a moment he'd turned and was walking smartly back through the small hall to the dining room.

I went upstairs in a daze hardly knowing where or *what* I was. One thing was clear, though, whatever the future held, I had already obtained my objective.

I counted for something in the house of Tremellick.

10

EARLY spring passed into young summer — a fitful period alternating with gales and storms followed by deceptively calm days flooded by sunshine which brought bushes and trees into bud, sprinkling brown branches with feathery pale green. Celandines and daisies starred fields and hedgerows. The moor was a patchworked glory of purple heather and the bright flame of gorse.

Between my determined attempts to keep myself always desirable in the eyes of Mark Tremellick I let my thoughts wander occasionally to the troupe and Dick, wondering if the circus players would visit the fairs at Skillan and Zaul. When there was no word of their coming, I tossed my head and shut the teasing memories of them away. What did it matter anyway, if I never saw Dick again? By then I was aware that Mark's desire for me was increasing. Whether he loved me or not I didn't know. What *was* love, after all? Once I had believed I knew. Now I realised that to different people it could mean different things.

Many times I could let matters between the Master of Boscarne and myself reach a crisis point — or rather forced the issue. But after that first passionate kiss, I was careful whenever possible to avoid intimacy of any kind — either by touch or in conversation.

"Hard to get," old Lady Susannah said one day. "That's the way to titillate a man, gal; keep him guessing. It's what this doleful house needs — a bit of intrigue, eh? Fancy him as a husband, do you?"

The direct question took me aback. I *had* visioned myself at exciting moments as becoming Mistress of Boscarne. But *marriage*. I'd not allowed myself consciously to look quite so far ahead. The old woman tapped her fan sharply on the table. "Well, what about it? He's not exactly the Adonis type, I grant you. Morose sometimes — stern, overbearing but that kind can make good lovers and breed well. Take it from me — I *know*." And she gave that certain sly laugh of hers that sometimes mildly repulsed me.

I decided to be quite honest.

"If ever Master Tremellick *asks* me to be his wife, I may consider it," I said. "Until then — "

"You're not going to cook your goose until it's hatched," she interrupted. "Wise girl. I like that about you. Down to earth when it's necessary. Yes — if it means anything to you — I suppose. You've got a head on you, *and* looks. Couldn't abear to have a plain pie-faced little miss fussing around."

She relapsed into silence. I'd have liked at that point to ask her more about her family background, including the strange dependent in his quarters above. But the next moment her old head had fallen against the pillows and she was asleep.

There was a storm that night. As evening approached the air became curiously oppressive under a yellowing sky. Before the first roll of thunder rumbled from the West, wind stirred the curious stillness, and the first drops of rain fell. Gulls rose screaming from the sea against the ominous rolling train of sullen black clouds; the line of moorland hills was lost above the wild and tossing sea.

From an upstairs window I saw Mark taking the side path to the open moor. He was wearing a cape and high boots, and strode with head thrust forward, full of purpose. I wondered what he was about — what mission drove him seawards against such fury of wind and rain. He was no farmer with livestock to attend to, and he did not normally frequent the kiddleywink in the dip of moors close to the precipitous cliffs. It was no business of mine, of course, but curiosity plagued me, keeping me rooted and watchful, peering hard as I was able, through the dripping glass of the window.

My glimpse of him was brief, quickly distorted by the stream of water then taken into the shadowed wet darkness of land and sky. Then I noticed something else; something that made me stiffen, alerted by a suspicion I'd sensed on previous occasions, but dismissed afterwards as a mere figment of my distorted imagination.

There was no moon that night, and

the first stars were obscured completely. Yet between intermittent lightning were other blurred glimmers of lights — quick flashes, no more, appearing, dying then reappearing again like contorted evil will-o'-the-wisps luring men falsely to their doom.

I was suddenly frightened — not only of what might be happening out there — but of my own monstrous thoughts. Something was taking place that concerned Mark Tremellick and uncharitably I sensed it had no good purpose. I had an irrational impulse to plunge out into the storm-ridden night and discover the truth for myself. Then reason told me I'd be discovered, and I could do nothing in any case. So presently I went downstairs to the parlour, and on the way met Mrs Pratt.

"It's a time for bad things to happen," she said ominously, then eyeing me shrewdly added, "You should thank your stars you're lucky not to be out in it. I've a fancy there could be drownings this night. Where have you been, Miss Tregeer, if I may ask? Mrs Delaney was saying that Lady Susannah was wanting you."

"Oh. I'm sorry. I'll go to her immediately." I rushed past the woman without another word, feeling her eyes following me as I made my way to the old lady's apartments. When I neared the door Mrs Delaney was already waiting.

"I'm glad to see you," she said. "The poor old thing — excuse me — her Ladyship, is — a little strange this evening. Due to the storm you understand? Thunder always excites her, and then — "

She broke off as a peal of wild raucous laughter and shouting penetrated and seemed to shake the very ceiling, from above.

I glanced up, half fearfully. The chandeliers were quivering, imbuing the portraits on the gallery walls with the fleeting impression of movement and life.

"Come along, my dear," Mrs Delaney's voice held a soothing note. "There's nothing to worry about — except my old lady. She *is* so very ancient, the poor dear. And that — that relative of hers — " she rolled her eyes upwards, "he's no help whatever. None at all, at all." She shook her head, urging me through the door, past the various rooms until we reached the bedroom.

When we entered Lady Susannah was sitting up in her mass of frills with the red wig perched on her head, her eyes gleaming bright as small polished buttons from her withered face.

"Come here, gal, come here," she commanded shrilly. "And let that woman go. Don't feel like Delaney tonight. Delaney! What a tomfool name. More suitable for a count than a mere attendant." She lifted a bottle to her formidable nose, breathed vigorously, while Mrs Delaney, mildly annoyed, but with extreme dignity, walked stolidly to the door and departed.

The old lady smiled, with her lips closed over her toothless gums. Then she said, "Think me a bit of a shrew, do you? So I am. So I am. Have to be with that foolish creature upstairs."

She pointed a finger upwards, causing the bangles on her thin wrist to rattle and quiver in the fitful light. Almost at the same moment there was a loud crash of thunder, followed instantly by a further reiteration of jumbled shouting and raucous bellowing. Yes, bellowing was the word — more like that of some caged up wild thing than a human being.

"Is he — is he often like this?" I ventured to ask. The old lady put a hand to an ear and said, "What's that, eh? Who? — speak up. Georges, d'ye mean?"

I nodded.

She gave me a quick shrewd glance.

"Georges ain't your concern," she said irritably. "Keep your curiosity and quick mind on your own business, and on *him* — the other one — Mark."

I said nothing, feeling that whatever remark I made might be wrong, and after a pause she quietened and nodded thoughtfully.

"Wants watching, *he* does," she continued. "Been in and out all afternoon. If you ask me he's up to something."

"In this weather?"

"That's *why*, gal. The storm. Storms can be very — lucrative. Oh, I'm no fool. If there's a wreck tonight, Mark'll be there. You see if I'm not right."

"But — "

"And no buts. Didn't want you here for arguing. Dance, girl — dance — "

I glanced down dubiously at my gown. It was a frilled muslin creation in a pale shade of buttercup yellow. "I'm not properly clad," I pointed out. "But if you'd like me to change — "

An angry touch of purplish-red mounted her prominent cheek bones.

"*Dance!*" she shrieked. I rushed to the bay window as a streak of lightning zig-zagged across the floor, and started on a gypsyish display of motion with arms and limbs rotating against the scene outside of lashing rain and windswept landscape. To the ancient old creature in the immense bed I could have appeared as no more than a gyrating shadow. Dimly, between the crashes of thunder weird haunting melodies from her music-box rose and fell, but their sound was intermittent and entirely subservient to the crashing and shrieking of the elements.

At last, exhausted, I stopped, and fell on to a nearby chaise-longue. When I'd recovered sufficient breath I walked to the bed. Lady Susannah was lying strangely quiet, with her eyes closed, and a secret small smile of triumph on her thin lips. I touched a wrist gently. It felt cold as marble. There was a flicker of her lids, and then they opened showing two slits of clouded weariness piercing dimly through the shadows.

"Good girl," she said. "Good girl," her throat rasped. "I liked that. Remember what I said though — " Her voice became a mere whisper, hardly more than a sigh. I bent down to hear what she was trying to tell me. "Watch him — " she said. "He has to be watched."

To whom she was referring I didn't know, except that it must obviously be Mark or the stranger above — her demented relative. A little later I had to accept that her intention must remain forever secret.

Lady Susannah Le Villemont was dead.

So were many more that night, for there was a wreck — a cargo ship driven off course with several passengers aboard, all of whom, and the crew, perished. Little of the valuable cargo was recovered; throughout the tragic hours plunderers — many of them natives of the district — were frantically purloining kegs of brandy, silk, lace — anything that was at hand, sometimes resorting to ruthless cruel acts on others in their greed.

Mark returned in the early hours of the morning tired and haggard, looking as though greatly distressed. How much of the emotion was genuine I couldn't tell. Only facts and commonsense could provide the answer, and facts were the unknown quantity. One alone registered uncomfortably when I thought back over the disastrous events — there had been amongst all the muddle and confusion of that tragic night a good deal of activity going on in the cellar of Boscarne. I'd *heard* it, from my room which like many in old buildings could carry echoes of sound in an uncanny way.

Where had Mark been at the time?

'Watch him,' Lady Susannah had said; 'he has to be watched'.

Had she meant Mark? I shivered involuntarily at the idea. If so, then I was dealing with and playing up to a very dangerous man indeed. Apprehension seized me in a rising cloud of self-revelation; in seeking to ensnare him — and that was exactly what I had been about — I'd lost sight of real issues and motives. Facing the truth squarely I hardly recognised myself as the innocent girl who had set off with her bundle and Delilah on her ambitious journey to Boscarne those many months ago. Oh yes, I'd had a mission, but the mission had been strangely mixed up with Dick's rejection. Where had desire and excitement taken over from the fairy tale? Everything concerning Boscarne for a few frightening moments seemed suddenly almost unbelievable — an over-coloured melodrama into which I'd unwittingly been plunged, and from which there was now no escape.

Even then I wasn't being quite honest. I wasn't *bound* there. I could don my old clothes, fetch the donkey from her field and walk away that very day if I wished, take to the roads again and seek my future elsewhere, forgetting the events of the past week: the terrible wreck and nightmare atmosphere while the storm raged, and Lady Susannah died; the ranting and raging of the lunatic in his towered premises; and of the ever-increasing desire in the eyes and heart of Mark Tremellick. The silks and satins, the vanity and wild achievement! Oh, what had happened to me? And why didn't I escape before it was too late?

The answer was simple.

I didn't want to.

I was already too committed to withdraw. I would continue with the charade until fate somehow resolved events with some sort of pattern. Only one factor would have the power to drive me from my course if Dick should miraculously appear again to claim his 'nymph'.

But he wouldn't. Every day that passed made me accept there was little chance of our ways ever converging again. Oh, I might one day see his face in a crowd at a fair, or passing by in some city street — perhaps even in London if Mark took me visiting there. *If.* There were still many 'ifs' to be considered. But in the strange instinctive knowledge I'd developed as a child, I felt that where Mark Tremellick was concerned they were soon to be dispelled.

I was right.

On an evening before Lady Susannah's funeral to be held at Zaul, two days later, I slipped out of the house, thinking a walk in the fresh air might help lift the pall of depression that had been with me all day. I would rather not have had to attend the sad ceremony, but convention and decorum demanded it, especially as the old lady had developed such a fondness for me. She had been difficult at times — and even rude but the imp of mischief in her had enlivened many boring periods, and I knew I was going to miss her. Still, she'd gone now, and her spirit was free, I told myself, making my way up my favourite moorland path — free as the gold rimmed clouds floating across the fading summer sky.

Several times, before nearing the first ridge, I paused, shaking my hair loose, allowing the cool drift of wind to stir my skirts and cloak, taking the lush sweetness of earth and air deep into my lungs. How pleasant it was, after the weeks of effort and sophisticated pretence, to be alone, *myself* for a time, however brief.

Except for birds' chattering and frail rustle of undergrowth in the gentle wind, all was silent, quiet, yet somehow alive with a sense of forgotten things, of ages past when early civilisations had placed standing stones and menhirs about the wild landscape either for the worshipping of strange gods, or as sacrificial monuments. The very air, I told myself, must be impregnated in some atavistic way with memories of the countless human beings who had once trodden the short turf smelling so sweetly of thyme and heather.

Death seemed a mockery, an anachronism, out there, in the lonely wilderness, for all existence was merely change — a constant rhythm of sleeping, waking, then turning to rest once more, with the approach of winter.

I was so lost in my own half-dreamy state, that I was quite unaware of anyone's approach, until a voice behind me said clearly, shattering the quiet, "Good to get away sometimes, isn't it?"

After a start of surprise, I jerked round, and in that same moment Mark's arms were about me, the warmth of his body close against mine, one hand smoothing the hair from a cheek. I made an ineffectual effort to free myself, but his lips were warm on mine; I could feel the thudding of his heart, as he continued, keeping his voice arrogantly cool, "The time for games is over, don't you think?"

"Games? Games — what do you mean? I — "

"You know what I mean well enough. And although the occasion may not be propitious, I think the old madam would approve. Oh, yes, she'd be exceedingly pleased. I can almost hear her laughing. Love affairs were quite her career once — "

"*Love* affairs?"

He touched my spine where the cloak had fallen from the shoulder, letting his hand travel sensuously beneath the soft silk of my dark-coloured gown, down the spine towards my buttocks, softly at first, while my whole body shuddered, half in rebellion, half response:

"Sari — Sari — " he went on, "witch, seductress, actress — thief — "

"I'm no thief. Let me go."

"How dramatic! How very, *very* naive. Well — no matter. The act's over." Once more his mouth burned my cheek, and neck, while my breasts, to my own self-disgust and anger, pricked towards him. "You've been wanting this for quite a time, haven't you? And much — much more. Did you really think I didn't see through the working of your cunning little brain from the start? Mistress of Boscarne. Well, why not? Your pouting ways and peacock clothes — damn bad taste at times, but effective, darling, though they cost a hell of a lot — "

"How *dare* you?"

He laughed, and when I made a rush to escape him, caught me swiftly up, and pushed me down, where I lay defenceless with only his wild dark face and the greenish glow of quickly gathering twilight above me. Something in me ached and longed for him — but something also of hatred and contempt.

"Don't touch me — " I muttered in a harsh whisper. "If you dare lay a hand on me I'll — I'll bite you — "

"And receive the beating of your young life," he told me relentlessly.

Then suddenly he let me go, got up, and pulled me to my feet. "Over here with you," he said. "The moor has eyes." He dragged me to a hollow overhung by heather, where, without more ado, he deliberately unclad and ravished me.

When it was over he fastened his shirt and breeches, bent down and pulled my bodice up over my bare breasts. "Now get up, darling, and don't say you didn't enjoy it — "

My eyes blazed as I struggled with my clothes. "*Enjoy?* Enjoy that, you brute?"

He smiled, and this time the smile was gentler, a little amused, but with something enigmatic about it I didn't understand.

"Oh, yes. And I can assure you as time goes by you'll begin to wonder how you ever got along without me. There'll be no thoughts or secret lusting for that pretty Dick of yours any more, because I'm the type of man who demands faithfulness from his wife — "

"*Wife?*" Still pulsing from the whirl of mixed emotions that had left my body hot and trembling, I stared at him in amazement.

"Of course. I'm no libertine — except only on very rare incidents such as this; and I must ask you to use a fraction of your astute intelligence to understand — at least in part. You've wilfully done your best to entrap me for months now. And you've succeeded at last. You should be proud of your victory, Sari, but it's a victory with a price. Marriage." He paused. "Well? Is that understood?"

I didn't know what to say. Suddenly, in a fit of unexpected fear I longed for Dick. Uselessly and stupidly. Yes, it was ridiculous to have any thought for him now. So with resolve suddenly strong in me, after all, I *had* planned for something of the sort, I said, "Very well, yes, if that's what you want — if you're really sure — I'll do it — marry you I mean." My tones were intentionally matter-of-fact, rather cold, though I still felt at a loss, bemused.

"Generous of you, darling, and so *very* romantic." The statement was sarcastic, but I sensed the hurt beneath the facade. And triumph filled me.

So it was, that without the slightest inkling of what I was going into, I agreed to be the wife of Mark Tremellick. I made no excuse to myself for either of us that we should have become so recklessly involved, so vitally concerned with the flesh, under the shadow of the old lady's death and the horror of the wrecked vessel. Life had been its own master proving its aptitude to flourish even through despair and decay. Later perhaps shame might register. It didn't occur to me at the time that Mark could have been acting under great strain, and suffering on account of his own personal loss, grabbing at any emotional outlet for release.

Only in the morning did I learn he had not been to bed that night, but spent it in his study with the whisky bottle beside him. However, he appeared later, sombrely clad, and in a fitting state for the funeral.

It was a dreary occasion, with thin rain enhancing the gloom, casting a grey shroud over the household and the procession of mourners following the hearse to the church. Luxurious flowers arranged in wreaths and crosses were massed on the grave and a thought occurred to me — quite irreverently — that Lady Susannah might have smiled grimly if she'd been permitted to see.

As the cleric muttered the solemn words of the committal I glanced round involuntarily, noting a few wild marguerites swaying in the thin wind; a lone gull screamed overhead, and it was as though her harsh old voice whispered, 'Wild I was, gal, wild in life as in love. I like 'em wild. Dance then — dance'

The breeze caught my veil, lifting it momentarily from my eyes. I saw Mark's gaze stray to my face briefly, enigmatic and searching. In sudden embarrassment I looked away.

After we'd returned to Boscarne following the sad scene, I went to my room not wishing to hear her will read, and spent the rest of the day in comparative seclusion, idly wondering and thinking back. Strangely, the swaying star-shaped daisies in the churchyard remained in my mind. When the exotic wreaths had faded, I thought, I'd return one day to the church on my own, and place a few on the grave. I might even replant a root. I knew in her own manner she'd been fond of me, and would have appreciated Nature's ballet of dancing wild flowers about her.

Just how fond she'd been I didn't realise till the next morning when I was told by Mark that she'd left me her extremely valuable ruby ring which in itself could be worth a small fortune. Also a legacy.

"So you don't come to me without a dowry, my love," Mark said wrily. "Convenient for us both. I shall quite understand if you decide to rescind our agreement and go in search of your handsome ex-love."

I could feel myself stiffen.

"What an unpleasant thing to say, or even think."

"Is it? I wonder. If so, I apologise. I was merely pointing out in my usual blunt way that you are now an independent young woman able to choose your own course."

"My my bequest — " I told him, "won't make any difference. As far as I'm concerned it's settled, unless you — " I paused questioningly.

He shrugged, and without kissing me, said a trifle awkwardly, "There's no need to go on. I know my own mind. We'll discuss the wedding shortly, at a more befitting time."

He went out of the room closing the door quietly after him.

I didn't know what to think. I was curiously bereft of feeling, but I knew one thing.

I would become the wife of Mark Tremellick and Mistress of Boscarne.

11

ONE day in autumn when the changing shades of summer's green had turned to molten bronze and gold, interspersed with patches of purple heather, between granite boulders and wider tracts of brown earth, Mark and I were married at Zaul Church, very quietly, with only a few members of the household present.

Mark didn't wish for ostentation or any display of wealth. The men and their families at Wheal Sally which was still working as the only Tremellick copper mine, but with a reduction of employment owing to poor loads and the increasing fear that the ore was running out, were going through a bad time. Mark's confidence that in sinking a new shaft with an adit opening to the sea, westwards, could prove profitable and give stability to the workers, had proved a failure. The fresh levels yielded a minimum of copper, which gave evidence of soon fading out completely. Men were laid off to face inevitable hardship.

"It can't be helped," he said to me once, when I ventured to plead their cause. "I've done what I can. The estate can't afford to run at a loss for ever — even Boscarne."

"But what will they do?" I asked, remembering days in the past when Uter had toiled so unremittingly to eke a living from a small patch of earth. "Most of them haven't even land to grow anything on."

"They'll have to leave, I suppose," he said with what seemed to me ruthless disinterest. "I shall do what I can when any particular case of distress crops up. But many Cornish families are taking off to America, and others have their unions — "

"Like Uter!" I exclaimed bitterly. "And of course there's always Van Diemen's Land, isn't there?"

He came towards me and placed his hands on my shoulders. "Now look here, Sari, the mine is not your affair. The people are free — "

"*Free?* When families like yours — "

"Ours," he interrupted. "You've married me, remember?" His voice was hard.

"Ours, then," I conceded, with indignation seething in me. "But it doesn't *feel* like it. The wealth, the means, the *power* — are still yours. I can't do a thing without asking your permission or have the chance to spend or give a little help sometimes when asked. I'm just a puppet."

"Don't be ridiculous. Anything you've wanted you've had so far: But get this into your head once and for all — I will not have a future wasted on futile efforts to prop up a failing undertaking. Wheal Sally's shortly on the way out, and nothing on earth's going to save it. It's for their own benefit. The workers should realise it and have time to plan life ahead. Isn't that what the unions were formed for? To advise, and co-operate?"

"*Unions*," I almost spat the word out.

"Sari — Sari" he made a conciliatory gesture and tried to draw me to him. I tore myself away defiantly. "Leave me alone," I said. "Go away. I don't want you."

"No?"

I turned my head facing him with the colour high in my cheeks. "Not now. Not at the moment. I want to be on my own.

"You've done quite a lot of 'wanting to be on your own' since you married me, haven't you? Well, if I were you, for both our sakes, I'd take a good look at the situation, my love. Up to now I've been pretty reasonable, I think, concerning any — marital obligations. You're still young — I knew from the beginning there'd have to be a time of adjustment. But don't goad me too far, Mrs Tremellick; and in future don't spend so much time visiting workers' cottages with your goodies and fine airs. Oh, I know what's been going on. Your gifts no doubt have been appreciated. But your patronage hasn't helped at all. The tinners are a proud lot, and any assistance forthcoming should be from the proper channels. Then again, there's a sickness going around; cholera. I don't want you taking any risks. The cock-fighting too, and this poking your nose into men's affairs — stop it, Sari."

"You mean the smuggling? The wrecking?"

He laughed, but the laugh held no humour. "Yes. I mean just that. Fairy tales mostly. But fairy tales can be dangerous and lead to enquiries where I'd rather matters were left alone, at peace."

"But you said — you said before we were married you were going to get things cleaned up at Boscarne," I reminded him.

"Did I? How unwise of me, in your presence. I didn't realise then what an interfering little baggage you were. Well — as I said just now, no more of it, and that's an order."

He walked away leaving me chagrined, and once more doubting his devious and extremely domineering attitude. Obviously he didn't want any questioning at all about business matters or motives. At the first opportunity I was put in my place and reminded that for women to be subservient to men in marriage was not only to be expected, but their duty. So far I hadn't chafed too much, because I'd been mostly silent and careful not to create an argument. In my determination to charm him completely I'd put aside my first rebellious ambition to thwart and defy, and the result hadn't been entirely unpleasurable.

On our marriage night Mark had been considerate, after my first attempt to tantalise and evade any display of passion. Following our experience on the moors, of course, it had been impossible to play the innocent, but driven by memories and mixed up emotions I *had* shown him very clearly that I didn't intend to be a mere possession for sensual enjoyment, and at one point had said, in what I'd hoped was a bored, sophisticated denial, "Oh, *please*, Mark! I do think I've had enough of this sort of thing tonight," had yawned ostentatiously and turned away.

The next second his lips had been on my shoulder; he'd forced me round and said in a cold voice, but with the temper hot in his dark eyes, "None of your haughty ways, Mrs. Tremellick, or you'll get slapped. And no lies, darling — no pretending I'm your precious Dick when you lie in my arms with your eyes closed. We'll have this straight from the beginning for both our sakes. You're my wife, understand?"

He'd not waited for a reply, but had taken me in passion to a wild fulfilment that had left me in no doubts that he'd meant what he said. Resentment, anger, mixed strangely with exhilaration and an unexpected primitive delight, had left me warm and throbbing, and so exhausted I'd fallen almost instantly into a deep sleep. In the morning, when I'd woken, he'd already gone downstairs for breakfast, and at our meeting an hour later he was once more the self-contained firm Mark Tremellick I'd known in the early days remote and polite, glancing at me appraisingly as though we'd just been introduced.

"I hope you slept well," he said formally.

"Very, thank you," I replied.

He'd looked at the window, commenting, "A grey day. Probably we shall have rain later. I have to go to Truro on business."

"Oh, so you won't be here for lunch."

"No." He'd smiled a trifle cynically. "That will give you plenty of free time to recover your — equilibrium. Last night must have been a trifle — wearing for you."

Unpredictably I found his cool statement disappointing. I'd felt cheated, with a silly impulse to sting him to life. But I'd kept my temper outwardly in check and replied as languidly as possible, "Last night? — oh, yes. I was so very sleepy I'd nearly forgotten. We didn't quarrel, did we?"

"Evidently your bridal night didn't register in accordance with the rules," he'd replied cryptically, but I'd known he was annoyed.

I'd smiled serenely.

"Rules are so often boring, and rather futile, are they not?" I'd said with affected politeness.

He'd laughed shortly. "Oh, Sari, don't be so ridiculous. And for goodness sake — "

"Yes?"

"You've put on far too much rouge, even for a bride. Tired you may be, but go upstairs and take a good look at yourself in the mirror. Rouge doesn't suit you, and rub that stuff off your lips."

That had been that. But with some irritation later I'd seen that he'd been right. Scowling, with my brows drawn together and my underlip thrust out, I did appear a bit of a dressed up hussy. How foolish of me when my prime intention had been to impress and reduce Mark Tremellick to shame. Dick would have laughed, I'm sure.

Dick!

Oh, botheration. *Why* must my thoughts constantly turn to him in moments of needing assurance? To him I'd merely been 'nymph', that's all; and in the end not even that. The result of Mark's criticism, however, did have some effect. I must be careful — *very* careful, I told myself — to retain dignity at all costs — to be elegant, though I doubted I was naturally the elegant type — if less colourful and impressive.

The weather during the next weeks turned grey and damp, calm one day, windy the next bringing rain from the sea. Sometimes I went walking, swathed in my new green hooded cape, occasionally I accompanied Mark to Falmouth or Truro in the chaise when his business

— whatever it was — was not too lengthy, and allowed time for a snack at a coffeehouse or fashionable inn. But for the most part I was left on my own, and made use of spare hours at Boscarne by experimenting with my appearance, trying new hair styles, and using the different lip salves and creams from the ivory box given to me secretly by Lady Susannah shortly before her death.

One day Mark informed me that Captain Ffaulks was once more coming to dine with us that same evening. The prospect was boring until I realised the occasion would give me a chance to exhibit the new dignified me.

I think even Mark was surprised when I entered the dining room. I was wearing an olive-green satin gown, simply cut, low, but not *too* low on the shoulder, with an amber pendant — one of Mark's gifts to me, at my throat. Instead of my hair being coiled and pinned softly with a butterfly ornament or entwined with ribbon, I had it discreetly and simply taken from my face to the back with a single tortoiseshell comb. I wore only the merest suggestion of pale pink lip salve, and used no rouge for my cheeks — nothing but a faint film of powder; the effect was tasteful — even slightly matronly, I thought, except for the glint of my green eyes that seemed accentuated somehow, giving me a hint of the wayward 'nymph' look so frequently commented on in the past by Dick.

If Mark noticed he probably assumed uncharitably, that I'd been using belladonna or something, but I doubted he was aware of such details. His main concern was obviously his business with Captain Ffaulks, and that I should play the part of a graceful well-mannered wife and hostess. A background, no more — I wondered once again why he was so intimate with the Captain for whom I felt instinctively he had no real liking. Was Ffaulks a part of the cleaning-up process that Mark had referred to more than once? Or was there some ulterior purpose to the apparent friendliness existing between the two men? It was impossible to know. Anyway — why should it concern me so much personally, considering I'd married him not for love, but for yes, there was no point in denying it, even to myself — but for power?

The dinner party with the captain was certainly a success from my point of view.

I knew it from the lascivious, slightly surprised looks in the men's eyes — Mark himself was impressed; for once, it was quite clear to me, he saw the seventeen-year-old girl he'd married in the role he'd envisaged but not entirely expected — as mistress of his household and a situation that for secret reasons of his own was important to him.

"I'm enchanted once more to have met you," Ffaulks said before leaving, kissing the tips of my fingers in the manner of any fashionable young gallant, though he must have been quite forty, his small eyes crafty and cold in his rubicund face. The bland smile on his mouth was entirely false. But I smiled in return.

"It has been most pleasant, Captain Ffaulks," I lied with a faint inclination of my head, and rustle of silk when I moved.

"And doubtless we shall meet again," he added. "And I hope one day to have the pleasure of entertaining you — and your husband."

"Thank you."

When he'd gone Mark pulled me to him and planted a kiss on my forehead.

"You were superb, Sari," he said. "And I am grateful."

I pulled myself away abruptly. "There's no need for gratitude. It's what I'm here for, isn't it? What I'm *supposed* to do — fit in with your plans."

He laughed.

"Plans? What *do* you mean?"

"I wish I knew. But one thing I *must* say — "

"Go on."

"I don't like that man. There's something cruel and greedy about him, and he's not even attractive."

"Did you want him to be?"

"Of course not. Men mean nothing to me."

"Men?"

Wondering whether he expected me to say 'except you' — I circled round the answer and replied, "I'm a married woman, am I not?"

He smiled, his dark eyes lit with mockery.

"'Are you not, indeed!' Oh, Sari,

you really sound — quite ridiculous sometimes. Don't you realise that only a ninety-year-old, or a little girl would use such a pedantic expression?"

Discomforted I turned away. "Whatever I do and however I speak seems to be wrong. You compliment me one moment and then somehow" I swallowed hard, searching for the right word, "deride me the next."

"No." All lightness left his voice, his tones became solemn, dark, on a lower key. "I never deride you. You're far too subtle and primitively schooled in feminine wiles for me to imagine I could."

He came close to me. I could feel the warmth of him — the touch of his hand travelling to the base of my spine and lingering at my buttocks for a moment then circling my waist and drawing me to him. I lowered my head in a half-averted movement. His mouth rested on my bare shoulder as a hand pushed the silk lower, till the nipple projected as a bud of a flower would project from its green sheath.

We were in the conservatory which

led one way from the dining room. The servants had finished clearing the table — only soft candlelight streaked from a hidden chandelier at the far end of the room across the shadowed floor. The scent of pothouse flowers and foreign blooms hung sultry-sweet in the warm air. An unwonted strange excitement caused a pulsing of my most secret physical self as his pressure increased, fondling me. Instinctively, because I knew and resented the fact that I had not and never could love this man — I made a feeble effort to extricate myself, and failed.

"Not here," I protested. "There are servants about. Not here, Mark."

I must be free, I thought, free to collect my wits and steady my nerves. At the moment I was on the verge of complete subjugation which might turn even to supplication, betraying me. By the time we got to the bedroom I'd have schooled myself to a sterner mood. He would claim me, yes, and I'd respond. But this dark, demanding flame would have steadied into commonsense reality. I was his wife, he could give something I needed, and I could be, equally, a vessel for his desire. But not his possession — never, *never*.

Somewhere — half alive, still struggling behind the leaping, hungry vitality that consumed me, the shadow of another hovered fitfully — the lost romantic dream of a girl's intrinsic virginity. Dick. Senses and brain fought in a wild effort for justification; but the battle was already lost.

Mark lifted me up and carried me to a seat at the darkest end of the fern-smelling interior; then cat-like on lightning feet, he'd sped to the door and locked it. I attempted to pull the green silk protectively over the bared breast, but my hands were shaking, my whole body already trembling with the force of a river about to break into flood. One foot reached the ground — a satin slipper from the other fell as though of its own volition before I could properly move.

"Darling — darling — " Mark whispered, " — brat — woman — come — " His hands were soft and sensuous and sweet, gathering force until my being was ripe and ready, fully open to receive him. Above, the velvet leaves spread their shadowed shapes moving in mysterious rhythm with the rhythm of our bodies taken to the ecstatic forgetfulness of intercourse. Time was lost, and well obscured by the wild fire of mating. When the heart's tumult had at last calmed, we lay for a time still in and of each other limbs entwined, until he slowly eased himself free. I didn't move, except to sigh. He bent down once, and kissed the sweetly damp triangle of golden hair, guardian of my womanhood, so recently ravished, then got to his feet. My gauzy cape, like the sheathed wings of an immense fragile butterfly, lay on the floor. He picked it up, and handed it to me.

"Now, dress, Sari. We have the night before us."

I did as I was bid, bemused and still palpitating, while he smoothed his hair, and got himself into some sort of order.

Satiated, at peace, I felt no guilt, though an inward reasoning told me I should have done.

'I don't love you,' I thought. 'This was mere — sex. It must have been.'

And I tried — tried hard to think of Dick, but in the end gave up — Tomorrow I would be able to assess everything better; tomorrow I'd know whether this taste of something that was more than lust, less than adoration on my part, had endowed me with more power or lessened it.

Yes. Tomorrow I would once more be myself — Sari Tregeer who'd married Mark Tremellick intending to be a woman of purpose.

Girl no more.

Which fact, from now on, Mark would have to accept.

The months passed from winter into spring again, with Nature's blossoming wild and sweet about the moorland hills. It was a period of uncertainty for me, filled with passionate physical longings and appeasement which left me still doubtful and prone to fits of resentment concerning Mark's activities and secret self.

Though our bodies were now familiar, our spiritual and emotional selves remained apart — separate identities that held individual criticism of each other. It would have been easier for me if I could have found somewhere evidence of Mark's duplicity — for duplicity I'm sure there was — but there appeared no practical facts to go on. Workers at the mine were dismissed through necessity, for which he produced figures for me on paper. Some were retained when it was possible to survive loss, though without profit. He put accounts and figures before me which I pretended to understand, but which really meant little to me.

Apart from the financial problems which he said faced the estate he went out of his way to help any family in individual distress. Many he encouraged to go north to the cotton mills, by paying their fares. Others took off to the Americas in a mood of defiant resentment. He put a stop to cock-fighting whenever possible, but avoided trouble when he could, because, he said, it was to the landlord's advantage and those working for him to be on as good terms as possible; without co-operation there would be no achievement or improvement in mutual relationships.

I believed and superficially had to

accept what he said, but I wondered why he had to spend so much time at the notorious nearby kiddleywink — why, when there was any loot or plundering from a floundered vessel, Mark was somewhere in the vicinity, and why he was still on such intimate terms with Captain Ffaulks. I hated deviousness and the personal innuendoes frequently exchanged in my presence, and as my confidence in the status of being Mark's wife steadily increased, took the chance whenever it arose of absenting myself from the two men's company.

"You still don't like Ffaulks, do you?" Mark said once, when he found me on the terrace following the Captain's departure.

"No."

"Don't show it too openly, Sari, if you please," my husband said rather coldly. "I rely on him quite considerably."

"So it appears," I answered, with mild sarcasm.

"And there's no need to take that tone with me. Watch yourself. I have a way of dealing with naughty girls you wouldn't appreciate."

"I'm your wife," I stated.

"A girl nevertheless, and don't forget it." He turned on his heel, walking away smartly, leaving me feeling curiously chastened and indignant, and realising he'd meant, and was quite capable of fulfilling, his veiled threat. I shrugged my shoulders, tossed my head, though he was not there to see, and with the muslin skirt of my gown lifted in both hands above my ankles, made my way down the terrace steps, taking a path to a copse at the bottom of the gardens. All was still and golden and hushed there, but alive and vibrant with the secret pulsing and stirring of growing things, filled with scents of thrusting grass, ferns, and froth of blossom from thorn and wild cherry.

I thought instinctively of winding lanes, and vans moving to hidden resting places by woodland and curling streams. Images from the past were reborn with imagined echoes of laughter. From the deep purple and green shadows of the undergrowth, a bird piped joyously, and I was remembering the comical antics and squeals of Mylora's monkey — recalling the nomad existence with

Mr Goodfellow, Fanny Petra, Tobias and Rom — and Princess Titania; oh all of them. Especially Dick.

Dick!

He was a young fair-haired prince again, and I his love.

A choky feeling filled my throat. I wanted to laugh and cry, lift my arms and rush into his own.

What was I doing here in the garden of the great stuffy mansion when the whole surging world waited for me to wander and dance in?

There was no answer of course. Life was an odd unpredictable business. No one knew what lurked just round the corner.

Certainly *I* didn't.

Because, next day, Dick himself arrived at Boscarne.

12

IT happened out of the blue, almost unbelievably, a complete shock, which took me by such surprise I stood rigidly after the door opened, unable for seconds to move.

"Sir Richard Flaherne," the servant announced before the tall figure stepped into the large parlour.

I had been having a short argument with Mark concerning a horse I'd been trying out in the paddock — a young mare that he'd told me I must not yet attempt to ride because she was still unpredictable. At the time I hadn't meant to flout him, but the day was so beautiful, and during the past few weeks I'd grown to regard myself as a capable horsewoman — almost. And anyway where was the danger in a few yards canter round with a groom nearby?

Of course, Mark had seen and ordered me back into the house for a confrontation. Like a chastened rebellious child I'd gone, knowing that most probably I was in for a scolding which might or might not, as the case might be, end up with a passionate reconciliation. It was some time now since we'd made love, owing to my husband's late business hours which meant he was out very often into the early hours of dawn.

So my devious womanly instincts had induced me to take the initiative which if he discovered it would inevitably produce some sort of personal reaction. Once we were in close proximity I'd learned from experience the way to rouse his senses and thus satisfy my own. Oh yes, as well as being older than when we married, I was certainly more knowledgeable in certain physical matters. He had not become a substitute for Dick, and never could be. The role Mark played in my life was quite different — more down to earth and worldly-wise, whereas Dick had been my hero, my very first love whom I'd trusted and looked up to with romantic reverence until his betrayal.

So when he appeared, tall, golden-haired, blue-eyed, and as handsome as ever, I could only stare speechless and bemused, with my heart missing a beat then racing ahead with my brain whirling.

"Ah! Richard," I heard Mark saying as if from another world — a world of make-believe or theatre. "Come in. This is a surprise, I must say. You look very fit, my dear fellow. And flush. How've the masterpieces been going?"

There was a quick pause, so short as to be almost imperceptible. Then Dick strode forward with his hand out to grasp Mark's — or the other way round, I don't know which. He was looking quite splendid in pale grey, with a clean satin waistcoat, and neckscarf. The blood rushed to my face in a tide of excitement. My riding habit irked me, although it was of green velvet, and fitted perfectly. But I should have been wearing one of my elegant new gowns, was the first conscious thought that occurred after the initial shock of surprise. It was the first time I'd seen Dick for so long, and I had to be like this — attired more as a boy or play actress with the troupe, than as Mistress Tremellick, lady of the house.

From those few moments of uncertainty

that seemed an age I was dragged to reality by Mark saying, "Sari — this is Richard — Sir Richard Flaherne — an old friend of mine, and very remote family connection. Dicky — meet my wife, Sari."

The old elfin smile touched Dick's lips. "Hullo, my nymph," he said.

With a sudden rush of delight I ran towards him; he laughed, and half pulled me off my feet to hug me, then suddenly desisted — took a step backwards, regarded me quizzically and remarked, "My — *haven't* we changed? You're quite a young — lady, shall we say? And those breeches certainly become you, sweet.

Through a conflict of emotion I was aware of Mark's stiff comments, "So you two know each other."

"*Know* each other? This is *Dick*," I exclaimed. "*Dick!* I've told you about him. You know — the artist who was with us, the circus."

"Yes, of course. Your puerile attachment. Or should I say paramour?"

Slightly taken aback by the terse comment, Dick, after a short laugh, said, "Now that's putting it rather strongly. Sari was just a youngster; a child. A wild fiery little thing who appeared one day with an old donkey called Delilah. I always knew she was different in some way, didn't I, nymph? She had potential and a way with her — we got on well. And knowing her I must say I'm not surprised she took you by storm; though *marriage*! — always thought you a confirmed bachelor, Mark. But it just shows. I suppose I'd have heard the news earlier if I'd been in this country. But for some months I've had a spell in France, painting. However, what about a late toast to the occasion now?"

Mechanically I watched Mark take decanter and glasses from a cupboard, and pour wine into three glasses. He was curiously silent, until after handing me one — only half filled, he remarked, "We'd had so little contact during the last ten years I'd rather lost sight of your activities — except, of course, from time to time of your growing success, among other things, as an artist under the name of Dick Loraine — a painter of gypsies and the demimonde."

"Oh yes. I chose a fictitious name to work under. Why?" He shrugged. "A sort of cover-up, I suppose — a help to freedom and self-expression."

"Double identity," Mark stated drily.

"You could call it that."

"Which is why you've never had the inclination to look me up before this."

Dick's eyebrows shot up. "Dammit, Mark, old lad, you sound peeved. Well — " his voice turned to mockery "can't say I entirely blame you; I suppose it's been a bit of a shock finding your new — so very young wife and I had been so well acquainted. I know her well of course. She was in our troupe. Don't worry, though — " His expression sobered for a moment, became curiously penetrating as he glanced at me, then quickly looked away again. "I can assure you our affection was entirely innocent — a brother-and-sister affair most would call it, although I admit I was tempted. Sari in her own way is unique." The banter though meant to lessen the strained atmosphere, seemed only to increase Mark's annoyance.

"I can imagine it, recalling your Oxford reputation."

"Ah! Oxford." Dick's blue eyes sparkled. "The little charmer at the Rose and Crown! Adorable, wasn't she? and your nose was properly put out of joint on a certain occasion. But again — there was nothing in it, dear fellow, not seriously. She *did* fall for me, I admit, but it was just a game, a lark."

"In which you certainly excelled," Mark agreed with a wry smile, "and have done so I presume ever since."

I watched Dick's face change from mischief to one of thoughtful retrospection that hovered on me speculatively, then lightened to casual nonchalance as he lifted his glass, and said brightly, "Now then. This toast. The very best to both of you. I do congratulate you, Mark. Sari, I know, will prove to be a gem in your household, and make a wonderful wife and mistress of Boscarne. I envy you.

Nice words, but too late to mend the damage he'd done. Mark's lips had tightened, the dark eyes narrowed, holding a cold glint of suspicion — or was it jealousy — that hurt and disconcerted

257

me. And yet I shouldn't be either. I knew that I'd done nothing wrong. It was not my fault that I'd suddenly been so excited at the unexpected sight of Dick. Mark had known all along that I'd admired and cared for someone in the past. It must have shown. I'd never attempted to deny it. It was natural for me to show pleasure — for want of a better word — and to be excited when his friend proved to be the Dick of my past. But why had Dick explained things so lightly? And that reference to the girl at Oxford — although he was not actually comparing me with her, the allusion was somehow cheapening. That was his other side, I supposed — the sophisticated dilettante — the *Sir* Richard Flaherne who had his own life apart from that of the wandering unconventional artist who had so captivated my imagination and heart.

He'd deceived me. Indulged and played with me, that was all. I'd already known rejection of course, and learned to accept it. But his attitude now, in front of Mark somehow added insult to injury and further humiliation.

258

Following the mockery of a toast, I managed to excuse myself and went upstairs to the bedroom lingering on the way to stare out of the window on the landing where the afternoon sunlight dappled the changing pattern of the moor to a fitful vista of gold and deep soft purple and green.

My head was still awhirl, my heart quickly beating with trepidation, excitement, fear, shock, and a sudden knowledge that shattered wildly all my preconceived notions of loyalties and affection. It was as though a great wind had suddenly swept cold and clear through me, leaving facts, shed of all illusion, blatantly imprinted on my mind. And the revelation, though shocking, was also a triumph, because for the first time I really knew and accepted the truth about myself.

It was not Dick I loved. Not any more. I'd thought so — oh how I'd believed it; but I hadn't known him — only the facade, the handsome knight errant of a young girl's imagination.

It was Mark I needed and cared for so passionately. Mark, the realist and whatever else he might be — smuggler, adventurer, tyrant or law-maker. Good or bad, respectable or devious planner for his own ends, it didn't matter. Or if it did, I still wanted and desired him as I could no other man. The superficial moralities and prim judgements of youth counted as nothing against that one supreme fact: the overpowering mutual need of two people destined for each other, shocked to recognition through a chance situation, totally unexpected and shattering in its impact.

How long would Dick be staying, I wondered? Had he merely dropped in casually, yet hoping to stay overnight? And ought I to warn Mrs Pratt of the possibility so the guest room could be made ready?

I decided to leave matters as they were. If Mark wanted me to be concerned he'd have made some suggestion in my presence. Perhaps I should have offered hospitality myself. But no — that wouldn't have done. Mark had obviously been resentful that his old university friend should have been the Dick of my adventurous period with Mr Goodfellow's company. How silly of him; or was it? I *had* at times been rather over-enthusiastic in recounting what Dick had said and done — how handsome he was, and how clever with his brush, and of his plan to make me famous one day as Undine in his painting. So perhaps my husband was jealous. The idea sent a quiver of excitement through me. It would be so wonderful, later, for me to prove to him there was no need, that Dick meant nothing at all to me any more. "Oh darling, my love I thought. "Please, *please*, hurry up and send Dick away. I want you so —

Life indeed was incredible; weeks, even days ago I'd still believed only the fair-haired handsome gallant of my adolescence would have any place in my heart. Now he'd become just a pleasant shadowy image brought back to me from the past.

A dream.

Yes, it was like waking up from sleep suddenly to all the vivid wonderful possibilities of human existence. Happiness and thrilling anticipation glowed in me, "Hurry — hurry" I almost said aloud, tapping with my foot on the floor.

Restlessly, I left the window, and went to my room, where I discarded my riding habit for a blue gown.

How long it was before I heard the tread of footsteps on the stairs gradually becoming louder as they approached along the corridor to the bedroom I don't know. But at last the door opened and Mark strode in.

I waited hopefully, with my breath quickening, heart thudding against my ribs — waited for him to approach with the flame of desire in his dark eyes, trying hard not to make the first move. Why didn't he? Why did he stand there for a second or two looking so stern, almost angry, before shrugging and marching past me towards his dressing room? He went in and came out almost immediately with a coat over his arm.

"Has Dick gone?" I said as casually as possible.

"Naturally. It was only intended as a flying visit, or so he said. But quite long enough, it seemed, to rekindle your undying passion."

I was not only bewildered, but shocked, and ran towards him catching at his coat sleeve before he went out.

"But Mark! *Mark!* What on earth do you mean? I don't — I was only young, I admired him terribly, yes. I was romantic I suppose. But you surely don't think — "

I broke off, seeing he did not believe a word I was saying.

"Go on," he said coldly.

"About what? What is there to say?"

"Exactly. The light on your face when you saw him was far more revealing than any words could be. Oh, I don't blame you. I should have expected it. All those fancy clothes of yours — your calculated elegant efforts to please — your little girl innocence and pouting pretty ways — they were for *him*, weren't they? Even when we made love you imagined it was Richard holding you. *I* was just an *incident* — a convenient stepping stone to ensnare him when the moment arrived." He paused, adding after the brief interim, "My God, Sari, you've been clever. Even with the old lady — you had her fooled. 'Such a pretty child,' she said, 'virgin too. And all for you — mark my words. Marry her. I know the sort; faithful once the right man comes.' But she was wrong for once, wasn't she? And the right man was bloody Sir Richard Flaherne — "

"No. I've *told* you. Why can't you believe me? You must! — you *must*!" I forced my arms up to his shoulders, he wrenched them away, and his hands were iron on my flesh.

"Spare me the melodrama, Mrs Tremellick. No doubt I shall get used to being the make-shift — substitute — so long as I don't see too much of you — "

"How horrible of you!" A lump of indignation swelled in my throat holding the threat of tears. "What an awful thing to say, and what a lie! You've always taunted me with being young — well, then, why don't you remember it now, and try to be fair! Remember what I had to go through and how I started — "

"How the devil do I know how you started? I've only your word for it. I know precious little at all where you're concerned except your peculiarly adept way of kindling a man's fancy when it suits you."

"But — "

"Stop it, do you hear?" He forced me to the bed where I sat watching him dumbly, shivering and cold with despair, as he strode to the door. He turned there once again, looking at me before leaving. "Don't worry," he said in hard remote tones, "I've no intention of discarding or divorcing you. I've no reason, have I? Not legally, and in time no doubt I shall be able to look on your so beautiful face and body without recalling so vividly your all-too obvious passion for Flaherne. We shall have to see, shan't we? In the meantime I find the sight of you beyond bearing. So I shall take off to town for a bit, and maybe when I return we can resume life dispassionately without any foolish notions of love, dutifully, in the way of most married couples. Yes, in the future I shall expect you to do your duty and beget me a son. Remember to ensure, though, that he *is* mine — or I'm afraid I may kill you."

With which such dreadful words he left, banging the door behind him. He didn't know, how could he, since I wasn't sure myself, that I already carried the small embryo of his child in my womb, or that during the following days there would be many times when I'd wish I didn't and could run away to freedom and peace, forgetting there was anyone in the world called Mark Tremellick whom I'd once loved.

The trouble was that I knew I couldn't. Whatever and wherever I was however far apart we were, I would never forget. *Never.*

I loved him; and it was as simple as that. Searching wildly for an answer I thought again of Dick. Dick was the only one who could help. He hadn't realised the harm caused by his light chatter. But Dick had already left. If I could only find him and explain, he'd make Mark see sense, I was sure he would.

I'd no idea of his destination, though. To join the troupe, perhaps, or on his way to an exhibition somewhere. Whatever the answer, as it happened it made no difference. In the morning, after sleeping in his study, Mark had departed and I was alone. Alone except for the great house, the servants, and the demented stranger in the tower room, Lady Susannah's relative, whose terrible laughter and shouting could be heard from time to time like an ominous herald of disaster to come.

A sense of uneasy depression seemed to encompass the whole house. From a mood of earlier delight and anticipation, dejection enfolded me. Everything following Dick's arrival could have been so different — if only Mark had understood. But his icy sarcasm and deliberate condemnation had flung me into an irrational sudden hatred of my surroundings. I remembered my first impression of Boscarne those many years ago when I'd been a child — the awe and wonder inspired by the shadowed turreted place emerging forbiddingly from its nest of trees, the lights, a pale figure rushing to her lover's arms along the terrace — a fairy tale vision of secrets and romance that I'd hugged to myself during the long sad days following Uter's conviction and deportation, but one, nevertheless, that had also cemented the youthful determination for vengeance on the rich folk who could live like kings and queens of their domains, shutting their eyes to

267

the fates of poverty-stricken, less exalted, human beings.

I'd tried, at first, but because of Dick, followed by Mark's sudden impact on my life — I'd been content to forget, simply because the joys of living and loving had swept me into a wilder, happier existence. How could it have happened? And how — *how* could I have allowed myself to become so enslaved during the few moments of comparison between the two men — by such a domineering proud, hateful creature as Mark Tremellick?

Yes, I vowed to myself, with tears of anger and despair rising from my throat to my eyes, half choking me — I *did* hate him now, for his ruthless words and cruel attitude — the same cruelty that had coldly, deliberately sent Uter to his death. And the hatred was intensified by the knowledge and memory of my previous passionate subjugation to him — how he'd ravished and possessed me. I couldn't stand this place any more — I couldn't, I just *couldn't*. But deep down I knew I could, for a time anyway, until I was quite certain of the baby. If I was having Mark's child it must have every chance of a comfortable beginning; then, when opportunity arose I'd go away and deprive him of it. He couldn't stop me. I'd have by then sufficient means to support a child. There was always the ruby — Lady Susannah's gift to me. I could sell it; Mark had told me several times that it was worth a small fortune, and once had said jokingly, "Keep it safely in its box, Sari — if you ever get into a rage and want to leave me you can buy yourself a ticket to the Americas and take off."

He'd laughed, because of course the idea had been simply teasing.

Now I realised it could well be true.

I went to my jewel case and opened it. The ruby was still safe and sound among other trinkets, rings and necklaces given to me by my husband. He really *had* been generous; but then, I told myself wrily, he had bought me, after all. I, like those poor creatures I'd read about — had been sold, just as poverty-stricken women were known to have been in the past by heathen husbands at sales in open market places. Only in this case I had sold myself.

I was playing with the jewellery when I nonchalantly came across the small bronze brooch, relic of my babyhood — that I'd not worn for months. For the first time I was seized by a truly avid curiosity. What did the design and strange lettering imply? Who *was* I, *really*? Dick had appeared at moments to be overtly interested whenever I'd worn it at my neck or bodice. Once he'd wanted to take it to an acquaintance of his for examination. But I'd refused and clutched it to me.

"No. It's all I've got of my own except Delilah. It was mine before Uter ever saw it. I shall keep it always. It isn't valuable, anyway. Joanna said so."

Dick had shrugged, and replied, "All right, nymph — don't worry. I'm not intending to steal it."

I knew that, but all the same I had been careful to keep it always on my person where no one could touch it without my knowing. Thinking about the charm, or whatever the strange emblem on the brooch meant, released some of my tension concerning Mark, and even made me recognise that I could have been over-melodramatic about the sharp verbal battle between us. A man who could have felt so passionately about me surely wouldn't lose desire so easily just because he imagined I'd had some kind of an affair with his friend?

I put the brooch back in the jewel case and regarded myself through the mirror. My eyes stared back at me brilliantly from cheeks that were too flushed to be becoming. I dabbed some rice powder on, and decided to go downstairs, determined to appear cool, aloof, and dignified, if Mark should still be about, and surely he would be, he could not have left for London so quickly.

But he wasn't there.

Mrs Pratt was hovering about the hall at the foot of the stairs when I got there. She had an envelope in her hand. Handing it to me, she said, "The Master left this for you. He was called away hurriedly, as I believe you know, ma'am."

"Yes," I answered mechanically. "I was well aware of it."

When she'd gone I opened the note. It simply said,

Sari, sorry it had to be like this. Your play-acting of the innocent was somewhat naive though; during your period with the troupe you should have mastered your art more efficiently. However, that's neither here nor there. As I said, in time, when I can bear the sight of you again we may be able, effectively, to resume an outer facade of connubial existence. Richard, I believe, may be calling at Boscarne in the not too-far-off future. If so, give him my regards. I trust you to conduct yourself with reasonable propriety in public. As to the rest I don't care a damn, my dear, I really don't. When I shall return I don't know. Take care of yourself.

I remain your husband in name,
Mark Tremellick.

I stared at the cold, condemning note moments before screwing it up and putting it in my pocket. So bitter, so cold — almost deadly. Nothing in the message of warmth or consideration but 'take care of yourself'. And that meant no more than mere politeness. But he had said

Dick might come. Well, let him. If Mark meant to treat me in such a reprehensible way, there was always a second best. With this defiant purpose I went upstairs again and applied an overgenerous amount of make-up before returning to the large hall and parlour to face the household and any suspicious ideas they might have of Mark's departure.

No one seemed to have any exact idea of when he meant to return. The bailiff of the estate was a competent man, busy at the home farm, and the manager of the mines, Joe Parish, was popular with workers, possessing a tactful tongue, and understanding of the precarious situation which enabled him considerably better than Mark, to deal with any unexpected problem. Oh yes; Mark had seen when he inherited Boscarne, that management was under adequate control to continue efficiently without him should it ever be necessary, which was why, I supposed, he hadn't been *too* harsh in dealing with any odious customs brought to his notice such as secret dog baiting and cock fights.

As for the wrecking — but I didn't

know about that, so could prove nothing at all. And in any case my enthusiasm for justice and righting wrongs, had worn so thin as to be comparatively non-existent during the personal misunderstanding that had arisen. How ironical that after so proudly and subtly enticing Mark to marry me — which, unpleasant as it appeared in words — was nevertheless the truth, he had in the end cast me off like any discarded and unwanted mistress.

During the days that followed I tried hopefully to believe that all might come right in the end, but I didn't really believe it. His words, and the bitter dislike on his face before he left for town still made me writhe in humiliation. Therefore when Dick returned in early October, I was more than willing to receive him.

He had wished to see Mark, he told me, on a certain matter, but as he was away would have to return later, some time before Christmas.

"You'll stay to dinner, though?" I said politely, in cool tones that belied the mixed emotions churning me.

"Yes," he agreed heartily. "A chance

to sup with my nymph in all her elegant splendour will delight me." His blue eyes were twinkling.

"Oh, don't be silly," I said. "I'm not your nymph, and I'm eighteen now. Not only that — I've learned a great deal since I was with the troupe."

"I'm sure you have. And it's not so bad, is it, Sari, leading the sophisticated privileged life?"

"I'm hardly sophisticated," I told him. "It's pleasant having money, of course, and not having to worry about circumstance and — "

"And your domineering jealous husband is able to fulfil your other needs very satisfactorily, I'm sure."

I flushed.

"I don't know what you mean. We're married, I'm *his* wife — I — I want for nothing," I lied.

He shook his head slowly regarding me thoughtfully. "Is that true, Sari? Really *true*?" he asked in quieter tones.

"Why would I lie to you?"

We were standing in the small parlour which was more primitive than the larger premises.

"Because I unintentionally may have hurt you," he answered. "But — can we sit down and talk about something between ourselves for just a little time, love?"

Ignoring the word 'love', I replied, "Of course. Although I don't see what you have to say now that can be important to me," I told him.

"That's why you must know."

"Know what?"

He held out a hand. "May I look at that brooch you're wearing?"

Mystified, I put a hand up to the little bronze ornament pinning the white lace at the neck of my green satin gown.

"*This?*" He nodded.

"You've seen it many times before," I added, as I handed it to him.

"Not closely enough."

He took the brooch and studied it carefully, then put his hand in a pocket and drew out a piece of paper headed by a small engraving which he compared with my memento.

"Have you got a magnifying glass?" he queried, after a full minute.

"No. But I think there's one in the

top drawer of the secretaire — over there, I've seen Mark using one." I indicated the chest at the far end of the room. Dick strode swiftly across the floor and jerked the drawer open. The glass was there. He took it to the window, and scrutinised the two objects while I stared on bewildered.

Then he murmured half to himself, "So it's true."

"*What* is?" I asked. "Oh, Dick, do tell me, what are you talking about?"

"Sit down, Sari," he said, as he replaced the magnifying glass in the secretaire. "I have a story to tell — a strange one, but true, nevertheless. I'm sure when you've heard it you'll understand *me* better, *and* other things, incidentally — things concerning how Uter came to find you by the wreck when you were a baby."

"*Uter?* Do you mean — ?" I broke off helplessly. He took me by the shoulder and eased me into a chair. Then he seated himself in another, nearby, and began.

I watched his face unblinkingly, noting the subtle changes of expression:

hesitancy, doubt, followed by a tightening of the lips denoting a determination at all costs, to reveal something pleasant or otherwise, that would have considerable impact on my life. When he spoke his voice was quick at first, gathering force as the narrative got underway.

"You've been thinking for some time now — years — " he said, "that I'd been playing with you in the past, that my feelings for you were light and worthless. Oh, yes — " when I attempted to speak "don't interrupt. I couldn't blame you, but believe me it was no joke to me. I *did* love you, Sari, although you were so young, and I still do. If things had been different there'd have been no need for us to be separated. But, my dear, nothing in the world could have made any union between us possible. And we were becoming too fond. Many times I tried to delude myself I was mistaken. There were days — moments when I thought — damn it, why not take the risk? No one knows — facts aren't proven; if it hadn't been for the brooch there'd've been no cause to dream of such a thing — "

"But *what* thing? *What* facts?" I demanded impatiently. "Dick, do explain, you're talking in riddles."

He sighed.

"Very well. I've now got all the proof needed. The truth is — " he hesitated for the fraction of a minute before stating bluntly, " — you're my niece, Sari, or rather my *half*-niece. Your mother was the daughter of my father's second wife. So you see — "

"But I don't. I *don't* see," I cried, with excitement rising in me. "How *can* I? How do you know? And what has the brooch to do with it?"

"The brooch bears the crest of our family. Alone it would not be sufficient to prove your identity. But following months — more than that — of research, and digging and delving, I've procured and have here an envelope with a letter in it stating the true facts of your birth. It was given to me by the aged brother of an old servant of our family now dead, and is an account of how you came to be found by your foster-father on the night of that terrible wreck eighteen years ago.

Still too dazed to properly comprehend what he was saying, I merely asked, "What *could* any old servant know about me and — and my mother, and Uter?"

"Uter simply happened to be at the scene of the disaster at the time," Dick continued. "Your mother had eloped and married an impecunious artist, much to my father's distress and anger. The man must have been a bit of a bounder, I'm afraid — charming and no doubt talented, but without conscience. He deserted her, leaving her practically penniless and expecting a child. After the birth she had sufficient money to make the journey to Cornwall where the old retired servant I mentioned lived. Her name was Sarah Geeke, and Marie-Anne, your mother, had been a particular favourite of hers. She'd hoped, according to this letter, that old Sarah would take the baby in, and that she herself *without* the child, might return home to her father — her mother was dead — and ultimately be forgiven."

"Unfortunately Sarah herself was almost on her death-bed, and could not take the responsibility of the little one.

Then, in the same week, there was the wreck. Desperately, Marie-Anne seized the opportunity of taking the child to the seashore and in the confusion leaving her in a comparatively safe place — where Uter found her. Now don't please blame your mother too much. She was young and frightened, and did not return to Sarah's cottage — it's derelict now, a mile along the cliff to the west — until she saw the child — *you* — rescued. In about a week she set off for Devon where our family lived, but the strain had been too much for her delicate frame and on the way she collapsed and died."

I stared at him blankly. Aghast. "You mean my mother — *my* mother could do that — "

Dick looked grim.

"My father, your grandfather was a very stern man, Sari. He *could* be terrifying."

"But how did you find out all this?"

Dick shrugged.

"Oh — there are ways. Devious methods. As I said, the brooch was the clue; Sarah's ancient brother proved to be the last vital link. I located him in a poor house run by kindly nuns, and after careful questioning he handed me the letter given to him by Sarah. The one you see here. It's an account of what happened on that tragic night so many years ago. The old woman had evidently worried about the affair, and when she knew she was dying had handed the information to old Joe in case it could ever be of use to you, Sari, in the future. There's no possibility of fraud about it. She'd got a young minister to witness the statement. He might have divulged the contents later, I don't know, but the same week he was drowned in a futile attempt to save a young boy who'd fallen into the sea. Joe, of course, should have given it up — the letter — long ago. If it hadn't been for the brooch with the family crest on it — well, you would almost certainly never have known your true identity a — " he paused whimsically before adding, " — Sari, daughter of Marie-Anne and Wilfred Crane, grand-daughter of Sir Frank and Lady Flaherne."

"*Lady*," I gasped.

"Oh, yes. My late father was a baronet."

"And you? That's why Mark introduced you as *Sir* Richard Flaherne?"

He gave an ironic, yet somehow amusing, little bow. "Exactly. But more important still, and you must remember this always. I'm a would-be artist, play actor, and adventurer — a dreamer of dreams, and companion to all, vagabonds, gypsies, rogues and kings. Another thing — "

"Yes?"

"Your father's paintings, Wilfred Crane's, have become more famous year by year. In his way he was a genius, Sari. I've a great respect for him as an artist — if not always as a man, considering his treatment of your mother. But at least you were born in wedlock."

I couldn't get over it, I simply couldn't.

For some time I couldn't speak following the astounding news, then at last I said, "And you're really my uncle?"

"Your half-uncle. So you see — however much I might have wanted you — in a certain way, it would have been wrong, nymph — " Oh, how I loved at that moment to hear the well-known words on his lips again, " — in fact, worse than that, incestuous which *could* have led to the most unthinkable outcome, concerning children, of course. Do you understand?"

I nodded, without speaking, trying hard to adjust myself to a whole new situation and relationship I would never have dreamed of.

Dick! — the man I'd loved, my uncle. But why hadn't he told me before? So much sadness and bitterness could have been saved. I would never have thought of him in terms of passion and romance. The love would have been there, but of a different kind.

Seeing the shock and bewilderment in my expression, he answered the question without my having to ask it.

"I only knew for certain last week," he told me quietly. "It's taken quite a long time, as I told you, to get the necessary information."

"But you must have *believed* it," I pointed out. "Then why did you let Mark think we'd been sort of — "

"Lovers? But, nymph, I didn't. He was so exceedingly stuffy I couldn't resist pulling his leg a bit. You know *me* — maybe I shouldn't have. But, mark my words, I got him on a soft spot. Every husband needs to be made a bit jealous on occasions, and I didn't *lie* at all. When he comes back from wherever he's gone to, he'll be at your pretty feet begging you to forgive his bad mood. Surely to goodness you don't imagine he *really believed* I'd gone into the great seduction act with a *child* — " He stared at me in amazement.

"I don't know what he believed," I answered, "but he was very angry with me, because you made me look *cheap* somehow."

"Well, then, I'm sorry. But after he's heard the true state of affairs everything will be all right." When I said nothing he queried, "You *are* happy I hope? You love him?"

"I don't know," I replied bluntly. "At the moment I'm not sure of anything at all."

And I really wasn't.

We chatted for another half an hour or so, then, after the meal, Dick left.

"I shall be calling back quite soon,"

he told me, kissing me gently. "And do buck up. Everything's going to be fine for you — I'm sure of it."

"And Mylora?" I questioned, suddenly remembering. "*Did* you marry her?"

"*Marry?* What are you talking about?"

"She said she was having your baby — it was when you went away that time and you were going to marry her. That was why I couldn't bear to see you again."

He sighed, flung out his arm with a gesture of exasperation, shaking his head in disbelief.

"Mylora and truth are often at war," he said. "What she says and wants can be very different to reality. No, I did *not* marry Mylora, neither did she bear my child. In the end Rom, who is quite an obliging fellow in his way, took her on, seeing the state she was in."

"You mean she's his wife — that he — ?"

"He may be the baby's father — it's a boy, incidentally — he may not. Who knows? Rom anyway appears to quite enjoy the responsibility. They're two of a kind in their casual infidelities and seem to get on well, with plenty of fights between them to brighten up the domestic scenc. As for marriage" Dick's eyebrows shot up, " — there was some sort of ceremony I believe, a kind of Romany affair to which I gave my blessing later and a handsome wedding present as help for them along the road."

I felt quickly ashamed, indignant at my own past naivety and Mylora's duplicity.

"How beastly of her to tell such lies," I said hotly.

"And how silly of you to have believed them. By the way — " he changed the subject quickly " — next month you'll be presented with a new aunt. The Lady Angela Frayne, daughter of an old friend of my late mother's. Yes, your roaming vagabond uncle has at last decided to take the plunge. I've kept her on strings long enough, poor girl. She's very sweet and charming, and will make an admirable wife, I'm sure, knowing beforehand of my liking at times for rogues and players, and wandering the world for brief periods with paints and brush on my own.

He smiled whimsically, and kissed me

again, lightly, on the tip of my nose. Then he turned and ran lightly down the terrace steps, looking back only once, to call, "You'll see me back very soon, nymph. We've still things to talk about, and with Mark too."

Then he was gone.

The next few days became sultry-sweet, with the sun only dim gold behind windless yellowing skies. I longed desperately for Mark to return, but he did not. The house itself held a brooding quietness disturbed only at infrequent intervals by the occasional heavy murmuring of Lady Susannah's dependant from above. I seldom saw Mrs Delaney, and Mrs Pratt herself appeared more irritable than usual, speaking only when she was addressed, in short jerky tones.

I longed for all the windows in the house to be opened enabling any air there was to clear the stuffy interior of lingering dust and atmosphere of things long gone. Once I took my mare from the stables and rode up the slope to the first ridge of high moors behind the house. Even there the sense of oppression — even menace

— lingered. Dolmens and standing stones assumed a curious identity of their own, emerging from heather and bracken as watchful guardians of their own primitive territory. Occasionally a bird squawked, or some small wild thing scurried through the undergrowth, otherwise all was quiet. Deadly quiet. In the distance to the east, the stark shape of an abandoned mine stood bleak and skeletal against the sullen sky-line. It was as though all nature waited. For what?

I turned my mount abruptly, kicked her to a canter, and presently cut down in the direction of Boscarne.

When I went into the house, after leaving the mare with a groom, no one was about, although from the kitchens I heard once the vague clatter of a kettle or pan being moved.

I went upstairs desultorily, and changed from riding kit into the coolest dress I had, of pale green muslin, patterned with tiny daisy spots. I knew it suited me, and felt resentful that there was no one to see me except the servant and Mrs Pratt. She passed me as I took the turn at the foot of the stairs towards the library.

"A pity the master isn't here or Sir Richard," she said in dull emotionless tones. "You look charming, madam, if I may be allowed to say so, fit for a dinner party." The last little statement held a hint of disapproval.

"I just wanted to be cool," I remarked with a brief glance at her before continuing on my way.

She muttered something. I think it was "Yes, it's heavy. Maybe we'll have thunder later," and disappeared into the shadows of the hall.

The library seemed very dark when I went in. No candles had been lighted, or lamps. But then it was still comparatively early, and as the room was seldom used except by my husband I supposed the housekeeper had thought there was no need. Three of the walls were completely filled with volumes, mostly travel books and the classics with a portion allocated to fiction including Samuel Richardson, Daniel Defoe and Miss Austen. After peering without much interest for a few moments I chose two books, and returned with them to my bedroom which was considerably more cheerful than the musty downstairs interior.

I read a few pages of *Pride and Prejudice*, but was disturbed by my maid coming to turn down the quilt of the large bed, and after that I found I couldn't concentrate. The sullen skies drew in to yellow-grey evening. Boscarne assumed the enveloping cloying atmosphere of a tomb. Try as I would, I couldn't shake it off; it was as though ghosts moved silently, unseen, along the vast corridors and rooms, predicting disaster. I considered at one point whether to ask Mrs Delaney for permission to enter Lady Susannah's apartment and have a tune from the music box which I knew would be in its usual place. Everything, I'd heard, had so far been kept in its usual place since her death, almost as though she was expected to return one day, having woken from a long sleep.

I shivered, abandoning the idea quickly. Better far, and less morbid, to settle down in the small parlour after dinner, and continue working on my needlework a sampler bordered by fantastic birds and sea-creatures.

I did try. But needlework or sewing

had never really interested me, and sitting for any length of period on a straight-backed chair wearied my spirit. So I went to bed early, hoping that I'd soon go to sleep and in the morning wake to find that the weather had freshened sufficiently for me either to take a walk, or possibly travel by carriage or chaise to Truro on a shopping outing. For a little while I glanced through the pages of a new fashion magazine before settling down. Then, when my eyes started to prick, I blew out the candles, removed the extra pillow, and very soon dropped off into a pleasant doze that gradually took me into deep sleep.

What startled me some time later, I never knew. But I woke up abruptly, with my heart racing, nerves on edge, knowing someone or something was about. I sat up listening. There was no sound at all, but what could have been the creaking of a door, followed by a faint shuffling movement.

The room was quite dark, except for a very thin shaft of quivering light streaking across the floor. I reached for the candle and matches on the bedside table, but my hand came against an obstacle, soft, rubber-like, followed by a low-throated chuckle that could have been from some strange animal or of human origin. It was obscene — horrible. I was on the point of screaming when a padded thick object accompanied by intensifying blackness, smothered my mouth. Light flared then unexpectedly, and looking up, I saw, terrified, a wide bloated face staring down on me, huge lips curved upwards in a leer. Small protuberant eyes stared from mounds of fleshy cheeks close to my own. I struggled vainly to escape, half-choking in an attempt to make myself heard. But it was no use. I was stifled and could hardly breathe. At the same time an enormous hand grasped one breast, then circled my back and lifted me close against a hot sweating body. Before I fainted I was aware briefly of a white wig half-tumbled from a bald head, and noted again the gross features — bulbous nose and heavy jowls with saliva trickling down the stout chins. Then mercifully darkness claimed me, obscuring terror into deep temporary nothingness.

When I recovered consciousness I was aware at first only of a glittering whiteness streaked with shafts of gold that finally resolved into an ornate ceiling encrusted with huge animal shapes and naked human beings, flowers, fruit and ornate trees.

From the shadows cast by flickering crystal chandeliers, the figures gave an odd impression of movement, and when I turned my head reflections of statues and gilt furniture confronted me from numerous mirrors. There were mirrors everywhere; mirrors, lights and — something else. Something large and bulky looming in a far corner of the room, the gross form of a bewigged man watching me. My heart quickened and thumped against my ribs as he approached the chaise-longue where I was lying, coming into full view under the brilliant blaze of the central chandeliers. He wore a crimson fitted velvet coat reminiscent of a past decade with knee breeches and cream silk stockings to match the silk cravat where a huge diamond blazed its white fire. His immense stomach was protuberant under a yellow satin waistcoat, reminding me of some rich villain of a fairy tale.

But it was no fairy tale. As my mind managed to register clearly I did not have to question who he was. It could be no one else but Lady Susannah's mad relative, the occupant of the tower room. Frenziedly my brain sought this way and that for the safest way to handle him — if there was any way at all. Instinct told me I mustn't argue. At the moment he appeared pleasantly inclined to me, but I sensed a wrong word could move him to violence.

I got up quietly, curbing a rash desire to run screaming to the door calling for Mrs Delaney. Where was she anyway? I wondered. How had the imprisoned recluse managed to reach my room and capture me without anyone knowing? As if sensing my thoughts the obese figure moved closer, smiling. Then he spoke, in curiously light high-pitched tones.

"Ah madam!" An arm showing tips of podgy fingers behind the lace ruffles of his coat was waved towards me in mock dignity. "You wish to rise no doubt? Pray allow me to assist you."

I shrank back. He frowned.

"Now, now. No tantrums, if you please. It is a great honour I do you. When a king such as I — a rich and noble king bestows attention on a — female — it is her duty, is it not, and her pleasure — to curtsey?"

"But — "

His mood changed suddenly.

"Get up," he shouted in almost a roar, "or I shall have to chastise you. With this." He picked up a small gold-handled whip from a chair, and raised it, waving it to and fro, so the motion set it writhing and curling like a thin snake through the air. "How would you like that, eh — *eh*?"

I gulped, too terrified to answer, and his temper eased slightly. "No, I think you would not like it at all, to be beaten about the buttocks like any common whore — " He let out a great sigh, and said sadly, "It would be hard, very hard. Because you see, I desire you. I've seen you from my window many times, and, yes, the king desires you very much. Is that not an honour? A very great honour indeed?"

I swallowed with difficulty and managed to say appeasingly, "Of course, sir. Of course. But wouldn't — wouldn't your man or Mrs Delaney mind? I mean — "

He threw his head back and laughed uproariously, "My man, Stockmore, has the day off, and as for *her*. That coarse common Irish besom?" He leaned forward so I could feel his hot breath on my face, and continued, speaking in a low voice, confidently, "To tell you the truth, midear, I've already dealt with the meddlesome creature. When my grandmother died she took too much on herself. Like a look at her, would you?"

"Is she — is she about?" I ventured to ask.

"*About?* Come — " He grasped a wrist and dragged me to a door slightly ajar, which led, apparently into some sort of dressing room.

"There!" he said, kicking it open savagely. "Such an ugly stupid creature. No breeding, and no idea *at all* of her place."

So you see, I had to do it. My duty." He took a pinch of snuff, as though to conclude the statement firmly.

I stared.

The body of Mrs Delaney lay pushed in a corner near a wardrobe trussed up like a fowl. Limbs were contorted and bound by cord, rope cut deep into her neck; her eyes were glazed cold and staring, and between blue lips the tip of her tongue emerged. There was a bruise on one temple and I knew from my first glimpse that she was dead.

Icy with terror and shock I glanced up at her tormentor. He was by then walking up and down, chest thrust out, muttering pompous senile words, the words of a maniac: "As I said, I had to do it. Duty is the essence of kingship — however unpleasant it may be." He paused as he drew near the victim, continuing contemptuously, "Poor thing. She should have known better."

With the toe of his shoe he prodded the bundle that such a short time ago had been a human being, then turned to me smiling his idiot grin, and remarked, "*But* you will be different; no sneaking and cheating and prying into my affairs. You will behave. I'll see to it, and even allow you a bon-bon when I feel like it. And never, *never* hide this from me, understand?" He took a large key from his pocket and waved it before my eyes.

When I didn't immediately answer he repeated, shouting, "D'ye hear me, eh? Answer, apologise, wench, or you'll rue the day. Get down on your knees before I take the whip to your back."

Trembling, feeling sick, frightened, and so disgusted I feared I'd vomit or faint, I bowed my head and made the gesture he demanded.

When I got up again he sighed complacently, replaced the key in his pocket, and eased himself into an immense plush-seated armchair with a high back surmounted by a coat-of-arms. He was breathing heavily as though the incident had tired him, and his complexion had changed from its rubicund hue to greyish purple.

I waited, wondering if I dared to move, trying to avert my gaze from the terrible vision of Mrs Delaney's dead body. The very air seemed to tremble with unseen forces of elemental energy, such as those governing the ebb and rise of the sea — of tremendous amoral action receding at regular intervals to passivity and quiet, then once more gaining strength and power. And as I stood there facing him, Georges' expression, even his features appeared to change. Hopelessness dulled the protruding eyes. The strong muscles of his large stout hands flagged, leaving them limp and flacid. He shook his head slowly.

"You'd better go," he said. "Very soon it will be over, and I shan't be sorry. It's a wearisome business, being king. But I could've been a good one if they'd let me. Understand? It's all mine — this place — " He stared at me almost pleadingly.

"Yes — yes," I agreed mechanically.

"All mine — " he repeated, "and no queen. Until now."

He heaved himself to his feet and moved an arm in a circular motion over my head. Then he placed a finger on my brow, and drew himself up to his full height towering over me like some legendary giant come to announce death or life. "Beautiful," he muttered, "eh, yes. And beauty must live. Not like the flies and black things contaminating the earth. That's what I meant, y'see? For beauty to live, the ugliness must perish. That's the way of it — what being a monarch means — to stamp out the bad such as that old crow lying there — "

His brow puckered suddenly into a frown. He swayed slightly, with the red blood mounting beneath his skin. Involuntarily, I made a movement, stepped back, and it was then, with a strangled cry, and clutching his own throat, that he fell. There was the crashing noise of a side table going with him, and the splintering of glass, followed by the echo of footsteps running along the corridor outside, and a thunderous banging on the door. With a great effort I warded off fainting and forced myself to fumble at his pocket for the key.

It was there, thank God. I rushed ahead, located the lock and turned the key in it. The door swung open catching me with a sharp edge on a temple. I fell, knocked senseless by the impact of flesh with wood and iron, into a world of blackness and swirling stars that became acute pain like the sharp agony of a hundred knives stabbing.

Then the world receded; I was aware only of faces looking mask-like from above, whether of angels or humans I didn't know or care. My one desire was for the cruel hurt to ease, and for sleep. But sleep did not come until a strong draught of some pain-killing drug had been forced down my throat. Even then there was no proper rest; all was a confusion of mixed impressions and illusions — of flying, running, climbing, and struggling for some unobtainable goal, while friends mocked and crowded upon me, throttling and sucking the breath from my lungs.

Examination of the two bodies confirmed that Georges Monterron had died of a seizure, following his brutal attack on Mrs Delaney which had resulted in her death. However, for more than a week after the tragic event, I lay in a half-coma, from shock in which nothing registered but a wish to be alone and free from any human company. Although it was still summer everything about me felt cold, even the warm bricks wrapped in blankets at my feet, and the hot liquids forced down my throat. I recalled nothing positive of the tragedy but horror — of having been in some kind of hell where bulging eyes and snakes writhed to the accompaniment of senile shrieks and laughter. Sometimes I cried aloud for help and was then told I had merely suffered from bad nightmares. Once or twice Dick called to see me. I recognised him, but remained rigid and aloof, wishing him to go away. The doctor came; he was a kindly, portly man with a red beard that looked like a straggly carrot. I laughed and pointed when I saw it. He looked surprised, but patted my hand and put something in my mouth — a thermometer. I had a wild fleeting desire to clench my teeth and bite it in two, but instead stupidly started to weep.

"There, there," he said. "Try and relax, Mrs Tremellick, you have a fever, and a certain amount of concussion. But it will pass in time. One day all this will be nothing but a bad dream to you. You'll have your baby to think of then. On the whole, you're a very lucky young woman."

I must have been getting considerably better in spite of delirium, to have understood his conversation. I was even momentarily startled by his reference to the coming child. Not that the idea of becoming a mother gave me any pleasure. I didn't want any baby of Mark's who could possibly develop into something like the dreadful Georges. Yes, suddenly I remembered; Georges, the lunatic relation of Lady Susannah who'd killed Mrs Delaney and imprisoned me in his dreadful apartment.

"I want to get away from here," I whispered once to a nurse who was attending me, "please help me. I know what happened. I can't bear this — prison any more."

"It's not prison, my dear," the kindly voice said, "and when your husband, Mr Tremellick, arrives, I'm sure he'll agree to take you away for a holiday once you're strong enough."

I tried to think clearly, but it was wearying. "When does he come then? Does he know what — what happened?"

She nodded. "Sir Richard left for London to inform him, and we had word yesterday that the master would be here in the shortest possible time."

"I don't want to see him particularly," I said coldly.

"Now, now, don't say such a thing. You know it's not true."

"It *is* true. I want — " I broke off, losing myself in an aching poignant vision of the past, of wandering with Delilah, my old donkey, down verdant summer lanes rich with the scent of honeysuckle and lazy sound of bees droning, of heathered purple moorland splashed with the brilliant golden flame of gorse and broom, and of never knowing what awaited round every corner — a shepherd, perhaps, vagabond, or the drift of blue smoke curling upwards into a fading evening sky by some gypsy caravan.

Freedom. This was all I wanted any more, to be done with the terrible problems and eccentricities of Boscarne for ever. Yes, that was what I truly believed in those early days of recuperation to escape and be free.

Until Mark arrived.

And then my bewilderment and

problems started all over again.

He appeared sympathetically concerned when he entered the bedroom immediately after his return from Town.

"I'm distressed and exceedingly sorry for what happened," he said, "and for the manner of our last parting. I was not very understanding, I'm afraid, but when you're quite better we'll make every effort at a new start together, and put the stupid business of Dick behind us. I met the doctor downstairs and he informed me you were with child," he paused; I turned my gaze from his not wishing to meet the softening expression in his dark eyes. "I'm — grateful. A son, or a daughter — it's of no great import which — should help heal old wounds. So you must make every effort now, to relax and regain strength — "

"I don't want your child," I said coldly, and very clearly. "And at the moment I don't particularly want to get better. I'm not ill anyway. Just — horrified and disgusted."

"Sari — " A hand touched my shoulder. I shuddered. "Go away. *Please* leave me."

His hand was withdrawn. I hoped I'd hurt him, but as I couldn't see his face I'd no way of knowing his reaction; but his voice was cold and remote as he said, "Very well. I've certainly no wish to intrude. Obviously you're still not yourself. I shall remain at Boscarne until you've regained a sense of proportion, then perhaps it will be possible to have an intelligent conversation.

I lay rigid and still, miserable because I realised I'd been hateful, yet infuriated by his obtuseness and fatuous manner of expecting a few conciliatory words could patch matters up between us. As for the baby! — didn't he realise what dreadful possibilities would be entailed by the birth of any child of his? Georges' insanity might be inherited — a taint running through the whole family. Suppose I bore a monster?

I tried to dispel the suggestion, but during the days that followed it lingered insidiously at the back of my mind, like a dark cloud preventing any normal relationship with Mark. We led separate lives maritally, although except for very rare occasions he appeared considerate doing everything possible to divert my thoughts from the terrible events leading to Mrs Delaney's death. We never spoke of it. Perhaps it would have been better if we had — then at least I'd have had the comfort of strain and tension released, of sharing my inward fears.

Autumn followed summer quietly, a serene period in which leaves drifted soundlessly from trees showering a carpet of bronze and gold over paths and lawns of the gardens. Silvered mists and early dew diamonded cobwebs draping hedgerows and furze of the countryside. The doctor pronounced me fit for normal life, although he didn't advise riding. Mark took me for drives and shopping expeditions. My waist had already thickened, but I took no pleasure in selecting my new wardrobe, and unknown to my husband spent much thought considering an abortion and how to obtain it. There was no one I could speak to on the subject; Mrs Pratt, I knew, would have been shocked and condemning; Mark too. If anything was done about it I knew I had somehow to settle the matter myself. In secret I did dangerous exercises, even rolled down a short flight of stairs on purpose, when no one was about — all to no effect. And deep down, behind my fears, frustrations, and terrors, love for Mark still lingered painfully — love that frequently became resentment and bitterness — even tinged with hatred for what he'd done to me.

So I firmly kept myself cold and aloof from him, and in those dark days took a cruel pleasure in hurting him. At moments I longed to strike out at him — confront him with any accusation possible; dislike of the Tremellicks that had first been installed during childhood was resurrected with renewed force. Suspicions of his secret business activities were reinforced in my mind. If he was discovered to be guilty of contraband or worse things, I decided determinedly I wouldn't lift a finger to save him. Rather the reverse.

Sometimes a glimmer of shame filled me, because deep down beneath my troubled emotions I knew I was being wrong and unfair. But my life temporarily, was quite out of focus and torn apart by the horror I'd been through.

Naturally, as September passed into October and early November, Mark retreated into himself and no longer tried to humour me. The weather changed, bringing stormy seas under sullen skies followed by rain and frequent flooding.

It was then that my husband absented himself from the house a good deal, and cunningly, remorselessly, I started to watch. Captain Ffaulks appeared on the scene more often, and common-sense told me some plot was brewing which I intended somehow to probe into and if possible discover the truth.

One day about this time I heard some fair people had pitched camp near Skillan, and that a dark woman who had second sight was appearing to tell fortunes for a penny a time. Generally such events as fairs or circuses had packed up for the winter by mid-November, and I wondered if the woman could have any knowledge of the travellers I had once known so well when I was with Barney Goodfellow's group. The idea was intriguing, a kind of instinctive feeling like the intuitions I'd had when I was a child, a sort of sixth sense that had warned me frequently when a disaster was about to occur — a mining accident perhaps, or a wreck at sea.

In this case, of course, I recognised the suggestion could be mere wishful thinking, but it persisted in my mind, and I knew I'd have to go to Skillan myself for the opening of the event. Mark was always either away at some place like Falmouth and Truro, or discussing business matters at the mine or in the company of Captain Ffaulks. Being alone so much wasn't good for me. I brooded deeply still on the horror I'd gone through, and longed for a word with any of my old friends, if possible. Even Mylora. If Mylora was the fortuneteller described, she might still have her little monkey with her, and it would be nice to see Rom. I could take a few guineas with me and give them both a wedding gift. That would put them in a good mood. Mylora might even have known a way for me to rid myself of the baby if I'd seen her earlier. She'd had gypsy blood in her and was very knowledgeable about herbs. Still, it was too late now, and my feelings, strangely, were beginning to change. If it hadn't been for the dark fear of inherited evil, I could have almost welcomed the thought of having someone small and helpless of my own to care for. I had to accept that the life of an unfriendly chilly union with only moments of selfish passion to enliven it was certainly not my idea of happiness. To be warm and glowing with the desire to give as well as take was surely the essence of any worthwhile existence. But Mark these days gave nothing save polite attention to my needs as formal mistress of his household. Once it might have been enough. But the challenge had gone; even my determination to avenge Uter was now appearing a rather ridiculous notion that could bring no fruitful result.

Colour, dancing, quarrelling and laughter — the sweet fulfilment of emotional as well as physical contact — of understanding, and the capacity to forgive human frailties their tears and hot tempers — oh, surely, these were for what we were born. The waking to spring following rest by winter's firesides, and upsurge of joy when early daisies stirred the grass and young leaves burst into tender green.

"Mark! — Mark!" I thought, "where are you? The *real* you! Where has our love gone?"

As always there was no answer. And I had to have response and contact somewhere — even from Mylora and Rom if they were at the fair.

So on that certain afternoon when the fair opened on Skillan's village green, I took the trap and drove myself to the scene, after a brief remonstrance from the head groom who said the master wouldn't like it.

"Like it?" I answered. "Master Tremellick? My husband? Phaw!" I snapped my fingers. "What does it matter? He won't know if you don't tell him. He isn't here — he's *never* here. What harm can it do?"

"The pony's not been out for some time, and — "

"Good! It'll give the poor thing a bit of exercise," I exclaimed, not waiting to hear the rest of his objections. He was a fuddy-duddy of an old man now, anyway, who didn't approve of a woman having a say in anything.

So we set off, after I'd had a brief

word with old Delilah. "Sorry we can't journey together, Del dear," I said, giving her a pat on her cheek, and a carrot I'd purloined from the kitchen, "but you couldn't carry me now, because there are two of us, and you're getting on, dear."

I pushed my face against her. I think she understood. Her brown eyes blinked and her lip quivered over her funny old teeth, where bits of carrot still showed.

The next moment I hurried away, and a minute later I had the pony's reins, and we were jolting along the moorland road to Skillan. The day was fine, crisp and cold, and I was glad I'd thought to wear my thick grey velvet coat and bonnet hat with veiling tied under my chin. When I reached the village there was a crowd of natives wandering about the site where a few vans and tents were pitched. As I'd expected that time of year, the fair was a comparatively small one. Only one or two booths displayed their wares; mostly the occasion had been arranged for the sale of livestock and poultry in view of the approaching Christmas season.

There was no sign of Barney

Goodfellow's van, but in one corner, a tent with the name 'Madam Zilla' scrawled boldly outside, was already attracting custom. I drew the trap to a halt, gave a generous coin to a youth to keep watch and take care of it with the promise of more when I returned, and crossed over to the tent.

I waited until a customer had left, then parted the canvas carefully and peeped in. A brown-faced woman with immense gold rings glinting from her ears through massed black hair, was crouched in a multi-coloured shawl at one side not far from the entrance. Before her was a small table with a crystal ball on it, and a pack of cards. Curious squeaks emerged intermittently from somewhere behind her shoulder, and I realised with a rush of delight it was Mylora's monkey shrieking — it must be. No other monkey could have such a chattering chirpy little voice — even though it was more cracked now. Older.

I was right.

As I went in the small creature sprang suddenly at my feet and doffed his red cap — probably not the same one — years had passed since I'd last seen him. But his button eyes were still bright in his puckered-up face, his teeth as large and yellow when he grinned, though one was missing. The woman gave a sharp command, and the monkey raced back to her. I stepped forward through the mysterious shadows into the rosy glow of lamplight, and she instantly straightened her back, staring. In spite of the stain, probably walnut, emphasising the darkness of her naturally olive brown complexion, I knew her immediately. And the recognition was mutual. After my little gasp of pleasure, Mylora in her familiar deep tones, said without the flicker of a smile, "So it's you. And quite the fine lady, I'm sure."

Beneath the narrowed lids her fine dark eyes regarded me shrewdly.

Determined not to be put off by her abrupt mood, I smiled. "Yes, Mylora. I heard you might be here, and I wanted to see you so much."

She gave a short laugh.

"Ha! It doesn't appear to me you want your future telling or to cross my palm with gold. Looks like you've met Lady Luck herself."

"I didn't come for that," I said, "I've brought you a present — your — your wedding gift. Dick said you and Rom were married — "

Her expression softened. "So you've met? You two. Well, I sh'ld've expected it some time. Yes, when the troupe broke up one way and another, Rom and I got together," she shrugged. "With the little one on the way it seemed best."

"Are they here? Rom, I mean, and the — your little boy?"

"He's in the van, young Robin is; Pom-Pom keeps an eye on him when I'm entertaining the ladies and gents here. Does a bit of a tumbling act and conjuring. The van's ours, Rom's and mine, and next week when this is over and I pack up, Robin and I'll be going up country a bit where his job is. It's a good one for the winter — forestry."

"Oh." I was a little disappointed. I'd wanted very much to see Rom. "Well, I'm glad for you, Mylora, that you've settled and — "

"*Settled?*" She flung back her head

and showed a flash of white teeth. "Me and Rom settled? We don't do that. Not our kind — it's here one day, there the next. But the money he's getting now is good and it'll see us through the bleak time.""

"I hope this will too," I remarked, handing her several guineas.

She stared. "*You* — doing this? — for *me*? And after what I said about Dick and the baby. Oh, go on, Sari! Put it back in your pocket. I was never a one for charity."

"It isn't charity. I *want* you to have it. Honestly. Please, Mylora."

She shrugged, and took the money. "Very well, but — " She screwed up her eyes more closely and peered at me questioningly. The glow from the fire lit her glance with spots of flame; it was as though hidden sources of ancient knowledge, visions of past, present and future came to life momentarily, blending with a mystic prophecy as darkly inevitable as the passing of time itself.

I waited, apprehensive, watching, with a kind of fearful excitement in me, telling myself whatever she liked to predict, either for good or ill, it would make no difference. I wouldn't necessarily believe it; she was merely Mylora, who had never liked me very much, but possessing all the same a strange gift, bred of her gypsy forbears, of sensing matters alien to others of the human race.

"You'll have your bebee," she said at last. "Either this, or another — but take care. There's a stranger there, in a flaring coat." She put a hand over her eyes. "Red — all red. Take care. Fire and water — great waves and pain. But the end — " Her voice wavered and faded.

"Yes? Yes?" I urged. "Tell me."

She shook her head, her eyes closed for a moment, then she turned them on the crystal ball.

"I can't see any more," she told me, wiping the sweat from her brow. "It's all clouded. But you'll be all right." She thumped her chest. "I feel it here — a rich fine lady with her silks and satins, and baby in its golden crib." Her voice held its old mocking note. She straightened up, re-arranged her shawl, and shook her cloud of hair back from her shoulders. "There's someone waiting outside," she said. "They're chattering. Listen. I must get on with my job, Sari, thanks for the gift. It'll help us. And take no notice of what I've just said. All in the act, you understand?"

I shook my head. "I don't know. I never know what to believe about you, Mylora."

She smiled, and in that moment looked strangely handsome with the ray of lamplight accentuating the fine modelling of high cheekbones, proud nose, chin and jaw. "That's as well," she said. "If everyone knew about *me*, there'd be no gold for my palm, would there?"

I nearly said, "I'm not everyone, I'm Sari." But just at that moment the narrow gap in the tent opened, and a woman's head poked through. Knowing it meant business for Mylora, I departed then, after a short friendly farewell and a shake of the hand with the little monkey, to make my way between the vans and booths in a search for Pom-Pom.

I was lucky to see him making his way to the shabby van, carrying a box and a sack, probably containing the props he used for his conjuring.

"Pom-Pom," I cried, running towards him.

At first he didn't recognise me. He stood perfectly still, watching me like some life-sized marionette in his baggy spotted trousers, doleful-looking as ever, with his ginger hair screwed into a comical corkscrew on the top of his narrow head.

"Why, bless me bloody boots!" he exclaimed, as we came face to face, "if 'tisn't the bane of me life, young Sari herself playin' the grand lady." His drawn-down mouth lifted suddenly, stretching almost from ear to ear. "Where you come from, girl?" he asked, "An' don't go expectin' me to bow an scrape an' 'madam' you just because you caught that rich fellow at the big house, I ain't that sort, as you well know."

"You'd heard?" I said, "About my marrying Master Tremellick, I mean?"

"What did you expect? News travels fast. Anyway come along with you, and meet young Robin. A real lively one he is. Seen Mylora, have you?"

"Yes," I told him, as we walked on

together, "and I'm glad for her — being married to Rom."

"That's right. Two of a kind they are; spit'n scratch, 'n love an' breed. By the time she's forty she'll be fat as a brood mare with a herd o' youngsters an' grandchildren about her knees. Maybe young Robin'll have his own then. He's a real lusty one, I can tell you."

He certainly was, but not particularly friendly to me. All the little boy did when I tried to be companionable was to scowl resentfully as though I'd no right to be there. To look at he was quite beautiful, with the olive-dark colouring of Mylora and the bright eyes of Rom. I soon discovered, after getting him at last to accept a bon-bon from my reticule, that he could smile winningly when he was pleased, and scream loudly for what he wanted, behaving outrageously if he didn't get it.

When I left he was pestering Pom-Pom for attention, which meant the old clown performing one of his tricks, and I was quite glad to get away.

The clear weather had dulled when I set off in the trap again for Boscarne, and

322

the wind had a sting in it. The distant sea held an angry darkness, spattered with white high-flung foam against the thrusting rocks of the jagged coast. I had stayed longer at the fair than I'd intended, and by the time the moorland road took the turn towards the house, yellowing twilight was slowly enveloping the landscape, imbuing the standing stones, twisted trees and humped tumpy growth of heather and gorse with sinister elemental identity. It was easy enough to rekindle ancient legends of the past, of witch, giant, and horned demon haunting bog and eerie moor. The whining of the wind became the drawn-out howling of the evil black horseman and the shrieking and creaking of branches in the cold air the moans of the dead, about to rise and attack harmless travellers.

I was relieved to reach the turn of the drive from the lane, and as I did so happened to glance up towards the ridge. I thought what I saw at first — the movement of a figure dipping with lowered shoulders down the slope towards a steep gully cutting to the sea — was just my own heightened imagination, due to the eerie atmosphere and quickly fading half-light, a bush blown willy-nilly against the onslaught of approaching storm.

But I was wrong. My sight hadn't deluded me; the form was human broad, almost squat, and with a bump of my heart I felt certain of its identity. Captain Ffaulks. What was he about? What was a Revenue Official lurking about for, like any furtive thief seeking to evade capture? I reined the mare, pulled the carriage to a halt for a few seconds, then, when the man had disappeared down a track not far from the ill-reputed kiddleywink, I loosened the reins and drove round the side of the house to the stables.

To my surprise Mark was already back when I entered the hall. He appeared unduly haggard and worried, and demanded irately where I'd been on such a foul evening.

"It wasn't foul when I started off," I answered shortly, "just dull, like me." With a casual air I added, "If you *must* know my destination exactly every time I go out, I'll leave a message each time in my little book so you know where to track me down. Actually I went to see someone I knew at Skillan — Mylora, she was with Barney Goodfellow's troupe and had a performing monkey."

"And you had a sudden desire for the company of a monkey. I see." His tones were dry, telling me nothing except that he'd been irritated by something which might or might not have to do with me.

"I had a sudden desire, as you put it, to see anyone or anything not connected with Boscarne," I answered shortly. "There's no one here to talk to about anything amusing or interesting — I find it difficult often just to sit stitching, or reading, or — or thinking about what happened. *You* don't know **what** it was like — what I went through with your terrible relative, and finding Mrs Delaney's dead body — " I shuddered. "You weren't there. It was me — *me* alone. I loathe this place sometimes, yes I *do*. *Hate* it. There've been three deaths since we were married, and you may think it silly, but sometimes — sometimes — " I gulped and broke off.

"Yes?"

"Well — I wonder who's going to be the next.

There was a pause in which Mark studied me thoughtfully, then he said, "You're not well, are you? Perhaps I've been a bit thoughtless — unduly concerned with my own affairs. I'm sorry, if so. But I *have* had very important business — and certainly not pleasant to attend to. I should have realised earlier you needed a change." He put a hand to his head, ruffling it wearily. "Well — it can be arranged. At the end of the week I should have time to think things out. In the meantime, do go up to bed and try and rest, Sari. I'll get Mrs Pratt to bring you a sedative, and you can — "

"I don't want Mrs Pratt or her sedatives," I interrupted sharply, "and I'm not ill. I'm just — " I was on the point of adding ' — frightened to death, because I'm going to have a baby, *yours*. And it terrifies me in case it turns out to be like that terrible Georges.' I kept quiet, however, and the opportunity for revealing my fears to him vanished.

"Very well," Mark agreed, with assumed nonchalance, his voice once more cold, aloof. "As no suggestion of mine appeals to you, you must try and rid yourself of your own morbidity. Death is generally a shock, and I'm quite aware of the fright you had with the old lady's pathetic grandson. *And* poor Mrs Delaney, of course. But they're both gone now — 'at rest', the Church would affirm. Just one thing, though — "

"Yes?"

"Do not, in future, refer to Georges Tremellick as *my* relative. Lady Susannah was a step relation, remember, which puts a very different complexion on things. The old lady had a daughter, Janette, by her husband, the Viscomte le Villemont. Georges, Janette's son by her husband Jean Louis Monterron, inherited unfortunately a family taint of insanity on the paternal side. Later Janette married my uncle John Tremellick, the second of the three Tremellick brothers. It was a speedy marriage four months before the birth of her son, Georges, conceived by her union with Jean Louis. He was, therefore, legitimate, and as William had no children of his own he was the true heir to Boscarne when John died. It sounds complicated, but under the circumstances I'm sure it's right now, that you should know, and have no outlandish notions that the poor creature, the old lady's cherished grandson, should have any blood tie with my particular family."

I flushed, that he could have probed my mind so clearly. "I *have* wondered sometimes," I admitted, "about your actual relationship with Georges and Lady Susannah. You called her 'Matriarch' and sometimes — " I broke off. " — I thought she was a kind of step-great-aunt. No one here ever said definitely."

"There's been no reason, nor is there now, to explain our family tree to every Tom, Dick and Harry," Mark said shortly, almost rudely. "However, for your information, since you're indirectly concerned, here it is. Following the death of her first husband, Janette — as I've already told you — married John Tremellick, my uncle. I was only a boy when he met his death in a riding accident not long after my own father died. Janette quickly took another husband, Sir Frank Flaherne. As far as I know they were happy, but Janette succumbed to a bout of fever the following year. His second wife was a girl of noble family, the Lady Dorothea Farne. In their four years together until her death she bore two children, a daughter, Marie-Anne, and a boy who lived to be only two. Richard was the son born of Sir Frank's third marriage. Marie-Anne came to a bad end when she was eighteen, by eloping and marrying an impecunious artist." He paused, then added significantly, "There was a child, I believe — Richard has been digging and delving, and throwing out strange hints."

"I see."

"Yes, I think you do. I think you can be quite a secretive character when you feel like it. However, that's nothing to do with Lady Susannah. The reason I took her under the family wing was partly genuine compassion — because she was left lonely with no one of her own any more but poor Georges — on whom incidentally, she quite doted — and partly finance. She was very rich; my side of the complicated Tremellick clan needed money — badly. So the arrangement was both humane and philanthropic. Now — " he stood very straight, staring at me challengingly, " — perhaps now you'll rid yourself of any preposterous calculations you *may* have been harbouring, and be quite assured there'll be no taint of hereditary mental sickness in any child you bear by me. I may seem a hard, devious character at times, but I happen to possess a conscience, and hope in future you'll remember it."

Without another look at me, he turned and strode quickly away.

"Mark — " I called once. But he did not hear, or if he did took no notice.

I stood in a daze, bewildered and quite unable to think clearly. Confused by the mixture of ancestral details including Dick's account and now Mark's, concerning events that seemed more suited to the pages of a book than real life.

I did not see Mark again until the following morning and then only briefly. He passed me as I was entering the parlour, and after a short greeting went out. There was obviously something on his mind. If only I could have cleared it, I thought, we might have come to a friendlier understanding and companionship. But the breach between us seemed to widen with every day that passed. It was not so much the memory of far-gone past events that angered me now, but a painful resentment of his cold attitude to me. So many times I'd felt an urge to break it — to fling myself desperately in his arms, begging him to soften and love me. But always the impulse was stifled the next moment by the rigid set of his countenance; it was as though a wall of hard ice had formed between us — something which, try as I would, I'd find it impossible to break.

So a fierce pride had developed in me, which made me feel far older than my years, and frequently desperate to escape to a more natural existence, thinking longingly of the period when Delilah and I had led the life of nomads with Barney Goodfellow's troupe. Those days though were gone for good. The child I carried and my lingering all-consuming passion for Mark, however bitter, held me at Boscarne, for good or for ill, and that day, with a strange sense of foreboding,

I sensed it might well prove to be the latter.

During the night the weather had worsened, and a high wind risen. The naked branches of trees in the gardens were swept creaking to the ground, and I guessed that at sea the hungry tides would be driving great breakers to the shore. I recalled Captain Ffaulks' suspicious prowling along the ridge the day before, when he had cut down towards the kiddleywink, and I couldn't help wondering if Mark had some devious assignation with him, and was even now on his way to meet him. For what? Perhaps I was being childishly over-melodramatic. *Was* wrecking a planned practice? Or was the plundering of a floundered ship merely a chance tragedy used by needy and greedy natives for their own ends? No one really was in a position to say except those concerned. Whispers had been put about, and accusations made, even in my own lifetime. But pirates were known to exist; their boats could well be used for wrecking others, and the loot salvaged by their accomplices under cover of a dark wild night.

A spasm of guilt shook me that I should even consider the possibility of Mark's being concerned in such foul goings on. Had he not insisted to me always, since our marriage, that his main purpose at Boscarne was to better conditions for the poor and so far as he was able stamp out cruelty? But then there were two sides to him as I'd already discovered, and I couldn't help fearing the domineering hard part of his character which could be relentless when he felt it necessary. Gain, though, from any financial source, was no necessity to him now. He'd admitted to me that his family had needed it in the past, but through Lady Susannah's death Mark had become a very wealthy man. No. Oh, *no* — I told myself, hating myself for my wrongful thoughts — he was no thief or murderer, and what was wrecking but murder? — adventurer he might be, and bored perhaps, with his unsatisfactory existence with me; but any secret other life he had would reach no further than a little harmless smuggling, and many of the gentry, as I'd always understood, indulged in that.

So I briefly rid myself of evil images,

and tried to concentrate on other subjects.

My efforts were practically useless. The house itself seemed devoid of life or friendship. The servants appeared grim and uncommunicative, the wide halls and corridors filled only by the creaking and moaning of the wind which, although the windows were closed, lifted the tapestries on the walls, and rustled the rugs, whining down chimneys, and even dampening the glow of logs in the great fireplaces. It was as though ghosts of the past shivered about the vast interior, casting greater gloom on my spirits. I tried once to quell the depressive atmosphere by altering ancestral portraits about — a stupid thing to do perhaps, but the sound of my own voice held a certain comfort, by saying, "You mustn't stare so, you're nothing — *nothing* but just dead images. One day I'll get you removed and have flower paintings instead."

But would that ever happen? Would Mark ever allow it? Would the great front hall ever resound with the scamper of children's feet and their laughter?

Children! the baby I was carrying might be the only one. It was hard during that long gloomy day to believe my husband and I could come together in love once more, almost impossible to visualise a time when the bitterness would be erased. Yet our periods of true passion in the past had been so wonderful, so abounding with rich delight and joy. How could either of us have allowed such a wide gulf to arise? So many small flaws had arisen, one by one, adding fuel to the miasma of misunderstanding. My own youth and determination to have power — Mark's jealousy, and initial taunts arising from my earlier relation with Dick; *Uncle* Dick. Oh, it was so ridiculous — as ridiculous as my childhood's vow to have revenge on the whole Tremellick family for Uter's death.

I was musing on such things and pacing about the small parlour restlessly when Mrs Pratt poked her head round the door. "Are you all right, ma'am — Mrs Tremellick?" she asked. "I thought you were in your bedroom and had a dish of tea taken up. But the girl said you weren't there. You'd be warmer upstairs. When the wind's in this direction you always get it cold here from the hall."

"I don't want to spend my life upstairs," I said rather shortly. "I'm not an invalid."

She appeared a bit huffed. "I didn't say you were; but in your condition — and pardon my mentioning it — it's good to relax as much as possible."

"How can anyone relax with this awful wind blowing?" I remarked, turning and glancing at the window. "Just look! — there's sleet coming now. Perhaps we shall have snow."

"It could be," she agreed stiffly. "It's happened before now at this time of the year. And *we're* the lucky ones at such times. Think of those poor folk out at sea — fishermen and merchant ships. Could easily be a wreck Craggan way, by the rocks. The lighthouse has been known to fail, and then there's no guide at all for any vessel off course."

I shivered. "You sound very gloomy. It doesn't help."

"Ah well! I was just trying to get you to forget yourself, ma'am, by thinking of others."

"I'm often thinking of others," I told her sharply. "I was brought up in these parts on the edge of the cliffs, as you very well know. I'm sure my background is no secret. The servants would have discussed it many times."

"I don't discuss your affairs with the servants, Mrs Tremellick. However much you may like to criticise me, there's one thing I *always* remember — to keep to my place at Boscarne, and to forbid gossip in my presence. Most of those who work here now are fairly new. But naturally — " she paused before adding, " — your arrival here with that old donkey of yours has become almost a legend, just as the old lady — Lady Susannah's moods and fancies for having you dance. You can't blot out any fantastic happening. And that terrible business over Mr Georges — "

Suddenly I could bear no more. "Please — *please* don't bring up the past," I cried in desperation, "especially that. Telling me to relax one moment, and then bringing everything back in such a sudden manner. Are you trying to frighten me?"

"*Madam!*" she sounded outraged. "To suggest such a thing is unfair and very cruel. If Mr Mark was here I'd feel like packing up and leaving — " She sniffed, and dabbed a handkerchief to her nose.

Realising the atmosphere and weather were affecting her nerves in a similar way to mine, I forced myself to say in conciliatory tones, "Mrs Pratt, please let us forget this stupid conversation. We're both on edge, and no wonder. Many housekeepers in your place would have said goodbye to Boscarne after what happened to Mrs Delaney and — me. You mentioned my husband just now; it's a pity he's *not* here. He should be. I know that in his absence you take your responsibilities very seriously. Thank you for doing it, and please don't mention leaving again."

"Very well," her voice was quieter. She smoothed her apron, drew a hand across her brow under the lace cap, pushing a strand of hair away, and with an air of dignity took a small bottle of smelling salts from her pocket. She had two sniffs, sighed deeply, and said in her usual formal way, "Shall I have tea sent in here then, madam?"

I nodded. "Yes, Mrs Pratt. Thank

you. Later I may settle to my tapestry work."

But I couldn't settle. In spite of my efforts with needle and wool, my ears were alerted all the time in listening for signs of Mark's return — the thud of his footsteps along the hall, or mounting the stairs.

They didn't come.

By evening, though the sleet and fine rain had eased, leaving the landscape clearer, the wind, if anything, had intensified. Even lamps throughout the house flickered, and candles caught in a rush of air by an opening of a door, frequently guttered out.

And still Mark did not return.

Mrs Pratt retired early to bed with a headache, leaving the other servants at any late tasks in the kitchen or huddled round the large stove. I waited for a time, then after taking a glass of hot milk from Mrs Jelly, told her I should need nothing more that night, and would presently be going to bed. She said she was doing the same, and after the serving butler had made his usual inspection that all the doors of Boscarne had been safely locked or bolted, I heard both of them plodding up the steep backstairs to their sleeping quarters.

By nine o'clock all was dark in the kitchens. No light flickered from anywhere except from the one lamp and candles in my own room, and a sudden quivering glare from a watery moon when it momentarily pierced the sullen line of black clouds. Between a thin opening of my curtains it zigzagged eerily across the floor. I jumped out and had to pull the blinds closer, and it was then I saw against the distant sea the blink of a light dangerously near the locality of the projecting Wyke Point, but not where it *should* have been — to the left on Craggan Rock Lighthouse to give warning of the treacherous underwater reefs.

What had happened to the keeper? And why wasn't the large light working? Any ship in the area could be misled to its doom on such a night. I tried to believe at first that my eyes had deceived me, and I'd got my locality wrong. But I knew I hadn't when another sudden shaft of blurred moonlight quivered across the waters. For a few seconds the dark outline of a brig was visible, tossing its way precariously to the massive Craggan itself where no warning registered at all, no guiding signal to avert disaster. And along the misted rim of moon and sea a line of shapes, whether horses or human beings — it was impossible to say with any certainty — moved to the gully cutting to the shore.

On impulse, and without thinking coherently — for what could I do on my own? — I dressed quickly in heavy skirt, boots, and woollen cape and with the hood over my head went downstairs quietly, and let myself out of a side door which though locked I knew would be unbolted until Mark returned. I found the keys hanging in the butler's pantry, took them along, and after discovering the right one, let myself out, leaving the door unlocked and the keys on the floor.

Then, bracing myself against the elements, I cut away from Boscarne and made my way to the high lane overlooking the coast. About a quarter of a mile along, a track led towards the gully. It was rough and narrow, but by then, luckily, the pale moon had risen above the clouds. As I stood staring, half-blinded by salt, wind and rain, I could make out, nevertheless, a line of men astride horses, riding in single file, like creatures of the ocean itself, along the shore to the left.

At the same time there was furtive movement a little below me on the moor, the breaking of twigs and undergrowth carried on the wind's moan, and then quite unexpectedly the broad dark shape of a figure rising menacingly in front of me. I was suddenly not only shaking from exhaustion, but terrified. The face for two seconds, clarified by the eerie light, was that of the man I'd detested and mistrusted from our first meeting. Captain Ffaulks, and fear too showed on his countenance. His eyes were wild under his tangled damp locks. I was conscious only of that — the wildness and menace.

For a second he stared at me, but obviously without recognition. The hood and hair had fallen over my face, and I made no move to deter or question him, noting that he was holding a gun. The muzzle glimmered for a moment, then with his other arm he pushed me savagely down into the undergrowth, and went on, scrambling, stooping, head bent, like some wild animal evading capture. It was then I heard the booming of the ship's siren from the sea. I eased myself up to a crouched position keeping my eyes fixed as firmly as possible on the Captain. He was about to dip behind a tummock of furze bordering a path leading seawards when a second figure emerged from the other direction, immediately facing me. He paused for a second or two glancing round and would no doubt have spotted me if he hadn't first seen Ffaulks.

I waited, petrified, as the Captain straightened up and the two men stood facing each other, enemies in confrontation, at bay. Then the second man stepped forward, and I nearly screamed aloud in fear; not because both had guns, but because through the flurry of rain, mist and driving wind, the fitful moon's light fell full on the set face of the newcomer, giving cold clarity to the lean features, set of jaw and fiery glint of eyes.

Mark!

I moved then, and opened my mouth

to shout, but no sound came — or if it did, I didn't hear. There was a shout, a sharp reply as Mark stepped forward, followed by the deadly crack of a pistol shot. In a moment of horror I watched my husband totter and fall with one hand clutching the air. As I rushed to his side, stumbling, falling, getting up again and going on, Ffaulks dived into the shadows of a nearby thicket and disappeared. I screamed and screamed then — screamed against Fate, the elements and the murdering captain for what they'd done that night. Looking at Mark's cold moon-washed face and the blood trickling from the artery of one arm, I had no doubts that he was dead.

Mercifully, however, I was wrong.

When at last help came, he was still breathing faintly, and in the morning I learned that he would live.

Later the doctor told me something else, something I had already guessed — the child I'd carried would never be born.

As if I cared.

"No matter," I said, "just let me see

my husband. It's only Mark I mind about."

It was then that I heard he had no wish whatever to see me, and that under the circumstances it would be better for him to have complete rest.

"He's very badly injured," the doctor told me sympathetically, "one of his hands, and arm below the elbow, were completely blown off. Shock, under such conditions, plays odd tricks with the mind. Leave him alone for the time, my dear, and when he's stronger, with the fever gone, he'll be more himself and look forward to your company. So be patient, and get some rest yourself. I've already ordered a draught for you. You understand, Mrs Tremellick?"

Yes, I understood. But *he* didn't. Somehow Mark had come to hate me.

And at that moment I wished I could die.

13

A WEEK passed before I was allowed to visit Mark in his bedroom. He looked weak and haggard, but I'd expected that. What I *wasn't* prepared for was the remote, almost mechanical way he spoke. My first impulse on entering was to rush to the bedside and let my lips rest on his — to show, somehow, how I loved him. But he merely stared at me unsmilingly, and remarked, "I'm sorry to have been such an infernal nuisance, and about your own — mishap. Perhaps all things considered, though, it was as well. A child would have complicated matters; having a one-armed cripple for a father would certainly have been no fun — "

"But, Mark, I — "

He waved his good hand in a gesture of negation to stop my flow of words. "Don't get intense, Sari. You're always so — impetuous."

"I'm sorry," I said, "I don't want to upset you. I — I hope you're feeling better now. Are you?"

"If you mean can I now eat, still use my two legs without difficulty, swallow pills to numb this damned pain of an arm which isn't there any more, breathe and answer questions fairly intelligibly, yes, I suppose in my limited fashion I show some improvement," he agreed bitterly.

I forced optimism into my voice and refusing to be rebuffed, I told him lightly, "The specialist was just leaving with the doctor before I came up. He said in time you'd be able to have another arm and hand fixed below the elbow — they're the latest thing and very efficient. You'd be able to — "

"Do everything within reason," he interrupted. "Spoon food into my mouth once the remaining muscles worked, even deliver a good left-hander to any probing thief or marauder about Boscarne. Oh, yes; I'm sure they'll do their best."

Tumultuous feelings of depression and futility surged through me. Temper and grief fought for outlet.

"Oh, Mark, *please* don't be so — "

"So what? Cold? Off-hand? Determined

not to let you cry your pretty eyes out on my behalf?" He gave a twisted smile. "I don't care for dramatics. I don't want your pity, or your smothering affection, Sari. Neither do I want a scene. They'll inflict someone on me when I go to London. Poor thing! she won't have an easy time."

"*London?*"

"Didn't they tell you? The plan is that in a week or so I'm to be removed to the capital where they experiment in such things like artificial limbs. I'm assured I shall have the best attention that wealth can buy. Hospital for a period, then back to life again becoming adjusted to my new state.

"But — " I floundered in my attempts to assimilate the news, " — how long will it be for? I mean how long will you be away from Boscarne?"

"Long enough for us both to put this whole wretched business behind us," he stated, "and start life all over again. Isn't that how they put it?"

"Together you mean? Leave Boscarne for good?"

"That's still to be decided. But

together? Certainly not."

"*Why?*" I could feel my heart quickening, and my cheeks flaming wildly.

"Because, my dear child, you're far too young for taking on the business of an irate wounded partner — you were too young when I married you to know what you were doing, and I should have realised it. The union was tricky from the first. No, it's impossible. The marriage in due course can be annulled — there are ways which shouldn't involve anything on your part, and I'll see of course that you are well provided for. One day when you've found some healthy young man to care for you and be in every way the kind of husband you're entitled to, you'll be able to look back on this period as just a very unpleasant patch in your life, no more. You can stay here of course for as long as you wish; I doubt if I shall ever have much interest in the estate again. Nominally it could even be made over to you."

"Stop, *stop!*" I cried. "I won't accept it. I don't believe it. Just because you've lost a hand — to take things in this way! Oh, I know you must have been in great pain, and I know, too, that I've made mistakes, often been a nuisance to you. But I *love* you, Mark. Don't you understand? Can't you take it in? Love — *love*!"

He shook his head. "You think you do, just as you *thought* you loved Dick, remember? But that was your youth talking. So is this, in a different way. You're sorry for your lame-duck of an old admirer, and I can't take that, Sari, I *won't*."

"It isn't *pity*."

"I don't care what it is," he retorted then. "Call it what you like. Our marriage hasn't worked, and never would, certainly not now. So please, for heaven's sake, stop the melodrama and allow me a little peace. I'm tired, and your protestations weary me all the more. I suppose I should thank you for your efforts to help me in the Ffaulks affair. You were quite right to doubt him, of course, but so did I, from the very beginning. In fact, my going along with him at all was merely a facade, a dangerous game of mine, to unmask him — I believe that's the old-fashioned term used. He was making a tidy fortune on the sly, and I knew it. I expect you've heard how he met his end though?"

"No," I whispered.

Mark laughed shortly. "Very undignified for a Preventative Official — took a mistaken plunge over the cliffs on the night of the *Mariana* disaster."

"After he'd shot you?"

"Naturally. Poetic justice. If he hadn't got me I'd have got him. They say the right always wins in the end, don't they? What a ridiculous, puerile statement."

"The ship was saved though," I said defiantly. "And through *you*."

"Through my men. They had everything ready that evening. Things happened according to plan. Everything was so absolutely *right* for a murderous plot like Ffaulks' — weather, the brig driven off course. It was a valuable cargo, you know — gold, and diamonds, bound for Falmouth. I ferreted it all out of that thieves' hidey-hole of a kiddleywink. Then when the force of my men were spotted riding from the west with rescue gear — everything — that devil made a getaway — " His voice started to fade.

"But he didn't *make* it — did he?"

There was a faraway look in Mark's eyes, words finally died. I ventured to touch his hand with mine. He gave a little sigh, and turned his head.

The next moment he'd drifted off into a drugged sleep, and after a few minutes I tiptoed away, and informed the nurse so she could take a look to see that all was well with him.

14

CHRISTMAS was a bleak one that year. Mark had left at the beginning of December for further treatment at a well-known hospital in London, and I was left alone at Boscarne with only the servants and Mrs Pratt to create any sense of festivity. Dick brought his wife-to-be, Lady Angela Frayne, for a brief visit. They stayed just three nights and then departed. I found little in common with the slightly patronising young woman, who, though pleasant enough to me, viewed me, I felt, as something of a curiosity, just as she regarded Dick's painting. I could picture her fitting well into his town life when he wanted an elegant hostess for presiding at his home there, and publicising his work; but somehow I found it hard to connect the sophisticated Sir Richard Flaherne with the Dick I'd known of the roads the whimsical roaming artist, friend of vagabonds, players and amusing rogues.

His attitude towards me was still affectionately teasing, but our new relationship struck no chord of true sympathy. That I'd ever thought myself in love with him seemed almost unbelievable. Perhaps the change and lack of warmth in me was due to Angela's presence. The fact remained that I was glad when they'd gone, relaxed, but lonely. If Mark had softened before leaving Boscarne, or even agreed to my spending a few days in town with him over Christmas, I wouldn't have felt his absence so acutely. But he'd told me politely but coldly that it was far better for him to lick his wounds in solitude under strict medical care.

"You mean you don't want me?" I'd enquired bluntly.

He'd bowed his head in affirmation. "Shall we say I don't think your presence would be beneficial to either of us at this moment, he answered."

"Very well," I'd said, "of course; naturally I wouldn't dream of intruding if you didn't wish it. I'd hate to hinder your recuperation." I'd smiled at him with bitter-sweetness. "I quite understand. Don't worry. I shan't *dream* of forcing my company on you unless you particularly demand it." I'd put on an air of casualness. "As a matter of fact it *would* have been a bit of a bore having to make such a long journey for just a short visit. In a way I'm relieved. It will be a change being on my own with no — "

"Crusty invalid to inflict his woes on you," he'd interrupted wrily.

"Oh!" I'd turned away impatiently. "Try not to sound so self-pitying. You've lost your hand. Well it's awful, I know. I've *tried* to understand, but when I offer sympathy you just snub me so what's the use? Anyway, when you have the new one fitted the doctor says you'll be able to do anything in reason in time. So why can't you be a bit cheerful, and not so — so — "

"Deadly irritating? And such a mournful hypochondriac?"

"I didn't say that."

"You implied it, and it's true. Now, for God's sake, Sari, leave me alone in my own little private hell. If I want to grumble and moan, that's my affair, not yours. So please drop the cheering-up act and get on with your own life in your own way. You've the money now and the power — "

"To do *what*?" The sharp question was out before I knew it.

"How the devil do *I* know? There are friends — acquaintances — "

"*Your* friends and acquaintances," I reminded him bitterly.

"Give a party — hold court for your admirers — your tumblers and clowns. I'm sure they'd appreciate it. And Richard! Get him to bring his high-born fiancée along. As you can't marry him, you can still tease and tempt and titillate him. Excitement, that's what you want, isn't it? Well, go ahead. *Anything* — so long as you maintain a reasonable sobriety."

"*Thank you*. Oh, thank you very much," I'd retorted, by then very angry. "Perhaps I'll do just that. Only I won't promise anything, and as for sobriety — if I *want* to get drunk I will."

For a moment the old fire had lit his eyes, and he'd said sharply, "I'd like to spank you for that remark, but unfortunately I no longer have the strength."

"Oh, Mark," I said, "I'm sorry. Of course I didn't mean it. And for your — your hand, for everything — I'm sorry."

"I know, I know. That's just the point — it's no use darling, we're not good for each other any more. I've told you before, I say it again, I shouldn't have married you in the first place. You were too young. Now *please* do drop the subject, I'm off to London, and maybe in a month or two — perhaps more — or less, who knows? — I'll become adjusted. In the meantime, there's simply no use in discussing the future. Please understand; — your life's your own now. Use it — Only don't put any onus on me. I'll oblige in any way I can — *when* I can — to make your lot less harassing. For the moment try and forget I exist, that's all."

I'd been on the point of further protestation but his sudden haggard palor and the complete exhaustion of voice and bearing had kept me silent. After that upsetting meeting, we'd had practically no personal contact before his departure.

So Christmas passed into cold January, with grey skies hanging their sullen pall over the moors and sea. Berries glinted red in the glossy leaves of holly trees in the lanes, and in sheltered spots of the garden a few snowdrops sprinkled the hard earth, like miniature ballet dancers in the wind. I did my best to occupy myself, riding and walking when it was fine, but I met practically no one, except a farmer's wife or tenant of the estate to talk to, and restlessness mingled with emotional insecurity gnawed at me.

I visited any distressed or poverty-stricken families I knew of, and made regular visits with gifts of food or other presents. But gifts didn't really help the morale of miners out of work.

Sometimes I felt myself resented, and this not only worried me, but put me on the defensive. I discovered there was a trouble-maker at Wheal Sally who'd worked there only a year. His name was Will Behenna; he was a burly, aggressive character with a considerable knowledge of mining, who'd become a prominent member of the local union — not the constructive type, but a man given to violence and certain practices such as cockfighting that were abhorrent to Mark.

By devious methods I heard such an event was to be held at a barn on Tremellick land towards the end of the month, and in a wave of disgust and hot resentment I decided I'd do something about it. Ellen Grose, a new kitchen maid at Boscarne, had let the news slip one day when I was enquiring what her father, one of the dismissed miners, did in his spare time.

"There's always the kiddleywink, bain't there?" she said sullenly. "That's where Ma's bit of money went what she'd hid in our Gran's teapot. *An'* her china cat what he did sell to ole Matt Prynne, the pedlar. Tedn' right. An' then those cockfights — always think's he'll win, but moren' not he picks the wrong bird. Oh, there's plenty goin' on, Mistress, but it don't do much good to such as we."

"Did you say *cock*-fight?" I asked, in a low voice so Mrs Jelly, who was in the dairy, wouldn't hear.

"Ais. That's right." The girl's pale

face glanced up suddenly with a half-frightened rabbity look on it. "Doan' you go lettin' on now, Mistress, not as *I* said anythin'; there's them that don' think it proper, an' me pa'd be mad. Tek a belt to me he would if he knowed."

I promised her that her name wouldn't be mentioned concerning the planned meeting and managed to get details later of the exact date and time it would be held.

When the evening arrived I went to the stables and bribed the boy for a spare pair of breeches and boots that the head groom kept in his kitchen. Luckily the man himself was away for the night visiting a sick sister. "Get my mare saddled," I said, "I'm riding astride tonight. And not a word to *any*one, understand?"

The youth nodded doubtfully. "If anyone got ter know," he said, "I'd get the sack for sure."

"By who? My husband? He isn't here. *I'm* mistress — "

"But that Mrs Pratt — "

"She takes my orders. Oh hurry up,

boy. There'll be no trouble for you. I'll see to it."

Still muttering, he obeyed, while I discarded my gown and petticoats for the breeches and boots. The latter were too large, but not unduly so. The breeches were baggy, but pushed into the boots could have been those of any farmer's boy. There was a wool cape hanging on a peg. I put it round me, and pulled my hair tightly back with a ribbon.

Then, feeling and looking something like an ill-dressed highwayman, I set off, with a sturdy horsewhip, and a revolver, which though unloaded, somehow provided a certain comfort.

It was a wild night of yellow moonlit skies and racing clouds, giving dramatic movement to the landscape. I let my mount canter on a loose rein, occasionally breaking into a gallop. I felt free and reckless for the first time in months. That I was on business in which I'd really no right to be concerned, didn't trouble me in the least. With the air cold, and stinging my cheeks, and a dangerous purpose in view oh, yes, I was quite aware of the danger in confronting a crowd of frustrated miners restraint and commonsense counted for nothing. If I was harmed, what then? What did it matter, since I had only myself to care about, having lost the love of the one person in the world I wanted?

However, when I neared the dumpy shape of the barn and saw light zigzagging from a gap in the door across the trodden furze, my heart quickened and muscles tensed.

The horse reared, alert and frightened by the ugly screeching and guffaws of male laughter, the cursing and yelling. I reined, and managed to quieten her, then swung myself from the saddle, and led her to the back of the building where I tethered the animal to a sycamore. The noise died temporarily into an uncanny silence. I waited, wondering if I'd been seen or heard. But in a few moments murmuring, becoming argumentative and aggressive, started up again.

Keeping well into the shadows of the wall, and gripping the revolver in one hand, the whip in the other, I made my way to the entrance. As I pushed the door wide the glow of a lantern lit a group of figures hunched round an odious scene of flying feathers, squawking birds, and blood — blood everywhere, it seemed to me in those first horrified seconds. Suddenly a dozen or so pairs of eyes were turned fully in my direction, astonishment on their faces giving place quickly to malevolent belligerance. One man got to his feet and approached me with a swaggering gait, small bright eyes assessing me craftily and with something else in them — lust as well as cruelty that made my hand tighten instinctively on the whip. I knew him by sight, the trouble-maker, Will Behenna, and in one quick instant I realised the foolhardiness of my mission.

"Well, missus?" he said. "Come for a bit o' pleasure have 'ee? Or is that for us, eh, seein' as how you're dressed in pants as a bit of a lad?"

Murmurs of assent mingled with grunts of disapproval rose and fell from the background.

"Let her be," I heard one voice saying, and another, "Mistress Tremellick, edn' et? From the hall?"

"Yes," I interrupted loudly and clearly.

"And in my husband's place I'm telling you to stop this foul business immediately. You hear? Or there'll be trouble — "

"Trouble? Eh?" Will mocked sneeringly. "It's you who'll get that, young wumman, unless you tek care. Or mebbe not. Mebbe a bit of a slap an' a tickle eh? A tasty dose o' what your man don' seem to fancy these days — " He took a further step forward, rolling up his sleeves menacingly. I raised the whip, and it was then, against the horrible background of the two birds mauling each other to death, that I heard it — the unmistakable thud of horses' hooves approaching, and a voice — a voice with a familiar ring about it, shouting, "Sari — what the hell's going on?"

Most of the men got to their feet, others cowered in the shadows, one threw a dead cockerel into a sack, followed by another. There was muttering and swearing as Dick's tall form approached, leading his mount by the bridle.

The lamp was suddenly put out, but the moonlight broke clear from a belt of cloud to reveal the whole scene in its full macabre brutality. Dick kicked the earth and feathers flew. Feathers red with blood. One dead bird lay near the entrance.

Dick stared for a moment, then asked, "Who's responsible for this? You know very well Master Tremellick's outlawed such wretched sport on his land?"

"And who're you?" Will Behenna demanded.

"The one as was with them players — the circus folk," a man said from the back. "I see 'im with en — "

"I'm also uncle to this young lady," Dick answered quickly, and unless you want the Law involved I advise you to clear this mess up, and get to your homes as soon as possible. Do you understand?"

At first I thought Dick might be attacked. But after further words, and following a discussion amongst themselves, the scene quietened. The small crowd started to disperse, and presently Dick and I, astride our horses, were on our way back to Boscarne.

"You were very stupid," Dick said to me later, when I'd washed and changed into a grey velvet gown that I knew suited me. "Heaven knows what might have happened if I hadn't appeared at Boscarne at that particular moment. It was lucky the stable boy was on the spot, and the girl, of course. She helped. Knowing you, I guessed what had happened."

"I'd no idea *you* were coming," I said feebly, "and anyway, why did you?"

"Because of a hunch I had."

"What sort of hunch?"

"That a silly temperamental young wife had no business to remain alone in such a benighted place as Boscarne while her husband was so far away mooning in a London hotels."

"Do you mean you came all the way from Bristol just to tell me that?"

"That exactly. I saw Mark a week ago too, and gave him a bit of my mind. You two are really quite *the limit*. Well, d'you hear me?"

"Yes — yes," I answered vaguely. "I was just thinking I mean — you said a *hotel*. Mark in a hotel! — is it true? I thought — "

"Of course it's true. Why would I lie to you? He left the hospital, but goes daily for some sort of treatment. Except for the hand, he's practically fit. But morose. He needs you, Sari."

"Did he say so?"

"He didn't have to."

"Well, I'm afraid until he does, I'm just not interested," I remarked coldly, assuming a manner of aloof dignity. "I am not — just *not* going to be played with and bossed about anymore. First it was *you*, and then Mark. I'm a woman, with feelings, not just a child any more. If you knew what it's been like this last year — " I swallowed hard trying to control my emotions.

"Oh, Sari — Sari — " Dick came over and took me by the shoulders. "*No* one's playing with you. As for bossing — " he laughed whimsically, "I doubt any man could — unless you wanted it — " He stared at me with the knowing look in his blue eyes that brought the past vividly back to me — the past when I'd really *had* been a child and done all I could to charm and bring him close.

"What do you mean by *want* it?" I asked with as much dignity as I could muster.

He paused before replying, then he said, "You gave me the answer a moment ago. You're a woman — Eve reborn as the immortal nymph men dream about. The ideal mate for a dominant male character like the Mark you married. The wayward creature longing to be possessed and wildly captured, the object of man's will, but the ruler of his heart. In other words, the queen behind the throne. But Mark is proud, Sari love. Because of his — injury, he feels insufficient, incapable of putting you in your place and retaining your whole-hearted admiration and love. I assure you you're wrong. Mark may be a silly bastard — sorry — blighter but he's no weakling. He *adores* and needs you, nymph."

Against my will I felt a warm relaxing glow spread slowly through my whole being.

"You mean — but he told me he didn't *want* me. He *did*, Dick, truly. He hurt and humiliated me terribly, like you in the past, only *worse*. Much, much worse — "

"Because you love him. And because you've grown up. Then try and understand.

Go to him. Don't listen to his stiff and starchy remarks. Fling yourself at him, *refuse* to leave if he orders you to, which no doubt he will at first. Infuriate him, stand your ground, until he'll no longer be able to resist you. Forget your damned infantile little girl's pride, and — " He broke off, shrugged, then continued in quieter tones, "It's the only way, Sari. He's a stubborn character, our Mark. It'll be a challenge for you. But more worthwhile, don't you think, than your ridiculous confrontation at a cock-fight?"

I hesitated. Weakening and pleading with Mark was the very last thing I'd contemplated or thought myself capable of doing, but as Dick put it, there *did* seem sense to it, in a queer kind of way. And so in the end I gave in, and once my mind was made up, I realised to my utter, excited astonishment, it was the only thing I truly wanted to do.

The next morning Dick and I set off for London, and a day or two later Mark and I stood facing each other, alone, in a hotel bedroom overlooking Hyde Park.

He looked a little older, thinner, but handsome as ever in his imperious way, though his dark eyes held a cold challenge, implying he was already on his guard against me. He was wearing a gold-coloured velveteen jacket with cream waistcoat, cravat, and fawn breeches. The mutilated arm was bound, and in a sling, with the coat sleeve hanging loose. No one would have known, that dressed as it was, the whole arm was severed halfway up to the elbow. My first reaction was how gallant he appeared, like some legendary hero from the wars. He gave a little bow — a mere inclination of the head, and said:

"This is indeed a surprise. And in such weather. Rather futile, don't you think? Under the circumstances?"

"Is it?"

I could see his jaws tighten.

"Of course. I thought I'd made matters quite clear at our last meeting. However — " he glanced round. "Do take a chair. Would you like a drink? A madeira?"

I shook my head. "No, thank you. Nothing. Except to — to — oh, Mark

— *please*! I ran towards him and would have flung myself against his hard unrelenting body, had it not been for fear of hurting his arm.

He stepped back.

"Sari — Sari — it's no use.

"What do you mean 'no use'? And how *can* you act this way without — without a sign of welcome or affection — when I've been so lonely, and miserable, and *longing* for you. *Why?*"

He sighed, went to a chair, seated himself on it, and sat there for a moment or two with his forehead resting on his one hand. I moved closer. When he looked up his expression was tortured, grim.

"Because, my dear, I've no liking or intention of being a burden on any woman — "

"A *burden*? What do you mean? Just because you've lost a hand? What's that? You'll have another — it won't be the same, but you'll be able to do most things, I *know* — the doctor told me. And anyway, even if you couldn't, it wouldn't matter, not all that much, because I *love* you, Mark. Don't you understand? *Won't* you? — *Love!*"

He smiled slightly, a faint bitter gesture. "You *think* you do, at this moment because like most women you've got the intuitive ambition to mother something — a husband, if possible, and in such a way possess him. That's the truth of it, whether you like it or not."

"Possess?" My voice rose. "But *you're* the possessor and always will be. That's what I want — to be *yours*, Mark — yours forever — your wife and love — "

He shook his head slowly. "You haven't changed, have you? You're still the wild half-child, half-woman who only a year or two ago was so impetuously in love with Dick."

"In love isn't loving," I said stubbornly, "and you were wrong to imagine there could have been anything serious between us. That was *stupid* of you. I was only a child."

"That's the point. I shouldn't have married you. Apart from this damned arm I'm years and years older than you. Oh, Sari — " a hint of temper showed in his eyes and voice, "leave me alone, can't you? For heaven's sake stop pestering me and go. I don't need you, and you don't *need* me."

I knelt down then, on the floor, and the action was so quick a comb fell from my hair leaving locks free to fall to my shoulders. "Don't pretend," I begged leaning my head against him. "We need each other, and you know it. And I won't go. I *won't*. So there!" There was a great lump in my throat — tears were already threatening to fall. I felt suddenly desperate as though flinging myself against a wall of granite. My determination was weakening; I knew I was coming to the end. I'd done everything I could — tried every way to touch his heart even worn the ensemble he liked of blue velvet, and a touch of the perfume he'd given me, Fleur-de-Lys. But it hadn't worked. Turning my face from him, I got up, adjusting my hair, and lifting a shred of lace handkerchief to my eyes.

"Goodbye then, Mark," I said. "If you don't want me, I'm sorry to have been a nuisance. It won't happen again."

My hand was on the door knob when there was the sudden sound of the chair creaking, and the firm tread of footsteps across the floor.

The next moment an arm was at my waist pulling me fiercely round, crushing me against him.

"Sari Sari — " he murmured, "you witch, you cunning, adorable creature. My God! What a fool I am. And don't look like that, or I'll — "

"You'll what, Mark?" I asked over-sweetly.

His lips were hot, sweet and demanding then on my mouth. Oh, never in all my life had a kiss been so rich, so heady with promise and longing.

"That's what," he said at last. "Not as I'd intended things to be — but — "

"As they'll be all our lives from now on."

"No. This is only the beginning, love. We'll have our ups and downs maybe, but that's life. Sometimes you'll be the winner, at others I'll have to teach you your place, I suppose. What matter? In future I'll see you have no chance for straying, and you'll make an idiot of me in your subtle fashion. The point is — we'll be together."

"Yes," I agreed, so happy suddenly, that joy seemed everywhere, filling the world. I knew then that Mark was right — our real life together was only just starting.

THE END

Other titles in the
Ulverscroft Large Print Series:

TO FIGHT THE WILD
Rod Ansell and Rachel Percy

Lost in uncharted Australian bush, Rod Ansell survived by hunting and trapping wild animals, improvising shelter and using all the bushman's skills he knew.

COROMANDEL
Pat Barr

India in the 1830s is a hot, uncomfortable place, where the East India Company still rules. Amelia and her new husband find themselves caught up in the animosities which seethe between the old order and the new.

THE SMALL PARTY
Lillian Beckwith

A frightening journey to safety begins for Ruth and her small party as their island is caught up in the dangers of armed insurrection.

WITHDRAWN
No longer the property of the
Boston Public Library.
Sale of this material benefits the Library.